"Don't you dare look at me like that,"

Amanda told Alvin sharply. "I'm *right* about this, and you know I am, Alvin. They have no reason to treat me this way, either of them."

The scruffy dog gathered himself together, cast her a bitter glance and marched from the room, his fat body swaying indignantly. Amanda made her bed, trying not to think about the hours of darkness in this room, when Brock's sweet lovemaking had sent her soaring to the moon and back. Nobody had ever made her feel the way Brock did.

But *why* did he contin   situations? It would o   briefest of commitme   to quail like a child in   her head high, assum   and smile at Millie w

It was a disconcerting feeling, knowing that another woman was in the house and could pop up at any moment. Ruefully, she recalled all her foolish day-dreams, in which Millie had been a grandmotherly type, eager to take Amanda's side in this strange, unspoken struggle with Brock.

Fat chance, Amanda thought bitterly. *She'd hate to see me married to Brock. It's probably the last thing she wants, and I don't even know why.*

Margot Dalton is acknowledged as the author of this work.

Special thanks and acknowledgment to Sutton Press Inc. for its contribution to the concept for the Crystal Creek series.

ISBN 0-373-82531-5

NEVER GIVIN' UP ON LOVE

Margot Dalton

NEVER GIVIN'
UP ON LOVE

Harlequin Books

TORONTO • NEW YORK • LONDON
AMSTERDAM • PARIS • SYDNEY • HAMBURG
STOCKHOLM • ATHENS • TOKYO • MILAN
MADRID • WARSAW • BUDAPEST • AUCKLAND

Dear Reader,

Reviewers were unanimous in their assessment of the thirteenth installment of the series, Margot Dalton's fourth Crystal Creek title, *Mustang Heart:*

"This one will melt the hardest hearts!"

—*Rendezvous*

Ms. Dalton takes us back to the Double Bar this month, for another visit with Brock and Amanda, and, of course, Alvin. While the rancher and the image consultant contend with the strain on their relationship imposed by Brock's awful aunt Millie, Alvin manages to befriend an exploring young couple and land in a hole he can barely survive!

Next month, Bethany Campbell, another favorite Crystal Creek author, returns with the enchanting story of Ruth's cousin Betsy, a cultured, shy, rather secretive young executive, and Hutch, her polar opposite, a tumbleweed with the extraordinary notion of setting up a chili parlor in Crystal Creek. Ms. Campbell dishes up the perfect amount of spice to inflame the emotions of Betsy's family, the McKinneys and, of course, the reader! Watch for *Gentle on My Mind*, available wherever Harlequin books are sold. And stick around in Crystal Creek—home of sultry Texas drawls, smooth Texas charm and tall, sexy Texans!

Marsha Zinberg
Senior Editor and Editorial Coordinator
Crystal Creek

A Note from the Author

The Hill Country of central Texas is a storyteller's paradise. There's so much to fire any writer's imagination...wonderful scenery, rolling vistas, cheerful, warmhearted people and a fascinating history. But that's not all! In lavish Texas fashion, the beauty of the Hill Country conceals a whole other landscape, one that's more subtle but every bit as spectacular. This hidden country isn't available to everyone, but it offers untold riches to those few who are brave enough to seek it out. The astonishing interior landscape of Texas is the one that's explored in this book.

Margot Dalton

Who's Who in Crystal Creek

Have you missed the story of one of your favorite Crystal Creek characters? Here's a quick guide to help you easily locate the titles and story lines:

DEEP IN THE HEART	J.T. McKinney and Cynthia
COWBOYS AND CABERNET	Tyler McKinney and Ruth
AMARILLO BY MORNING	Cal McKinney and Serena
WHITE LIGHTNING	Lynn McKinney and Sam
EVEN THE NIGHTS ARE BETTER	Carolyn Townsend and Vernon
AFTER THE LIGHTS GO OUT	Scott Harris and Val
HEARTS AGAINST THE WIND	Jeff Harris and Beverly
THE THUNDER ROLLS	Ken Slattery and Nora
GUITARS, CADILLACS	Wayne Jackson and Jessica
STAND BY YOUR MAN	Manny Hernandez and Tracey
NEW WAY TO FLY	Brock Munroe and Amanda
EVERYBODY'S TALKIN'	Cody Hendricks and Lori
MUSTANG HEART	Sara Gibson and Warren
PASSIONATE KISSES	J.T. McKinney and Pauline
RHINESTONE COWBOY	Liz Babcock and Guy
SOUTHERN NIGHTS	Lisa Croft and Tony
SHAMELESS	Rio Langley and Maggie
LET'S TURN BACK THE YEARS	Hank Travis and Mary

Available at your local bookseller, or see the Crystal Creek back-page ad for reorder information.

CHAPTER ONE

LATE OCTOBER SUNSHINE glimmered on the glass-fronted cupboards in the kitchen, and highlighted the Boston ferns with an emerald glow. Amanda Walker paused near one of the latticework fern stands, an empty coffee mug in her hand, and pulled out a frond that was withering.

She wandered across the kitchen to look into the big living room, smiling as she recalled the way this room had looked the first time she'd ever seen it, more than a year ago. Back then, the whole house had been in wild disorder, littered with construction equipment and the haphazard clutter of a cheerful bachelor existence.

But now it was a different story. Brock Munroe's gracious old ranch house had been almost completely restored in the months since he'd met Amanda, and they'd done most of the work themselves. Amanda had consulted catalogs and books on interior design, spent long hours drawing diagrams and floor plans, searching through pattern books and coming up with ideas. Brock had labored good-naturedly, working hard to implement her dreams, demonstrating surprising skill and resourcefulness as a craftsman.

Still smiling, Amanda moved into the living room and reached up to touch the gleaming oak plate rail. At Christmastime, she was planning to wind holly and mistletoe all along the plate rail and up over the mantel of the fireplace, and hang antique Christmas ornaments from the archway. The place was going to be so beautiful....

Amanda sighed with pleasure and sat down on the old slate hearth, pulling the skirt of her blue silk dressing gown close around her knees. Her smile turned a little rueful as she thought about her apartment back in Austin, and the urban-minimalist decor she'd affected before she met Brock.

He'd been so coldly critical of her home the first time he saw it, and rightly so. Brock had sensed immediately that the starkness of her apartment wasn't a genuine expression of Amanda's personality. He'd realized that she was merely searching for someone to be, reflecting the tastes of a man she'd left behind. And because Brock wasn't capable of insincerity, he'd made his disapproval uncomfortably obvious.

But this big old house, with its leaded glass and rich wallpaper and polished wood, was actually a much stronger and more individual statement of Amanda's personal tastes. She loved the feeling of warmth and continuity, of family values and heritage and deep, lasting love and security.

In fact, Amanda was finding it harder all the time to leave the ranch on Monday mornings, drive back into the city and her lonely apartment, even though she was genuinely surprised and gratified by the unexpected success of her business. There were a lot of times when she cheated and slipped back out to the ranch a couple of nights during the week, although she and Brock had agreed that this was impractical and that so much driving was too tiring for her.

Amanda got up, feeling suddenly restless and a little sad, and wandered back into the kitchen to refill her coffee mug. But her spirits were lifted, as always, by the sight of that room, her favorite in the beautiful old house.

She squinted at a shelf Brock had recently built above the table, thinking that it would look nice to have a row of china ornaments placed up there.

Porcelain dogs, she decided. That was what the shelf needed. The ones she had in mind were terribly expensive, but they'd be perfect for the character of the house. And dogs were such warm, lovable creatures. Although, Amanda told herself with a private grin, it was certainly a little strange for anybody who lived with Alvin to retain sentimental emotions about dogs.

Alvin was Brock's dog. He was a small, ragged mongrel, largely of Australian blue heeler extraction, but with a few other indeterminate breeds mixed into his genetic background as well. Amanda and Brock both recognized that Alvin had some serious personality flaws. He was lazy, greedy, cowardly, and ill-mannered, but still there was something about the fat little dog, a touching kind of clumsiness and vulnerability that made Amanda love him with a fierce, secret love she would have been embarrassed to confess.

She took her fresh cup of coffee and wandered over to the window, drawing aside a ruffled paisley curtain to peer out into the ranch yard, hungry for a sight of Brock and Alvin. But the yard was still and deserted in the early sunlight, and Brock's truck stood quietly at the gate. They must be doing chores in the barn, she thought, dropping the curtain.

She looked up at the shelf again, feeling a fresh glow of pleasure when she pictured the row of beautiful china dogs. Maybe she'd buy one this week, she thought with sudden excitement. Her bank balance had surprised her on Friday, soaring to dizzying new heights with the addition of a deposit on a contract to do costumes for the local theater production of *The Phantom of the Opera*. She could certainly afford to give herself a treat.

Amanda continued to gaze at the shelf with narrowed eyes, trying to remember what kind of dogs she'd seen in the delicate painted china. Maybe she could even find one that looked like Alvin.

"Probably not," she murmured aloud, though she was still enchanted by the image of Alvin's fat body modeled in fine china.

Suddenly her smile faded and she shook her head, sinking into a chair by the table.

This was the same kind of conflict she'd been through a hundred times in the past months. There were so many things Amanda still wanted to do to the ranch house, special items that she wanted to buy, little touches she was yearning to add. But they were the kind of things a woman just didn't do until she was actually married and living in the house.

For instance, how could she have all her own and Brock's old family portraits mounted in matching antique frames to hang together in the stairwell? How could she buy monogrammed towels for the guest bathroom, or invest in something as costly as those porcelain figurines for the kitchen, when she and Brock still weren't married and there was no sign that they were ever going to be?

Amanda sipped moodily at her coffee, trying to push the troubled thoughts from her mind and recapture the happiness she'd been feeling on this bright autumn morning. There was no point in dwelling on the problem. Brooding about it only made her unhappy. Besides, she kept hoping that perhaps Christmas, with all its warmth and family closeness, might just be the impetus that Brock needed to...

Her wistful thoughts were interrupted by the opening of the back door and the noisy arrival of Brock and his dog. Alvin entered precipitately, as always, hurtling into the room and then skidding on the polished hardwood, his claws skittering along as he tried to stop himself before hitting the cupboard.

Amanda laughed and the dog rolled his dark eyes at her in sorrowful reproach, then twisted his body awkwardly to gnaw at one of his hind legs.

Amanda looked up to see Brock lounging in the doorway, his eyes sparkling with amusement. Her heart gave a lurch and began to beat unsteadily, just as it always did when she saw him, no matter how recently they'd been parted.

Dear Lord, how I love the man! Amanda thought in despair.

Brock was tall and rangy in his jeans and plaid work shirt, with dark hair and eyes and a weathered, rugged face. He still had an engaging, disheveled look, despite Amanda's best efforts to see that his clothes were neat and fresh and that he got his hair cut regularly.

When he met her gaze, his face kindled with a boyish look of adoration that touched her deeply, almost bringing tears to her eyes.

"Mornin', sweetheart," he said gently, still smiling at her.

"Good morning, Brock. I looked out the window a minute ago and couldn't see a trace of you two. What do you want for breakfast?"

"Not much. I'll just make us some toast while you get dressed. You'll be late if you don't start getting ready."

"I know," Amanda said gloomily. "I don't feel like going to work this morning," she added, as rebellious as a small child. "I wish I could just stay here and play with you and Alvin."

Brock grinned. "If you stay here, I won't get any work done, either," he told her. "Not when you're looking so pretty."

Amanda smiled at him and bent to pat Alvin, who had apparently forgiven her cruel laughter and was now expressing a warm interest in breakfast.

"Poor baby," Amanda murmured, caressing his ragged ears. "He's so hungry, isn't he? Poor darling, nobody ever feeds him."

Brock snorted and came across the room to place some papers and envelopes on the table.

"Oh, that's where you were," Amanda said. "You went down for the mail."

"I'm still waiting for the check for those calves I sold," Brock told her. "Things are getting a little tight at the bank."

Amanda paused in the doorway and glanced at him, concerned by the serious note in his voice. "Did it come? Your check?"

"Not yet, but the auction yard says it's in the mail. I'll give it a couple more days," Brock added grimly, "and if it's not here by then, I'll have to go into the bank and beg Cody for mercy."

Amanda looked down at her slippered feet, feeling awkward and tense. "Brock..." she ventured.

"Don't even say it, honey," he warned her. "We'll just have another fight if you say it."

"But, Brock, *please*... I have all that money just sitting in the bank, and it seems such a waste. I'll charge you interest if you like. We can even draw up a loan agreement through the bank, completely businesslike. Why won't you let me—"

"Forget it, Amanda. I don't need your money. I've got my own money, lots of it. I don't have any problems. It's just a little glitch in the cash flow, that's all. As soon as the check comes, I'll be right back in great shape."

"Brock . . ."

But she knew enough not to argue further. His face had taken on the set, distant look that she knew so well, and her heart sank.

Brock turned away to open the storage closet and dragged out a sack of dog food while Alvin groveled by the counter, thumping his tail ecstatically on the polished floor. Amanda paused, her eyes fixed in helpless silence on Brock's tall muscular body, his set jaw and the clean, tanned line of his cheek. After a moment, she left the room quietly and climbed the stairs to get dressed for work.

Brock was reading the mail when she came back down, and the table was neatly set with little pots of jam and marmalade, a jar of bronze chrysanthemums from the kitchen garden and a fresh pot of coffee. Alvin lay near the table, replete, his fat belly bulging alarmingly over the furry curve of his legs.

Brock, too, looked cheerful again. His brief dark mood had already lifted, as Amanda had known it would. Brock was just too sunny and optimistic to stay glum for very long.

When she entered the kitchen he looked up, startled, then gave a low whistle of appreciation.

"You like it?" Amanda asked him, feeling self-conscious but delighted as she whirled around and held out her skirt to display the new outfit.

It was a two-piece design in crimped silk, about the same color as the flowers on the table, and Amanda knew how beautifully it set off her delicate complexion and dark hair. But the nicest thing about the garment was the fact that it fit like a glove, and Amanda, with her small, slender body, had a hard time finding designer clothes that were suited to her shape. Most of them, she often told Brock in despair, were apparently cut for women about a foot taller.

"It's beautiful, darling," he said with warm approval. "Where'd you get it?"

"Edward sent it down from New York last week," Amanda said casually, glancing over Brock's shoulder at the mail. "He had it in a show up there and thought I might like it."

"For free?"

She chuckled. "Edward likes me, but not that much. Still, he gave me a really good price. And it's a terrific wardrobe piece because I can wear it all year round."

To her relief, Brock nodded absently and returned to his letter. Amanda would have been painfully embarrassed if he'd pressed her for details and she had to confess just how much she'd paid Edward for the bronze silk outfit.

Not that she couldn't afford it. She was doing so well these days that she could afford practically anything she wanted. But it seemed a little insensitive to spend that much on clothes when poor Brock was waiting anxiously for his money from the auction yard to ward off disaster....

"Who's that from?" she asked with sudden curiosity, noting his intense concentration on the letter in his hands.

He glanced up from the closely written pages, his expression puzzled. "My aunt."

"Which one? Grace, in Arkansas?"

"No, that's my mother's sister. This is from Millicent, my father's sister. Millicent Munroe."

"She never married?"

Brock grinned faintly. "At least a couple of times. She just never took her husbands' names."

"That's sort of unusual for a woman of that generation, isn't it?"

"Well, Millie's sort of an unusual woman. She was the terror of Crystal Creek when she was growing up. My daddy had some hair-raising stories to tell about her, that's for sure."

Amanda looked at the letter again, intrigued. "How old is she?"

Brock leaned back in his chair with a thoughtful frown and munched on a slice of toast liberally smeared with marmalade. "I guess Millie must be about sixty by now," he said finally. "She went to school with Virginia Parks."

Amanda poured a half cup of coffee and settled in the chair across from him, reluctant to leave the warmth of the kitchen and head out to the city. Alvin wandered over, sighing with contentment, and lowered himself onto the floor next to her. He began to gnaw cautiously on the heel of her shoe, glancing up at intervals to see if she noticed.

"Where does she live?" Amanda asked. "Alvin," she added sternly, "if you don't stop that, you're going out on the porch. I mean it!"

Alvin tensed and dropped his chin onto his folded paws, gazing off into space with a look of soulful innocence.

"Last I heard, she was living in Oregon. She had a little farm, I think, raising chickens or something. I haven't seen her for years, not since I was a boy. She used to send a card at Christmas, but she stopped after my daddy died."

"So why's she writing to you now?"

Brock shook his head, still looking bewildered. "She wants to come for a visit."

"Here? To the ranch?"

"Yeah, that's what she says. No explanation or anything, just says she's coming out to spend some time at the ranch if it's all right with me, and would I please write back and let her know."

"How long is she planning to stay?"

"No mention of that. Seems like maybe she's considering an extended visit."

Amanda glanced at him, startled and a little worried. She treasured her weekends at the ranch with Brock and Alvin. In fact, she probably couldn't go on living if this part of her life was taken away. How would it affect their relationship to have an elderly aunt moving in for an indefinite period of time?

"What...what do you think about that?" she asked Brock cautiously.

To her surprise, he grinned and reached for more toast. "Having Millie come out here for a visit? I'd love it."

"Really?"

"She's a terrific person, Amanda. Or she was, what I remember of her. Like I said, my daddy told stories about her that would stand your hair on end."

"Like what?"

"Well, let's see." Brock poured himself a cup of coffee and stirred cream into it. "One year when she was about seventeen, I guess, she got herself dressed up in a skimpy little two-piece bathing suit. Not too exciting these days, but it was pretty daring back in the fifties. Then she galloped down Main Street when everybody was lined up to watch the Fourth of July parade."

"That's pretty daring, all right."

"That's not half of it," Brock said, his dark eyes sparkling. "She was Roman riding."

"Roman riding? What's that?"

"Two horses, bareback. You stand on their backs, one foot on each, and hold the reins in your hands."

"Oh, my goodness," Amanda breathed, staring at him. "Wouldn't that be terribly dangerous?"

"Not if you know what you're doing. Millie Munroe was the best horsewoman in the Hill Country, back in those days."

Amanda shook her head in amusement. "This place has certainly produced more than its share of colorful characters."

"It sure has. Must be something in the water."

Amanda got up and moved around to kiss him, leaning against his back and dropping her arms around his neck. "And you're the nicest character of them all," she whispered, nuzzling his crisp, dark hair and his tanned cheek. "You're just the nicest man in the whole world, Brock Munroe."

He twisted around to return her kiss, smiling up at her. "Oh yeah? And how do you know? You've checked out all the men in the world?"

"As many as I care to," Amanda told him with dignity, gathering up her jacket and handbag. "I hate to leave," she said wistfully. "I really do, Brock."

"Come on, sweetheart. You love your job. Once you're on the road, you'll be all excited about getting back to the office and seeing what's going on."

Knowing that he was probably right, Amanda nodded reluctantly and moved toward the door. "Are you going to write her a letter?"

"Millie? No, I think I'm going to call her today. She seems anxious to get here as soon as she can. Says she'll fly into Austin once she hears from me."

Brock ambled out onto the porch beside Amanda, his arm resting familiarly on her shoulders. Despite his words of encouragement, Amanda knew that it was hard for him to watch her drive away, leaving him to face another lonely week at the ranch with just Alvin and his daily chores to keep him company.

If they were married, Amanda told herself, she'd sell her business in a flash and stay here with him all the time, working with him to make the ranch a success. Or, if they couldn't afford to get along without her income, at least she'd scale down a lot, make arrangements to run the business from Crystal Creek and only go into town for one or two days a week.

But it was the same old story. She couldn't start to reorganize her life until Brock made some kind of commitment, and that seemed to be the furthest thing from his mind these days.

Maybe it would be different when his aunt came, Amanda thought, suddenly hopeful. Maybe a tactful bit of family pressure was just what he needed to prod him into action. She pictured the wild young girl, half-naked as she galloped her horses in tandem before the shocked townspeople.

Amanda's optimism increased. A woman like that, she thought, could turn out to be a really valuable ally. "I'm looking forward to meeting your aunt," she said, smiling up at Brock.

"That's good. She might even be here when you come back on Friday."

Amanda stood on tiptoe and gave him a lingering kiss, thrilling to the firm softness of his lips, the masculine smell and feel of him. Finally, she pulled herself away and bent to pat Alvin. The little dog sat at Brock's side looking stricken, as he always did when she left.

"Bye, guys," she said with forced cheerfulness. "Take care of yourselves. I'll see you soon."

"Call tonight?" Brock asked wistfully, his determined cheerfulness suddenly giving way so that he looked as miserable and bereft as Alvin. "I'll tell you what Millie says."

"Of course I'll call. You know I can't get through a whole day without talking to you."

Still wearing a bright, artificial smile, Amanda turned aside and almost ran to her car. She shifted into gear and pulled quickly out of the ranch yard and onto the highway. As she drove away she stared straight ahead, knowing that if she allowed herself to look back at the tall man and the fat little dog on the porch, she'd probably start crying and smear her makeup.

Brock watched her drive out of sight, and a bit of him curled up and died as it always did when she left. He stared at the curve in the road where her car had vanished, gazing into the distance with fierce concentration as he pictured her face and tried to wrap all of her safely within the protection of his loving thoughts.

"If anything ever happened to that woman," Brock told his dog, "I don't know what I'd do. Truth is, Alvin, I can't imagine living without her."

Alvin gazed up at him in mournful agreement and dropped heavily onto the floorboards of the veranda, burying his chin in his paws with a disconsolate expression.

Brock, who felt just about the way Alvin looked, lowered himself to sit on the steps next to the miserable dog. He fondled Alvin's fur absently, still thinking about Amanda.

In sudden longing, Brock conjured up her image again, her delicate face and wide blue eyes, her tousled haircut and small curving form, her grace and gaiety. He moaned and stretched his long body in a hot storm of yearning, and wondered in despair if he was ever going to have enough of her.

It was the same thing, every weekend. No matter how many times they made love, how many hours they lay together in each other's arms, whispering and laughing, he was never satisfied. As soon as she left, he wanted her back. And by Friday when she drove out to the ranch, his hunger had grown so terrible that he was sometimes tense and irritable with her, entirely without cause.

Brock shifted restlessly on the hard boards of the veranda and stared off into the distance, his face brooding.

He knew that all this pain was entirely his own fault. He had it in his power to solve the whole problem, just by saying the word. If he asked Amanda to marry him, she'd accept in a minute, and if he asked her to give up her business and stay at the ranch with him all the time, she'd do it without hesitation.

Brock knew this to be true, but it was still something he could never bring himself to ask of her. For one thing, her business was so damned successful.

Brock remembered the early days of their relationship, when she'd been struggling and uncertain of herself, terrified to go to the bank and ask for an extension on her loan. Now, with dazzling speed, her business had grown until she was the image consultant for a large circle of prominent Austin residents. That alone earned her a good living, but she had also been offered several commissions to buy fashions for some of the trendy boutiques in the city. Brock still couldn't believe how much money somebody could earn, just by deciding that teal blue and burgundy were going to make a comeback this season....

And as if all that weren't enough, she'd recently expanded into another business, supplying costumes for special parties as well as theatrical groups and tourist associations. The costume business had started small but mushroomed, just like her other ventures. Now she employed seven seamstresses.

Brock sighed, thinking about Amanda's meteoric rise. The whole thing was hard to explain, because she wasn't really a businesswoman. She wasn't good at negotiating deals, and she still had no clear understanding of balance sheets and cash flow. She didn't have to, Brock thought with a bleak smile, because everything she touched turned to money.

He frowned, thinking about the recent conversation he'd had over a drink with J. T. McKinney, when they'd edged cautiously into a discussion of women and relationships. J.T. had confided a few of the problems in his own marriage, how his wife had wanted to be involved in the business and J.T. had held out and stubbornly resisted until he'd come close to losing her.

But the two situations weren't really similar, although Brock and Amanda occasionally had tense little scenes like the one this morning when she'd tried to lend him money.

Amanda wasn't trained and knowledgeable in financial matters like Cynthia McKinney, and she felt no urge to involve herself in business decisions. She'd be quite happy to live with Brock at the ranch, have a couple of babies, play with Alvin, walk in the hills, pick flowers from the garden and busy herself around the house.

In fact, despite her glamour and success, Amanda was probably the most domestic, contented woman he'd ever met. It was one of the things Brock loved best about her, her childlike delight in the simple, everyday pleasures of life.

Automatically, he leaned over to scratch Alvin's soft pink belly, causing the little dog to whine in ecstasy and pump his legs with a strange, jerky motion.

The whole problem between himself and Amanda, Brock mused gloomily, was that she had a Midas touch and he didn't. And how could a man explain that to the woman he loved? *I'd really like to marry you, sweetheart, but I'm afraid that you're always going to be more successful than I am, and I don't think I can stand it*… No, Brock thought, shaking his head. There was no way to tell a woman something like that.

He continued to scratch Alvin's belly, trying hard to look on the bright side.

Maybe things would pick up for him next year, and he wouldn't be so intimidated by her success. After all, the Double Bar Ranch had been doing well in recent years, and most of his current problems were just a combination of bad luck and poor timing.

For one thing, he'd spent more than he could really afford on the house, mostly because he was anxious to make everything the way Amanda wanted, and he was reluctant to confess to her that money was tight. And then the calf crop Brock had been counting on hadn't materialized. His cow herd had developed some kind of mysterious infection, utterly baffling to Manny Hernandez, that had resulted in almost half of them delivering stillborn calves. This was a crippling blow for any rancher, and hiding his troubles and worries from Amanda had been the hardest thing of all. Then, as if the sickness weren't devastating enough, beef prices had dropped again over the summer so the calves that he'd managed to raise were hardly going to cover expenses, let alone supply a profit.

Brock turned away from Alvin, who crept closer and inserted his nose under the big man's hand, whimpering insistently.

Things had to pick up, because another year or two like this one, Brock thought miserably, and he'd be forced to sell the ranch. He'd have to move to the city

and get a job selling cars or something. What right did
he have to propose marriage to an elegant, successful
woman when his own future was so uncertain?

He glared down at Alvin, who looked up at him with
a dark, inscrutable gaze.

"You think I should let her help, don't you?" Brock
asked his dog. "That's just like you, Alvin. You think
I should marry her and let her keep working and throw
all her cash into my account, just to keep the ranch
afloat. Don't you?"

Alvin coughed and thumped his tail uncertainly on
the floorboards.

"Well, that may be your style," Brock told the dog
firmly, "but it sure isn't mine. I'll marry her when I can
support my family without my wife's help, and not before. I'll marry her when I have something secure to
offer."

He got up with sudden decision, startling Alvin, who
was drifting off to sleep, and strolled back into the
house to call his aunt.

THE FOLLOWING MORNING, Brock drove his pickup
across a rutted trail through cactus and limestone
boulders, with Alvin bouncing beside him on the front
seat. In the valley below he could see the Gibson ranch,
where a few of the ostriches paced along the wire of
their enclosure, looking lofty and serene. "No wonder
they act like royalty," Brock told his dog with a sour
grimace. "They're worth a king's ransom, the ugly
suckers."

Alvin nodded agreement, peering cautiously down at the big, ungainly birds. He was even more frightened of the ostriches than he was of Mary Gibson's ruthless black tomcat. He began to whimper in terror if Brock drove anywhere near the Gibsons' ranch yard.

Brock pulled through a barbed wire gate and got out to haul it shut behind him, thinking about ostriches and exotic game farms, dude ranches and wineries, all the things his neighbors were doing in an effort to operate their ranches at a profit.

Amanda had all kinds of suggestions for expanding his profit base, but they seemed harebrained and senseless to Brock. For instance, she talked about opening a bed-and-breakfast for rock hounds, buying a team of draft horses and offering hayrides to tourists, contacting Hollywood about using the ranch as a set for movies.

Nothing that had any practical merit, as far as Brock was concerned. But if he ever weakened and allowed her to go ahead with one of her schemes she'd probably muddle along in her usual haphazard manner and wind up making a million dollars the first year.

What an annoying woman, he thought ruefully, aching with loneliness and love for her. A single day had passed since she left, and already it felt like a year....

Alvin barked abruptly and Brock looked out, frowning at the sparse, rocky land where they were searching for a missing bull. "What is it, Alvin? Did you see him?"

Alvin barked again, jumping up and down on the dusty seat in an agitated fashion. He stared out the window, his ears raised alertly.

Brock gazed past the dog's ragged head and saw a solitary figure approaching from behind a stand of mesquite that crowned a rocky cliff.

"What the hell . . ." he muttered, parking the truck and sitting for a moment before he got out and started toward the man, with Alvin trotting aggressively at his side.

Brock watched the man descend the steep path. He felt tense and cautious, wondering what anybody could possibly be doing out on these barren acres of limestone. It was the most useless piece of land he owned, far removed from his ranch buildings and from any kind of grazing, and certainly not a scenic area for hiking. Brock seldom came here except in search of strays, like the big Angus bull that had gone missing over the weekend.

But on closer inspection, the trespasser didn't seem at all threatening. He wore faded jeans, hiking boots and a down-filled jacket, with a well-worn backpack resting against his shoulder blades. He was young and tanned, with curly, dark brown hair that glistened with ruddy highlights, a cheerful smile and eyes of sparkling hazel.

"Hello," Brock said, pausing with Alvin at his side and waiting for the stranger to introduce himself.

Alvin barked a couple of times, but made no move to leave the safety of Brock's side.

"Hello," the young man said with a smile. "I guess I'm trespassing."

"I guess you are," Brock agreed, but he liked the man's looks too much to be stern about it. "I'm Brock Munroe," he added, extending his hand.

"I'm Clint Farrell. Nice to meet you. You own this land, right?"

"Yeah, I do. Not that it's worth much. There's not even enough grass to run goats out here on this limestone."

"It's an unusual bit of territory, all right. Sorry about the trespassing," Clint added. "I got your name from the county office and tried to call a couple of times last week, but there was no answer."

"I'm not in the house much," Brock said, falling into step beside the young man and moving back toward his truck, while Alvin gazed up at them suspiciously.

"Your dog doesn't like me," Clint observed, reaching up to adjust his pack.

Alvin's ears pricked hopefully and he edged closer, his tail wagging.

Brock grinned. "Alvin's not a real great judge of character, Clint. He tends to like anybody who'll feed him."

Clint reached down to pat the dog's ears and then tore off a length of beef jerky from a cellophane pack he extracted from his pocket. When he handed it to Alvin, the dog's eyes widened in amazement.

Alvin fell to his haunches on the path, tearing at the spicy bit of meat. He growled low in his throat with pleasure, and his tail rotated like a windmill.

The two men laughed and moved off toward the truck again. "What were you saying," Brock asked after a brief silence, "about this being an unusual piece of territory?"

"The limestone mantle is almost fully exposed up here," the young man said. "There's not many places in the Hill Country where that's the case. It makes the terrain easier to study."

"I see. Why would anybody want to study this god-forsaken terrain?"

"Well, I'm involved in a branch of science known as speleology."

Brock grinned. "No kidding. And you think there's a cave under here somewhere?"

Clint Farrell looked in surprise at the rancher. "You know what a speleologist is?"

Brock nodded. "I read a lot," he said briefly.

It was his stock answer to questions like this, which he tended to encounter frequently. In fact, Brock Munroe was a voracious reader with wide-ranging interests, and his mind was stocked with an amazing fund of information on a great variety of topics.

The young man continued to look at him with lively interest for a moment, then smiled. "Well, you're right," he said at last. "I think there could be a cave under here, Mr. Munroe."

"Call me Brock. What makes you think so? I've never heard of caves around Crystal Creek, though I know they're scattered all over the Hill Country."

"This whole area is part of the Edwards Plateau, which was laid down over ninety million years ago from sedimentary limestone. There's caves everywhere in the region. The whole territory is essentially porous, like a huge sponge. It's just a matter of finding an entrance to the caverns that must be down there."

Brock looked at the younger man. "How do you go about doing that?"

Clint turned to smile at Alvin, who had trotted up behind them and was sniffing earnestly at the stranger's hiking boots.

"There are a few specific things to look for," he said, "if you want to find a cave entrance. A piece of exposed limestone like this is good, especially if it's an area that shows signs of extensive water erosion and quick runoff. I noticed after that rain we had last week that the water seemed to run out of here in a flash. It has to be going somewhere."

Brock looked around, fascinated. "And you think it's going underground? Into a cave system?"

"I think it probably is. I'd like to find the entrance. I hope you don't mind if I hike around and keep looking?"

Brock paused by his truck and opened the door. "I don't mind a bit. I'd sure appreciate it, though, if you'd come down to the house and let me know if you find anything."

Clint Farrell grinned, a sudden warm smile that lit up his boyish face and made his hazel eyes dance. "Brock," he said solemnly, "if I find a cave entrance up here, I'll tell the whole world about it. At least the whole scientific world," he added. "It'll be an incredible discovery."

Brock smiled back at him, then called sharply to Alvin, who was showing considerable reluctance to leave the young man's side. He sat near Clint, thumping his tail in the dusty path and looking with intense concentration at the pocket where the rest of the beef jerky was hidden.

"He's a real loyal dog," Brock said cheerfully. "Won't leave his master for anything. Get in the truck, Alvin," he added. "Move!"

Alvin's ears lowered and he hurried into the truck, giving Brock a reproachful glance as he scrambled up onto the seat.

Brock got in behind him and turned the key in the ignition, then looked out the window, resting his arm on the sill.

"Hey, Clint," he called to the young man, who was already turning away, preparing to hike back up the face of the cliff toward the mesquite. "Have you seen a big Angus bull out here anywhere? I had one break out of the corral a couple days ago, and I've been looking for him ever since."

"There's some kind of animal all by itself over to the west," Clint said, waving a hand in that direction. "I was looking at it through the binoculars a little while ago. It's too far away to make out details, but it could be a bull, I guess. It's standing near the windmill over there."

Brock nodded. "That's likely him. Thanks a lot," he called.

He watched as Clint toiled up the cliff face, setting his hiking boots carefully on the rocky path, his sturdy body full of purpose. Then Brock turned to grin at Alvin, who was regarding him suspiciously.

"Wanna play cowboys, Alvin? Let's go round up that pesky bull."

Alvin hated situations where strenuous action might be demanded of him. He gazed out the window, ignoring Brock with icy dignity. At last he settled on the vinyl seat and lowered his head onto his paws with a sigh of resignation as the truck bumped across the dusty trail toward the windmill.

CHAPTER TWO

ON THURSDAY AFTERNOON, Brock drove into Austin to pick up his Aunt Millicent at the airport. He would have liked to use the trip as an excuse to catch a glimpse of Amanda, maybe take her to lunch before Millie's plane landed. But Amanda had caught an early commuter flight to Dallas to attend a fashion show and wouldn't be back until evening.

Brock was startled by the change in his aunt's appearance when she came out into the reception area. Of course, he reminded himself, it had been years since he'd seen her. Back then her hair had been as dark as Amanda's, worn in a thick, heavy braid down her back so she looked like an Indian princess. Now it was mostly white, piled in a carelessly elegant fashion on top of her head.

Millicent Munroe was still erect and proud in her bearing, a striking woman with a chiseled face and wonderful dark eyes, wearing a long dress of Indian cotton and an impressive array of gorgeous silver and turquoise jewelery.

Brock smiled as she approached, feeling a surge of affection for her. Brock's mother had died when he was young and he'd had no brothers or sisters, just a haphazard upbringing by a hard-living, alcoholic father. He'd spent his life starved for family warmth and a mother's touch, and many of his fondest childhood memories were centered around this beautiful, eccentric sister of his father's. "Hi, Millie," he said gallantly, moving forward to gather her into his arms. "You look just beautiful. Haven't changed a bit."

"Liar," Millie said, pushing him away. She held him at arm's length and studied him, her face softening with affection. "You've turned out all right, I guess," she said in a grudging tone that belied the glow in her eyes. "You look a little the worse for wear, but sturdy."

"I'm real durable goods," Brock said good-naturedly. "Let's go get your luggage. Are you hungry, Millie? Want to grab a meal before we head for home?"

She shook her head. "I want to see the ranch. I want to go right now."

Something in her tone caught Brock's attention, a kind of restlessness that seemed coupled with a sudden look of bleak sadness in her eyes.

"Is anything wrong?" he asked.

"Of course not," she said crisply, as if the fleeting moment of sadness had never happened. "If you start fussing, boy, I'll rent a car and drive out there by myself. I do hate people who *fuss*."

Brock grinned. "Okay, I won't fuss," he promised, taking her arm and steering her toward the luggage carousel.

Millie, he thought with relief, was just the same as always. She hadn't changed at all.

But when they were in the truck heading back to the ranch, he recalled that strange mood and glanced cautiously at her withdrawn profile. Millie sat quietly with her hands in her lap, gazing out the window at the brown hills. "Must have been a hot summer," she said finally, not looking at him. "The hills look real dry."

"It was pretty hot. We've had a couple of good rains over the past week or two, though. Freshened things up a bit."

"What's been happening?" Millie asked. "What's everybody been doing?"

Brock searched his mind to tell her all the news, about the marriages in the McKinney family and Bubba Gibson's jail term, about the restoration of the town carousel and the new businesses that were springing up on local ranches.

"Who's dead?" she asked abruptly.

"Beg pardon, Millie?"

"Dead," she repeated impatiently. "People are always dying, aren't they? Somebody must have died since last time I was here."

"Well, Dottie Jones died of a heart attack last year, and old Hank Travis died this summer after he got to be a hundred years old, and—"

"A hundred years old," she interrupted, staring moodily at a field of placid Hereford cows. "God, imagine living for a hundred years."

Something about her words and manner was troubling to Brock, though he couldn't put his finger on it. "I think old Hank had a pretty good life," he ventured. "He always seemed to enjoy himself."

"He enjoyed complaining," Millie said. "He was the most ornery old devil I ever met, and I've met a few in my life." She was silent a moment, looking away so Brock couldn't see her face. "What's Virginia doing?" she asked finally.

"Don't you keep in touch? I thought you always wrote to Virginia."

"We used to write, but it kind of trailed off when I married Percy and we were overseas so much. I haven't heard from her for years. Is she still at the Double C?"

"Not anymore. She retired a few months ago."

"*Retired?*" Millie echoed in disbelief. "Virginia? That's hard to believe. She's only sixty."

"Well, she's not exactly sitting on the porch with her feet up. She moved into a little house in Crystal Creek and she's got a couple of girls living with her, sort of boarding there, I guess, so she's still got somebody to look after. She seems real happy."

Millie nodded without speaking. Brock gazed down the highway, concentrating on his driving as he pulled out around a truck hauling a long stock trailer filled with horses.

"How about you?" she asked finally. "What's new in your life?"

Brock thought about Amanda and felt his heart warm and soften.

"I see," Millie said briefly.

"What do you see?"

"I see that silly grin on your face. Gone and fallen in love, have you?"

"Yeah, Millie, I sure have. I've gone and fallen in love."

"My God, I hope you're not *married!*" his aunt said in sudden horror. "I never thought to ask. Is there some woman living out there at the ranch?"

"No, I'm not married. I have somebody in my life, but she lives in Austin and comes out to the ranch on weekends. Matter of fact, she'll be there tomorrow to meet you. Her name's Amanda Walker. She's a sort of fashion consultant. That means she..."

Millie waved a hand to cut him short, clearly not interested in the roles and functions of a fashion consultant. "She lives in Austin? Where?"

"In an apartment. But she spends a lot of time at the ranch. We've been—"

"Doesn't sound like much of a love life," Millie observed scornfully, letting her head fall back against the seat and closing her eyes. "Living in two different places and visiting on the weekends. Doesn't she want to marry you, or what?"

Brock hesitated, suddenly uncertain how much to tell his aunt about his personal life. "It's kind of... kind of complicated," he said lamely.

She snorted and turned away to examine the high stone gates of the Double C Ranch. "Look at that," she said. "J. T. McKinney's certainly got this place all spruced up, hasn't he?"

"The Double Bar's been spruced up a bit, too," Brock told his aunt modestly.

She turned sharply to look at him. "Spruced up? What do you mean?"

Brock shifted under her piercing gaze, feeling tense and uncomfortable. "Well, Amanda and I, we've been . . . remodeling the house," he said.

Millie continued to stare at him, her eyes darkening. "I see," she said at last in a toneless voice. "You and Amanda. Isn't that nice."

"There's the dude ranch," Brock said to distract her. "Remember, it used to be the old Kendall place?"

"Of course I remember," Millie said coldly. "Jim Kendall was crazy in love with me once upon a time," she added, her face softening briefly with a reminiscent smile. "And what's happened to it, did you say? It's a *dude* ranch?"

Brock nodded. "A lawyer from Austin bought it and rebuilt the whole thing. It's quite an operation, I guess. I've only been there a couple times for barbecues and such."

Millie observed the sleek modern buildings and shuddered with distaste. She turned to look at Brock and he was troubled again by that look of sorrow and grim despair in her remarkable eyes.

"If you've gone and changed the ranch house, Brock Munroe," she said with sudden passion, "I swear I'll never forgive you!" But when they arrived and Millie was shown around the old house, she had to confess that Brock and this unknown woman had done a fair job on the old place. They hadn't installed any modern atrocities like wall-to-wall carpeting or stippled ceilings, and there had been an obvious attempt to preserve the charm and character of the house.

In fact, Millie thought grudgingly as she moved about, touching the gleaming wood trim, studying the creamy plaster and polished floors, the house probably looked much the same as it had when it was first built, long before the Munroe family fell on hard times and gave it such rough usage over the years. Not that Millie was inclined to feel any more charitable to the unknown woman who'd invaded the ranch and imposed so much of her personality and taste on the home of Millie's childhood.

She has some nerve, Millie thought, fingering the new white muslin curtains in her own room and looking at the bouquets of tiny pink roses on the watered-silk wallpaper. *Coming into a place and acting as if she owns it, when she lives in the city doing something ridiculous for a living . . . .*

"Fashion consultant," she grumbled aloud to Alvin, who lingered cautiously near the door, keeping an anxious eye fixed on this formidable stranger. "What the hell is a *fashion consultant?* And why are you looking at me like that, you ugly creature? What are you staring at?''

She advanced on the fat dog, who tucked his tail between his legs and scuttled off with a terrified backward glance over his shoulder. Millie watched him tumble downstairs, wondering ruefully if she was really that frightening, then wandered back into the sunny bedroom where she'd spent her girlhood.

She stood gazing at herself in the old oval mirror on the oak washstand, and behind the softly wrinkled skin, the silver hair and aging body she saw the lovely girl she'd once been. It was a strange feeling, almost dreamlike, seeing herself against the background of her youth and beauty, her fiery courage and the lofty disdain she'd once had for any kind of human frailty.

With a sigh, Millie stripped off her long cotton dress and wandered into the little bathroom next door, carrying a robe over her arm.

The bathtub hadn't been changed, she noted with pleasure. They'd left the roomy old monstrosity, standing on its cast-iron claw legs, that had been Millie's bathtub all through her childhood. But the bathroom had been carefully restored in a green and white decor, wallpapered with lively peppermint stripes of rich forest green.

Millie looked around while the tub filled, studying the bright little room. Again she felt that strange mixture of grudging admiration for the woman's taste, and annoyance with her for daring to mess with the old ranch house.

Millie knew that she was being irrational, probably really unfair to Brock's sweetheart, but she couldn't help the way she felt. She lowered herself into the steaming tub and sighed, still thinking about Amanda Walker, whom she would meet tomorrow. Brock's fashionable city woman had wrought all kinds of changes in this house, and Millie knew that most of them were marked improvements.

But Millicent Munroe wasn't in the mood for change, not just now. In a world that was spinning far too rapidly, hurtling and lurching out of control, she wanted to feel that one thing was safe and serene, unchanging in the face of life and death....

Tentatively, Millie's fingers crept down and touched the swelling in her lower abdomen. She felt the same brief jolt of childlike disappointment that always shook her for a moment, and realized that she never stopped hoping it would somehow vanish, that one day she'd look for it and it would be gone, and this would all turn out to have been nothing more than a bad dream. But the swelling had been there for more than a month now, and it never went away. Millie ran her fingers over it with a kind of horrified fascination, trying to determine if it was any bigger. It was a soft, firm mass, yielding gently beneath her fingers, and it caused no pain when she touched it.

The lump still didn't hurt at all, Millie thought bitterly, sinking down in the bathtub and gazing with brooding eyes at a polished oak shelf on the opposite wall that held folded green towels and a basket of dainty white guest soaps. It didn't hurt, this lump in her abdomen, and yet Millie had never in all her life known such bewildering pain.

NEXT DAY, Millie rang the doorbell of Virginia Parks's cottage in Crystal Creek, then stood looking around at the shady yard with its yellow lawn swing and plant-filled terrace.

A nice little place, she thought. It suited Virginia, this house.

The door opened and Virginia stood there, beaming, her sweet blue eyes filled with joyous tears. "Millie!" she exclaimed. "It's really you! Come and let me give you a hug."

Smiling down at the small plump woman, Millie submitted to a warm hug. Virginia Parks was her oldest, dearest friend. Just the sight of her brought a wistful flood of emotion, memories of sunny long-ago days filled with girlish happiness. "Come inside," Virginia said with a breathless little laugh. "We're all dyeing."

"*What?*" Millie stopped in her tracks and stared down at her friend, her face draining of color. "What did you say, Ginny?"

"We're dyeing," Virginia said, holding out her hands to display large greenish-blue stains on her fingers. "Neale bought a packet of dye to do one of her cotton shirts, and then we all started finding things we wanted dyed. We're doing practically everything in the house."

Millie shook her head, still feeling dizzy and numb with shock. "Good Lord, you always were as crazy as a bedbug, Ginny," she told the woman with a shaky smile.

"It's teal blue," Virginia said breezily. "Amanda says it's going to be a big color this winter. We're just being really fashionable, that's all. Come on, Millie," she added, tugging at her friend's arm. "Come and meet the girls."

Millie allowed herself to be hauled into the sunny little house, following Virginia into a bright kitchen with an adjoining laundry room, where two young women stood next to an opened washing machine that was steaming gently.

One of the girls was slim and quick-moving, with shining light brown hair hanging to her shoulders. She wore blue jeans and a ragged college sweatshirt. The other, in a purple silk caftan, was plump and had a beautiful face. Her dark hair was pulled smoothly back from her face, tied with a purple ribbon, and she wore huge gold hoop earrings. Both girls had their sleeves pushed back, and were stained blue all the way to their elbows.

"Millie, this is Neale Cameron," Virginia said, indicating the girl with the light brown hair. "She's a writer."

Millie looked at the girl with interest, liking the direct gaze of her dark eyes and the easy warmth of her smile. "Hello, Neale," she said. "Did you know your elbows are blue?"

Neale grinned, holding up her slim arms. "It's a pretty color, isn't it? Hey, Marj, should we do our bathing suits?"

The dark-haired girl frowned thoughtfully, then smiled at Millie as Virginia drew her forward. "Marjorie Perez," Virginia said. "Girls, this is Millie Munroe, my dearest friend."

Both young women nodded and murmured greetings, then turned around in alarm as the washing machine began to agitate, sending little blue sprays of hot water bubbling into the air.

"Don't let any of that splash out on the floor," Virginia warned. "We'll never be able to scrub it off." She hesitated, looking with interest at the loaded washing machine. "Neale, are the sitting room curtains in there?"

Neale nodded. "And the rug from the upstairs bathroom. We thought that since it was pink to start with, it might turn a really interesting shade of mauve, or something."

"Or something," Virginia echoed ruefully, but she was smiling as she led Millie back into the kitchen. "They make me feel young again," she confided, settling her friend at the table and rummaging in the cupboard for her teapot. "They're so much fun."

"Where did you find them, Ginny?"

"Well, Marjorie came to town to take a job as Martin Avery's secretary, and..."

"Brock told me he married his other secretary," Millie said with a grin. "Who'd have thought it? Martin Avery, the original button-down man, marrying a girl young enough to be his granddaughter.''

"Not quite. Besides, they're very happy together," Virginia said. "Everybody was a little horrified at first, but it's working out really well.''

"I'll have to see it to believe it," Millie said dryly. "So," she prompted, "this girl came to town to be his secretary..."

"And she was looking for a place to live. That was just after I'd moved to my house, and I'd been planning to take in some boarders anyway, so it worked out just perfectly. Marjorie is a lovely girl.''

"And the other one? The writer?''

"She's Marjorie's best friend from college. She's very talented," Virginia added in a lower tone. "She writes articles for big national magazines.''

"Really?" The kettle began to sing and Millie watched as her friend crossed the kitchen to make their tea.

"Really. But Neale's been going through some hard times lately. Her father died after a battle with cancer that cleaned the family out, used up all their savings, and she's been trying to help her mother get back on her feet. Poor girl, it's a lot of responsibility for someone so young.''

"So you're letting her live here rent-free, I suppose," Millie said in a humorous tone, though she was still a little shaken by the story of the young girl's father dying of cancer.

Virginia shook her head, smiling. "No, I'm not. I offered, but she wouldn't hear of it. Neale wants to pay her way. I don't know how she manages, but she does," Virginia added, frowning. "She even writes articles for the *Claro Courier,* anything she can find to bring in a few dollars, and then I'm sure she sends most of it home to her mother."

At that moment the two girls entered the kitchen and looked hopefully at the teapot.

"The machine's rinsing now," Neale announced. "Pretty soon we'll be able to see how everything turned out."

"I'm worried about my rayon blouse," Marjorie said with a brooding expression. "Can you dye rayon?" she asked Millie.

Millie shook her head. "I'm afraid I don't know much about dyeing," she said, feeling a cold little stab of terror when she heard her own words.

Virginia smiled and put cups out on the table, then hurried back to boil another kettle of water. "Millie's had a really interesting life," she told the girls over her shoulder. "Her second husband was a foreign ambassador, wasn't he, Millie?"

Both young women looked at her with interest, and Millie nodded. "We lived in a lot of different countries. Then we retired to a chicken farm in Oregon and had a few peaceful years before Percy died."

"Do you live there all alone now?" Marjorie asked, her blue eyes gentle with sympathy.

"Except for the chickens," Millie said with a smile. "My neighbor's looking after them while I'm away." Her smile broadened as she turned to Virginia. "Remember Mr. Willard's chicken coop, Ginny?"

Virginia giggled. "We smoked our very first cigarettes in there," she told Neale and Marjorie. "It was so stuffy and hot, and the chickens kept squawking and flying all over the place, dropping feathers on us. To this day, the smell of cigarette smoke makes me feel hot and sticky."

"You were always such a Goody Two-shoes," Millie said, giving her friend a fond, scornful glance. "You wouldn't even try that bottle of whiskey when I swiped it from Daddy's liquor cabinet, remember? I had to drink it all alone, and I got so sick."

"Millie was a terrible influence," Virginia said with a dreamy smile. "She taught me everything I knew, back in those days."

"And God knows, that wasn't much," Millie said, smiling at the girls. "It's incredible to think how sophisticated we felt, and how innocent we actually were."

Virginia carried a plate of fresh oatmeal cookies to the table, and both young women fell on them enthusiastically.

"Virginia makes the *best* cookies," Neale told Millie solemnly.

"How long are you staying, Millie?" Virginia sat down and poured tea all around.

Millie shrugged. "I don't know. I just...I had a hankering to see the old place one more time," she added, with another bitter twist of pain in her heart. "But it's not the same. The house is all spoiled."

"Oh, Millie, don't say that. Amanda's done such a good job on that old house. I think it looks marvelous."

"What house is that?" Marjorie asked.

"Brock Munroe's ranch house. He and his girlfriend have been restoring it, and the place looks just wonderful."

"I think *Brock Munroe* looks just wonderful," Marjorie said wistfully. "I love those rugged, handsome guys who look like they need some tender loving care."

Millie snorted. "He's my nephew," she explained to Marjorie. "I remember when he rode a stick horse around the ranch yard. It's a little hard to think of him as an object of desire."

"Well, he must have something to offer. His girlfriend is the classiest lady in the whole county," Neale observed, gazing at the plate of cookies. "Should I have another one?"

"Of course you should," Millie said, beginning to relax and enjoy herself in the warm, friendly atmosphere of Virginia's kitchen. "You're just skin and bones, child."

She paused, watching as Neale gave her a shy smile and selected another cookie.

"What's so classy about Brock's girlfriend?" Millie asked after a brief silence.

"She's gorgeous," Marjorie said with another sigh. "She's tiny and graceful, and she dresses with such flair, and she has this wonderful pearly complexion and short dark hair. . . . When I stand next to her, I always feel like my hem's dragging and my makeup's smudged, and I'm at least two years out-of-date."

Millie shuddered. "She sounds awful."

"Well, she isn't," Virginia said firmly. "She's a very nice person. Everybody likes Amanda, don't they, girls? I can't imagine," she added with a frown, "why Brock doesn't just marry her and move her out to the ranch as soon as he can. Somebody's going to steal her away if he doesn't hurry up."

Millie looked unconvinced. "How's everything over at the Double C?" she asked, deliberately changing the subject. "I hear there's been a lot going on out there. Weddings and such."

Virginia smiled. "There certainly has. It was all real interesting, but Lord, it's been tiring, working there these past two years. I'm so happy to be retired."

"J.T. got married again, did he?"

"Yes, and they have a little girl just a year old. Jennifer Travis, they called her."

"I still can't believe it," Millie said. "J. T. McKinney's just a few years younger than I am, and he's starting over with a whole new family."

Virginia smiled at her friend. "It just goes to prove that we're not all that old, Millie. We've got lots of good years ahead of us."

"Do we?" Millie asked, staring into the depths of her teacup while the others around the table exchanged troubled glances.

"So, how's Brock feeling these days?" Virginia asked, her voice deliberately bright. "I never see the boy anymore. He and Alvin used to drop out to the Double C for a visit every now and then, but since I moved to town we've hardly had the chance to say hello."

"Alvin!" Millie said with contempt. "What an animal *that* is. He's got a face only a mother could love, that dog."

Neale chuckled. "The other day when I was in the drugstore, Alvin slipped in behind Brock and pulled out the corner bottle in a display of shampoo. One of those pyramid things, you know?"

She looked at the others, who nodded, smiling and waiting for the rest of the story.

"The whole thing came crashing down," Neale went on. "It made the most awful noise, like bombs falling. Poor Alvin was just terrified. He ran and hid under the candy counter, and Brock had to get down on his hands and knees to coax him out. I think Alvin knew that Mr. Wall was ready to kill him."

"Born to trouble," Millie said sadly. "Brock's all right," she added in response to Virginia's question. "Just real busy. The place seems so different now. I guess running a ranch is a pretty complicated business these days.''

"It's getting more complicated all the time," Virginia said. "Did you know that the Gibsons are raising ostriches?"

Millie grimaced. "I've seen them. And there's some scientist wandering around on Brock's property, looking for caves or something.... It's all so strange."

"Caves?" Neale asked, suddenly alert. "What caves?"

Millie shook her head. "God knows. I never heard of any caves around Crystal Creek. But Brock says he met a young fellow out in his east pasture...you know that rocky bit of limestone over at the edge of the ranch?" she asked Virginia.

The other woman nodded and poured more tea.

"Well, this fellow says he's looking for a cave entrance out there."

"What's his name?" Neale asked. "The cave hunter, I mean."

Millie frowned, trying to remember. "Farrell," she said at last. "Clark Farrell, something like that?"

"Clint Farrell," Marjorie corrected the older woman, her pretty face brightening. Marjorie clearly took a lively interest in the young men of the region. "Martin introduced me to him last week in the coffee shop. He's staying at the dude ranch," she told Neale. "And he's just the most yummy thing you've ever seen. Hazel eyes, dark curly hair, gorgeous tan..."

Neale grimaced, obviously not the least bit concerned with Clint Farrell's appearance. "What makes him think there's a cave entrance out there?" she asked, turning back to Millie. "Has anybody ever talked about it before?"

"Not in my lifetime. But this fellow is apparently college-trained, and knows what he's doing. I forget what Brock called him. A spellist, something like that?"

"Speleologist," Neale said absently, her dark eyes looking faraway and thoughtful. "I wonder..." she began slowly.

"Wonder what, dear?" Virginia asked.

"I wonder if there's a story in this somewhere."

Marjorie giggled. "You see stories in everything," she told her friend with a teasing smile. "Not that I'd mind interviewing the man for you," she added. "Just say the word."

Neale continued to gaze at the other girl with an absent look, then shook her head and got to her feet. "The machine's stopped," she announced. "Come, on, Marj, let's see what we've got."

Laughing breathlessly, the two girls hurried into the laundry room and began to remove dripping masses of blue-green fabric from the washing machine, while Millie and Virginia sipped their tea in the sunlight and smiled across the table at each other.

CHAPTER THREE

BEVERLY TOWNSEND SAT on the couch in Amanda's glamorous city apartment, sipping a diet cola and leafing through a magazine.

Amanda smiled at her friend, who looked as beautiful as ever in her slim leather pants and sweater. Beverly had been through a lot in the past year, and it showed in the shadows on her face and the new maturity in her eyes. But, Amanda thought fondly, the woman was never going to lose her interest in fashion and appearance.

"Are you and Brock doing anything for Halloween, Mandy?"

Amanda grimaced. "I can't even stand to think about Halloween. We've been so busy these past few weeks working on costumes, you wouldn't believe it."

In fact, all of Amanda's seamstresses were up to their elbows in silk and velvet, leather and fur and plastic, making outfits for the Halloween parties that would be happening across the city next weekend.

"You're busy all the time," Beverly complained. "I never see you anymore."

"I guess that's true. Bev, I hardly know what to do about my business. It's all getting so crazy." Amanda took a sweater from the pile of clothes next to Beverly, folded it and put it in her suitcase, feeling troubled.

Sometimes it was difficult for her to grasp just how much her little businesses had grown. She felt like the old woman in the shoe, with a brace of unruly offspring pulling her in all directions.

The Halloween orders alone were going to bring in a tidy profit. Then, when November came, most of the seamstresses would be turning their attention to costumes for the production of the *Phantom of the Opera,* while Amanda would be busy with a couple of buying trips to New York and discussions with clients about their winter and holiday outfits. The final-quarter profits were going to be incredible.

She should give the seamstresses a raise, Amanda thought absently, considering the neat pile of sweaters and jeans on the couch.

Her employees worked so hard and cheerfully, and they were all so talented. And they had to put in such long hours, because nobody had ever expected the orders to pour in like this. Especially not Amanda, who was supposed to be in charge of the whole operation....

While Amanda was packing, Beverly got off the couch and wandered into the kitchen to peer into the refrigerator.

"Hey," she said with enthusiasm, "look at all the fruit in here!" Beverly was spending the weekend at Amanda's apartment, while attending a two-day semi-

nar on the organization of play activities for children
in hospital.

"I knew you were coming," Amanda said, following her friend to the doorway and smiling at her. "And
I could hardly bake a cake, could I? I'm too busy, and
you're always dieting."

"Not anymore," Beverly said. "I just can't seem to
gain weight since Jeff . . ."

Her voice trailed off, while Amanda watched in
helpless sympathy.

"So," Beverly said briskly after a moment, breaking off a small cluster of grapes and giving Amanda a
glance over her shoulder. "Are you looking forward to
a weekend with your sweetie?"

"I sure am." Amanda sighed, thinking about the
blissful weekend ahead.

No client appointments, no flying trips to Houston
or Dallas or Corpus Christi, no fittings or consulta-
tions with fashion buyers. Just sunshine and cattle,
friendly breakfasts and cozy evenings by the fire with
Brock and Alvin. . . .

"And Millicent," she muttered aloud.

"Hmm? Have a grape, Mandy. They're really deli-
cious."

"Thanks. I was thinking about Brock's Aunt Millicent. Did you ever meet her, Bev?"

"Oh, sure, about a hundred years ago, I guess. From
all accounts, she's a real character."

"So I've heard." Amanda frowned, thinking about
Brock's houseguest.

"Have you talked to her?"

"No, I haven't talked to Brock since she arrived. My flight from Dallas yesterday was delayed about six times, and it was too late to call him by the time I got home."

"He left a message, though, didn't he?"

Amanda nodded, still frowning. Brock's message on her answering machine had been noncommittal, telling her only that Millicent had arrived and that they were all looking forward to Amanda's visit on Friday.

But Amanda, who loved the man so much that she could almost feel his heartbeat across a crowded room, had sensed something troubling in his voice on the tape. There had been a cautious note that disturbed her, made her wonder if everything was all right out there at the ranch.

She shook her head to dismiss the wayward thoughts, smiling at her own foolishness. Brock Munroe was a grown man, thirty-five years old, and he certainly didn't need her constant protection. But the thought of him being sad or worried was almost more than she could bear.

Beverly was watching her in silence. "You really love the guy, don't you?" she murmured. "I mean, you're just nuts about him, right?"

Amanda hesitated, feeling uncomfortable. Like any woman in love, she longed to talk with her friend about the man she adored. But Beverly's loss was so new and terrible, it didn't seem right somehow for Amanda to flaunt her own happiness.

"Look, it's okay," Beverly said, clearly reading her thoughts. "Truly it is. I don't mind if you talk about him. It's not going to bring Jeff back if everybody's careful not to be happy around me, you know. I like to hear you talk about Brock. Now, sit down for a minute and tell me what's happening."

Beverly moved back to her seat on the couch and Amanda followed, sinking into the armchair near the open suitcase.

"Sometimes it really scares me, Bev," she said at last, her voice low and troubled. "I love him so much. When we're together, the feelings are so powerful that I feel ... kind of small, you know? Like a person trapped in a volcano, or something."

Beverly nodded and munched grapes with a faraway look. "I know," she said softly.

"I've never felt like this," Amanda went on. "It's like there's no ... no edges to it, you know? No boundaries or safe limits. Whenever I see him again, even if it's just been a few hours, as soon as he touches me and kisses me, I'm lost. It's like drowning."

Suddenly embarrassed by her confession, Amanda got up and returned to her packing, wishing she hadn't said so much.

She'd always prided herself on being a rational, controlled woman, fully in command of her emotions, and she couldn't quite adjust to this kind of wild passion. It was troubling and confusing, like the sudden overwhelming growth of her business. She didn't know what to do with either force in her life, how to bring things back under control so she didn't feel dazed and troubled all the time.

But Amanda had a strong sense that what she needed most of all was simply for her and Brock to be married. Once that simple thing was accomplished, she had a feeling that everything else would fall into place. She'd know who she was and where she belonged in the world, and she could plan her future with a renewed sense of continuity and security.

When they were finally married, she could put Brock and the ranch first, and let the business find its own place in her life. She wouldn't have this sensation of spinning out of control, drifting crazily around the edges of Brock's existence like some bizarre satellite with an unpredictable orbit. She and Brock would be together at the center of things, solid and firm, and everything else in their lives would be secondary to their love and concern for each other.

Beverly was eyeing her thoughtfully, and Amanda was suddenly afraid of what her friend might say. But Beverly surprised her by switching the conversation back to the topic of Brock's houseguest.

"I'll bet," she commented thoughtfully, smoothing the magazine on her knees, "that Millie's giving poor Brock a hard time."

"Why?" Amanda asked, staring at her. "Why would she be giving him a hard time?"

"Why, about getting married," Beverly said calmly. "I reckon Brock and Millie have already had a couple of serious discussions on the subject. After all, that's what our mamas and our aunties like to talk about, isn't it?''

"My mother sure likes to talk about it," Amanda said dryly. "She's always pestering me about my relationship, dropping little hints and remarks about the importance of building a stable future, and asking about Brock and his 'plans.' It drives me crazy. Especially," she added, suddenly gloomy, "when Brock doesn't seem to have any plans to speak of.''

"He's got plans, honey," Beverly said gently. "He just needs a little push, is all. And who knows? Millie might be the one to provide it."

Amanda's spirits rose as she contemplated this prospect. It would be so wonderful to have somebody on her side, working to overcome Brock's inexplicable reluctance to get married. Just the thought of it was enough to give her a flood of affection for the unknown woman at the ranch.

She finished packing, hugged her friend and gave last-minute instructions about the apartment, then hurried out the door and down to the car, almost giddy with happiness as she looked forward to the weekend and the thought of seeing Brock in less than an hour.

AMANDA DROVE through the gates and up to the ranch house, her throat dry and tight with yearning, her hands trembling on the wheel. Alvin waited on the porch, gazing earnestly at the driveway. He tumbled down the steps to greet her in the gathering darkness, barking crazily with excitement.

Amanda laughed softly and knelt to hug him. "Alvin," she whispered, smiling at the dog, who was jumping up to lick her face. "Alvin, it's so nice to see you again, sweetie. Were you lonely without me? Were you..."

She paused, wrinkling her nose in distaste, suddenly aware that Alvin didn't smell at all pleasant. In fact, his body exuded a ripe, foul odor that made her eyes water.

"Phew!" Amanda muttered, holding the wriggling furry dog at arm's length. "Alvin, what on earth have you been doing with yourself?"

"He got into something rotten up in the pasture by the Gibsons' place," Brock commented unexpectedly from behind her. "He came home just before supper smelling like a landfill, and I haven't had time to give him a bath."

Amanda got to her feet and smiled at the rancher, her heart pounding crazily.

"Hi there," she whispered, loving the way the starlight glimmered on the fine tanned planes of his face, the way his body looked so lean and strong in the worn denim clothes, the way his teeth flashed when he smiled at her....

"Hi yourself," he murmured, reaching for her. "What's a classy girl like you doing out here with a poor old cowboy and a smelly dog?"

Amanda moved into his arms with a sigh of relief and a blessed feeling of homecoming. "I'd rather be here," she told him simply, "than anywhere else on earth."

Brock kissed her hungrily, running his hands over her body with a rising passion that left them both breathless and shaken. "What shall we do first?" he whispered in her ear. "Shall we give Alvin a bath, or go say hello to Millie, or make love right here in the dirt?"

"Let's make love right here in the dirt," Amanda said recklessly, making him laugh aloud.

"What a woman." He leaned back to grin at her. "She's just an animal. And she always used to be so prim and ladylike."

"See what you've done to me?" Amanda smiled back at him and reached up to kiss the brown column of his throat, right below the chin, where his skin was unexpectedly smooth and silky. "You know, considering how badly I've been corrupted, the very least you could do is..."

She caught herself on the verge of saying that the least he could do was marry her and make an honest woman of her. But Brock always grew tense and silent when she mentioned the subject of marriage, even in teasing, and she'd learned not to do it.

"What?" he asked, bending to peer at her face in the darkness. "What's the least I can do?"

"You can take me to bed and make me feel better," Amanda told him. "It's been a long week, darling. I've missed you so much."

"Okay. Let's go to bed. We can bath that dog in the morning. Serves him right to have to live with himself all night, anyhow,'' he added, glaring at Alvin, who hovered uncertainly near the car.

"I think he probably likes the way he smells," Amanda said thoughtfully, watching as Brock hefted her suitcase from the back seat. "Probabl~ that's like good cologne to him."

"Eau de garbage," Brock agreed with a chuckle.

Arms entwined, they moved off toward the lighted expanse of the ranch house. Alvin trailed at their heels, his head and tail drooping, miserably conscious of his disgrace.

"Well, you're about to meet my aunt," Brock said. "That's a real experience, honey."

"What's she like?" Amanda asked, hugging him with pleasure as they walked. "Is she the way you remembered her?"

Brock frowned and paused near the veranda, looking down at her in the shadow of a pecan tree by the house. "I don't know," he muttered. "She seems pretty much the same, but there's something about her...."

Once again she was aware of that strange troubled note in his voice. "What, Brock?" Amanda whispered, leaning close to him. "What's wrong?"

"I don't know," he repeated helplessly. "Maybe I'm just imagining things. You'd better meet her and judge for yourself."

Amanda nodded and moved toward the veranda steps, but he caught her arm and drew her back into the darkened pool of shade beneath the big tree. "Sweetheart," he said cautiously, "before you go in there, I should warn you about Millie."

"What about her?"

Brock's face was hard to see in the darkness, but she could feel the tension of his body. "Millie's a little . . . eccentric," he said.

"I know that, Brock. You've told me all about the wild exploits of her youth. I think she sounds wonderful."

"Well, she's always been pretty wonderful, all right. But she's different now, somehow. She seems . . . kind of irritable and upset about things. She never used to be that way."

His tension communicated itself to Amanda, and she gave him a quick glance. "Really? What kind of things is she upset about?"

Brock shifted awkwardly on his feet and moved the suitcase to his other hand. "I guess I'd better just let you meet her," he repeated finally. "Come on, sweetheart. But don't take her too seriously. She doesn't even mean half the things she says."

Amanda gave him a brief smile and climbed the steps. "Your aunt sounds as terrifying as old Hank Travis used to be."

Brock grinned back at her, his face illuminated by the soft glow from the living room windows. "Yeah," he agreed in a hushed whisper. "Sometimes she is."

Alvin had retreated beneath one of the wicker chairs on the porch. They could see his eyes shining from the depths as they passed, looking sad and humble even in the darkness.

They entered the house, and Amanda summoned a bright smile when she saw the silver-haired woman seated by the hearth. Millicent Munroe stood up, turning to them with a cool, enquiring glance.

Amanda gazed at the woman, surprised by her appearance. She realized that after hearing all of Brock's stories, and knowing that Millie now lived on a farm, she'd been half expecting her to be a weathered, hardbitten cowgirl type, a kind of elderly Calamity Jane.

But Millie Munroe was beautiful, with fine sculpted features, flashing dark eyes and a regal bearing. She wore a dressing gown of pearl-gray quilted satin that shimmered in the firelight, adding to her queenly appearance.

Of course, Amanda thought in confusion, Brock's aunt was no backwoods countrywoman. Her second husband had been an ambassador in Spain and France, and she'd dined with heads of state from all over the world. How silly Amanda had been to expect something so different! She should have been prepared for an impressive personage like this, and then she wouldn't be standing and gaping like an idiot....

"What a lovely robe," Amanda said shyly. "The color is perfect on you."

"I suppose that's high praise, coming from an expert in the field."

The words were cordial enough, but there was something in Millie's tone that chilled Amanda. With

a woman's sure instinct for the nuances of relationships, she realized in hurt amazement that Brock's aunt
didn't like her at all.

Amanda turned to him. Brock, a sensitive and per-
ceptive man, also seemed uncomfortably aware of the
undercurrents swirling through the room. He moved
forward, still carrying the suitcase, and smiled cheerfully at both women.

"Amanda, this is my aunt Millicent. Millie, this is
Amanda Walker, the woman I love." He came close to
Amanda and put his free arm around her shoulders.
She leaned against him, intensely grateful for his pres-
ence and support.

"How do you do?" Millicent said with exaggerated
courtesy. "I feel that I know you already," she added,
giving Amanda another of those level, appraising
glances. "After all, I've seen so much evidence of you
around here."

Amanda gazed back at her, chilled and puzzled.

"The decorating," Millie said, waving a glittering,
ringed hand at the old house. "Your touch is everywhere, isn't it?"

Amanda continued to stare at the silver-haired
woman, searching for words.

So that was it, she thought.

Millie didn't like the house being tampered with, especially by some upstart that she'd never met. These
old Texas families were so predictable, Amanda told
herself wearily. Their roots were so deep and solid, and
there was no way to penetrate the solid wall of their

defenses. You could marry into one of these families and fifty years later you'd still be considered a newcomer.

Like Cynthia McKinney, she thought with sympathy, recalling the struggles the woman from Boston had been having over there at the Double C. But Cynthia was weathering the storm, gradually making a place for herself just by being pleasantly firm and refusing to be intimidated.

And if she could do it, so could Amanda.

She lifted her chin and met the woman's gaze steadily, trying not to quail before the anger and dislike that glittered deep in those remarkable dark eyes.

"I've tried to keep the house very authentic," she said calmly. "I think all the things Brock and I have done have been improvements, and have been in keeping with historical accuracy."

"The younger generation always thinks change is an improvement," Millie observed, bending gracefully to pick up the book she'd been reading. "It's not always so, of course, but what can we older folks do about it, if you all just keep running roughshod over our wishes and values?"

Amanda stared at her, stunned by her abrupt manner and the unfairness of her words. With a wry smile, she thought about the foolish daydreams she'd been entertaining ever since she heard about Millie's upcoming visit. She'd actually pictured this woman forming an alliance with her, imagined cozy woman-talk in the kitchen and all kinds of gentle pressure on Brock to make his situation permanent....

"Millie," Brock said with a cold edge to his voice, "you're not being fair to Amanda. What she says is absolutely true. This old place was falling down around our ears, and something had to be done with it. In fact, I'd started on the renovations before I even met her. Amanda just put a whole lot of time and effort into doing the job right."

Millicent ignored him. "I'm going to bed," she announced, taking her book and moving toward the door, her silvery gown trailing behind her. "I hope you two don't plan to be up half the night. I'm a very light sleeper." And with that ominous warning she mounted the stairs and vanished from their sight.

AN HOUR LATER, Brock and Amanda were cautiously preparing for bed in his comfortable book-lined room on the main floor. Amanda sat on the bed and watched in silence as Brock lifted the suitcase up beside her and began to strip off his shirt.

But tonight she couldn't take her usual pleasure in the sight of his lean, muscular body, the breadth of his shoulders and the black hair curling densely on his chest.

"Brock," she whispered, "do you think this is a good idea?"

"What do you mean?"

"I mean...us sharing a bedroom like this," Amanda murmured awkwardly, her cheeks flaming.

"Yeah." He grinned at her as he unzipped his jeans and stepped out of them, then tugged off his socks. "I think it's a great idea, sweetheart."

"But she said she's a light sleeper. She was very deliberate about it. Maybe I should..." Amanda hesitated, looking down at her folded hands. "Maybe I should sleep upstairs in the other guest room. She's probably listening."

"Let's not talk about her anymore, honey. I'm tired of talking about her."

"But she hates me, Brock!"

"She doesn't hate you. I told you, she's just acting a little strange right now. She'll come around in a day or two. After all, how could anybody know you and not love you?"

"Oh, Brock, you just don't..."

He stood in front of her and gripped her shoulders, his nearly naked body gleaming softly in the lamplight. "Amanda," he said gently, reaching down to unbutton her shirt.

She still refused to look at his face, concentrating instead on the hard, flat abdomen that was just in front of her. But that was a mistake, because the sight of his body made her weak with desire, ready to forget all about the stranger in the house and fling herself on him with reckless hunger.

He touched her hair, then pulled her gently forward so her face was pressed against his bare skin.

"Amanda, I live for these nights with you," he whispered huskily. "I couldn't bear to have you under the same roof and not be close to you. I want you here in my bed.''

Then marry me! Amanda thought in anguish. *Marry me and make it real, so people like that awful woman can't look at me sideways and imply that I've got no right to be with you in this house....*

But she didn't say anything, just burrowed closer to him and tried to keep from crying. After a moment, the nearness of him began to work its sweet magic and she gave him a misty smile, pressed her lips against his skin, began to tease him gently with her tongue. He shifted his weight and pulled her closer, groaning with desire, his muscles tensed as she continued to caress him. The moon climbed higher in the autumn sky, Alvin barked fitfully on the veranda a few times, and before long the two people in the dimly lighted bedroom had forgotten completely about the strange, hostile woman upstairs.

WHILE BROCK AND AMANDA were renewing their love by the soft glow of lamplight, and Millie was lying sleepless in her room, gazing at the stars beyond the muslin curtains, Clint Farrell was also wide awake and not too far away from the Munroe ranch house.

He lay in his sleeping bag atop an air mattress on the expanse of rocky limestone, watching for bats.

Clint had spent a lot of time hiking and exploring on Brock Munroe's land, and this wasn't the first night he'd slept out on the limestone, huddled contentedly in the warmth of his sleeping bag. He could still remember his elation the first time he'd seen one of the tiny winged creatures flitting past in the glow of his lantern while he lay propped on one elbow, studying his research notes.

The presence of bats was the surest indication of a large underground cavern somewhere beneath this barren piece of land. There wasn't enough tree cover to provide adequate roosting for the little nocturnal creatures, and no other caves or shelters in the limestone that Clint could discover. If the bats were present at night in any numbers, then they must be flying off before the first light of dawn into a hidden cave beneath the level of the rock and cactus. Clint intended to let the bats lead him to the entrance of that cave. As he lay tensely in the darkness, he could almost hear the beating of tiny wings overhead. A swarm of bats was passing above him in a small cloud, heading south, swooping and feeding on insects as they went.

He caught his breath, staring upward at the dark mass of them against the starlit sky, gripped by a wave of anticipation that left him breathless with excitement. A bat colony the size of this was indisputable proof that he was right about the underground cave.

He set the alarm on his wristwatch to wake him a few hours after midnight, then nestled down in his nylon bag, oblivious to cold and discomfort, preparing to sleep until the predawn hours, when the bats would be returning to their shelter.

Clint fell into a fitful sleep, troubled by restless dreams about a woman he didn't know. He couldn't see her face or form, just the essence of her. She was slim and laughing, graceful and quick-moving as sunlight on water, and he had never wanted anything as much in his life as he wanted to hold her. But she turned and drifted away, her eyes smiling a promise while she vanished. Clint stumbled after her, shouting in anguish, feeling his heart being torn from him as she whirled off into the distance with a peal of silvery laughter and left him standing with cold empty arms.

HE WOKE before his alarm sounded, still chilled by misery and loneliness, and looked around at the silent darkness, where stars glittered like pale sentinels in the vast black sky above him. The stillness was deep and eerie, almost palpable in its intensity. The crescent moon that had hovered above the cliffs earlier was gone now, leaving the stars at their most brilliant.

Clint lay in his sleeping bag, thinking about the woman with the shining eyes.

He liked women, and had enjoyed casual, friendly relationships with many of the girls he'd known at college. A few of those friendships had grown serious for a while, and once or twice he'd even imagined himself in love, but something always happened to make him feel disappointed or disillusioned. And, he had to admit, he was usually so involved in his research and exploration that he had difficulty sustaining a relationship for any length of time.

The years had passed swiftly while he was exploring caves in Mexico and South America and traveling to the Austrian Alps to visit the world's deepest caves, endless icebound chambers honeycombed within the vastness of the mountain range. Now he was closer to thirty than twenty, and sometimes he felt a profound, wrenching yearning for someone to share his life and be his partner in work and love.

But no woman had ever made him feel like the woman in his dream, with her laughing sweetness and tantalizing, quicksilver movements. She was the essence of everything he desired in a mate, that unknown woman. Clint realized that his body was still taut and aching with sexual desire. He gave a rueful smile in the darkness.

"Bats, old boy," he muttered aloud, reaching to turn off the alarm on his watch. "You're supposed to be thinking about bats."

He rolled out of the sleeping bag and stretched in the starry darkness, then ran in place a little to get his circulation going. His sturdy, muscular body was already fully clothed except for hiking boots, which he laced on swiftly, casting a worried glance at the starlight, which was beginning, almost imperceptibly, to flicker and grow pale.

As if on cue, tiny creatures began to fly overhead, diving and swooping. This time Clint could actually hear the soft beating of their wings, accompanied by a chorus of clicks and squeaks as they passed. He tugged on his jacket, grabbed a handful of trail mix, a jug of cold tea and a lantern. Then he began to follow the swarm, heading off to the north over the rocky, treacherous ground.

There was no way he could keep up with the bats. But earlier they'd come from the north and now were heading back that way, so his area of search was narrowed considerably. And if he kept alert and moved quickly enough, he might be able to get an idea where the stragglers were disappearing before the sun came up.

Hours later, Clint was several miles to the north of his camp, still searching but well satisfied with his day's work, though he hadn't even had breakfast yet. He knew where he was going to concentrate his search, and was confident that he'd discover the cave entrance within the next day or two.

Now that he was in the right area, there would be lots of clues to guide him to the actual cave entrance. Runoff patterns, depressions in the terrain, the presence of cave crickets... all kinds of things would signal the nearness of a cave. Of course, the entrance could easily turn out to be a vertical drop of five or six hundred feet, impassable even to the most experienced cavers, and all this effort would be wasted. But that was part of the excitement of his quest.

Clint's stomach began to rumble in protest and he turned back reluctantly toward his camp, glancing at his watch. He probably had time to pick up his belongings and shift camp before noon. Then he could spend the rest of the day searching for the entrance. But he couldn't sleep out another night. He had to get back to the dude ranch tonight and restock his provisions.

Clint frowned in sudden thoughtfulness as he swung off across the sunlit limestone with a long, practiced stride, watching automatically for cactus spines and loosened rock.

It was expensive staying at the dude ranch, and the money from his research grant was going to run out soon. Clint had a good deal of his own money, part of the legacy from his parents. It was invested carefully in stocks and bonds, and he could always use it if necessary. But he shied away from the thought of touching that money.

The funds from his inheritance were to be used when he finally settled down, took a job somewhere teaching and doing research, assumed a mortgage and the other responsibilities of adulthood. In fact, a life-style like that was beginning to look more and more attractive to Clint.

Especially if he could ever find the graceful woman with the shining eyes . . .

Meantime, he financed his strange, nomadic existence with grants from research foundations and earnings from private companies that could afford to hire a geological engineer trained in speleology. Oil companies, in particular, were a good source of revenue, but Clint hadn't applied to any petroleum interests to finance this expedition. If there really was an undiscovered cave in this area, he didn't want it to become just another commercial phenomenon, something for oilmen, tourist bureaus and land developers to wrangle over. He wanted it to be protected and guarded, kept pristine in its loveliness, and he intended to fight to make sure that this was the case.

Clint grinned as he walked, his square, tanned face lighting with happiness in the early rays of the sun.

"Haven't even found the damned thing," he murmured aloud to a horned lark, which sat on a prickly pear cactus nearby, watching his passage with bright eyes. "It might not even exist, and already I'm fighting to protect it."

Suddenly he paused, squinting into the distance, his eyes narrowed with surprise. Somebody was hiking toward him, moving quickly and easily across the broken rock in the field below.

As he looked down, the distant figure waved an arm and began climbing in his direction. Clint frowned, then moved on reluctantly, wondering who would be out in this barren place so early in the morning.

It wasn't Brock Munroe, the owner of the property, whom he'd met a few days ago. Brock was a tall, broad-shouldered man, and the person approaching at such a brisk pace was small, slim and boyish in appearance.

As the newcomer drew closer, Clint could make out more details. The boy wore faded jeans, serviceable, well-worn hiking boots and an old baseball cap jammed low on his head. He had a denim jacket slung over one shoulder, and his shirt was a really strange color, a rich bluish green that glimmered in the morning light.

The boy drew near enough to call out, then approached with a smile and extended a slim brown hand. "Hi," he said in a sweet, husky voice. "My name's Neale Cameron. You must be Clint Farrell."

Clint shook the small hand, feeling puzzled and strangely shy. There was something odd about this boy, something that troubled him. He realized what it was when the newcomer swept off the cap with a casual gesture and a mass of shining light brown hair came tumbling down.

"You're a girl," Clint said, feeling stunned and foolish.

"Last time I checked," his visitor agreed cheerfully, rubbing her forehead and then bundling up the mass of hair to fit her cap back in place. "What did you think I was? A cow?"

"I thought you were a boy," Clint said, still amazed by this slender woman in front of him. There was something about her—something sweetly elusive, quick-moving and intangible, that kept reminding him of something. . . .

Suddenly it dawned on him. She was the woman he'd dreamed about the night before. He'd been distracted by the rough boyish clothes and the straightforward manner, but there was no denying this woman's sweetness and grace, or the tantalizing promise that was hidden deep in her eyes.

Recalling his dream and looking into those laughing brown eyes brought all the nighttime feelings back, so hot and strong that Clint felt another embarrassing surge of sexual arousal. He shifted uncomfortably on his feet.

The woman gazed up at him with calm interest. "I heard that you're looking for a cave out here," she told him. "I've come to help you."

CHAPTER FOUR

"THAT DOG still reeks," Millie said, wrinkling her nose in distaste. "Put him outside, Brock."

Brock hesitated, glancing at Amanda, who sat quietly across the breakfast table. Alvin huddled beside her chair, trying to make himself small and inconspicuous while the older woman glared at him.

"He's not nearly so bad this morning," Amanda said calmly. "I can hardly smell him at all, and he's right next to me."

"I turned the hose on him when I went out to do the chores," Brock said, avoiding Millie's eyes. "I'll scrub him later with soap, but I think Amanda's right. He's a lot better now."

"He's a disgusting animal," Millie said briskly. "He's fat and lazy and useless."

Alvin gazed up at her anxiously and pressed closer to Amanda, who looked down at him with sympathy and handed him a piece of crisp bacon. His tail began to rotate in ecstasy and he fell on the tasty morsel like a starving wolf.

Millie watched him a moment, shaking her head, then turned her attention to Amanda. "So, Amanda, how do you fill your time when you spend the weekend out here?'' she asked.

Brock could sense Amanda's sudden tension. "What do you mean?'' she asked, getting up to carry the coffeepot to the table.

Millie waved her hand expansively. "Well, there's not much out here to interest a city girl, is there? Do you put on blue jeans and follow Brock around while he does his chores, or what?''

Brock watched nervously while Amanda poured coffee, then seated herself across the table once again. She looked especially lovely this morning in her yellow cotton housecoat, like a slender flower in the autumn sunlight. Amanda always reminded him of flowers, Brock realized. There was a rare kind of delicacy and fragrance about her that he'd never encountered in any other woman. Brock's throat went tight and dry as he recalled their hungry lovemaking the previous night, saw her breasts gleaming in the moonlight, felt her slender nakedness in his arms and heard her broken whispers of love and fulfillment.

Dear God, how he adored the woman!

She was the whole world to him, utterly satisfying and endlessly exciting. He found himself wishing that Millie would disappear and leave them alone, so he could gather Amanda in his arms once more, unbutton her housecoat and kiss her breasts, lose himself in her silken sweetness. . . .

"Actually,'' Amanda was saying quietly, "I spend quite a lot of my time working on the house. That's what I'm planning to do this weekend, as a matter of fact."

Millie raised her eyebrows in amused surprise. "Working on the house?" she echoed. "What more could you possibly do to this house?"

"Oh, there's a lot left to do," Amanda said, sipping her coffee and frowning at Alvin, who had apparently forgotten his fear of Millie in his lust for more bacon. He was resting his front paws on the seat of Amanda's chair and struggling to haul his fat body into her lap.

"Down, Alvin!" she whispered urgently. "Get down this instant!" Alvin tumbled back onto the floor and looked up at her reproachfully.

"I meant to tell you," Amanda went on, turning to Brock with a bright, forced smile, "they finally shipped the wallpaper we ordered for the dining room, Brock. It's out in the trunk of my car. I was hoping you could find the time to help me tear off that old stuff later this morning."

Millie recoiled in horror. "You're surely not planning to take off that beautiful old paper in the dining room!"

Amanda's shoulders tensed a little, but she gave no other sign of emotion. "We have to take the old paper off," she said. "It's flocked velvet. The new paper would never stick to it."

"My grandfather had that paper shipped from San Francisco," Millie said, her cheeks flushing with anger. "It's absolutely unique. They don't make wallpaper like that anymore."

Brock munched his toast and glanced uneasily from one face to the other, wishing devoutly that he could be out in the barn, or in the corral, anywhere but sitting at this table between two women who obviously disliked each other.

"Millie," he began after an awkward silence, "Amanda and I have both—"

"It's a *crime* to tear off that paper!" Millie interrupted, her eyes flashing dangerously. "An absolute crime!"

"The old paper is stained and faded practically beyond recognition," Amanda said, making an obvious effort to keep her voice level. "I spent weeks searching through catalogs and found a flocked brocade that's almost identical, except that it's the original maroon, not a faded, dirty brown. It's going to be beautiful, and we're going to put it up this weekend."

Millie pushed her chair back and got to her feet, looking grimly elegant in her gray satin housecoat. "Over my dead body," she announced. "There are limits to what I will tolerate. This home was a showplace before *you* were ever born or thought of, my girl," she went on, glaring at Amanda, who looked back at the older woman steadily, her face pale with tension. "And I simply won't allow you to tear off paper that's been hanging on those walls for sixty years or more."

She marched from the room, leaving Brock and Amanda sitting in miserable silence at the table. Amanda sipped her coffee and gazed moodily through

the kitchen archway at the faded brown walls of the old
dining room, while Brock glanced at her uncomfortably and cleared his throat.

"Sweetheart . . ." he began.

Amanda turned to look directly at him, and Brock
realized with a sinking heart that she was deeply hurt
and very angry, not only with his aunt but with him as
well. She said nothing, however, just reached for a
fresh slice of toast and began to butter it with quiet
deliberation.

"Sweetheart," Brock pleaded, "don't be upset.
She's just talking. She doesn't really mean it. It's been
a shock to her, that's all, seeing the house looking so
different after all these years."

"You think she doesn't really *mean* it?" Amanda
asked him in a shaking voice. "Well, Brock, I think she
means every word of it. I think she hates me, and she
hates what I've done to the house, and if I try to take
off that old paper there's going to be a war. And then
you'll have to make up your mind whose side you're
on, won't you?"

Alvin perked his ears hopefully and looked at the
toast in her hand with sudden attention. Amanda broke
off a buttery piece and handed it to him, murmuring
gently and patting the dog as he pressed close to her
chair.

Brock found himself battling an irrational tide of
jealousy. He wished that she would smile at him with
the kind of warmth she gave to Alvin, instead of regarding him across the table with such cool appraisal.

"So," she asked quietly, after a moment of tense silence, "what's it going to be, Brock? Will you help me with the wallpaper today, or not?"

Brock shifted miserably in his chair, understanding with sudden clarity that there was lot more to this conflict than the question of wallpaper.

She was asking him to declare where his loyalties lay, to announce his intentions once and for all. Brock sensed that this incident, seemingly so trivial, was actually a momentous occasion, the culmination of a long, silent struggle. Amanda wanted her lover to clarify his feelings and his plans. She wanted him to tell Millie and all the world exactly what position Amanda Walker occupied in his life.

Brock felt a growing panic as he looked into the stormy blue eyes of the woman he loved. He knew that he was in terrible danger of losing her, and that life without her would be intolerable.

But, he realized in despair, there was nothing he could do about it. Something deep within Brock made it utterly impossible for him to gather Amanda in his arms, tell her how he adored her, ask her to marry him and be the mistress of his house.

The irony, of course, was that he wanted all this as much as she did. He ached for her all the time, missed her desperately when she was away, yearned for the settled comfort of a home and family and this woman at the center of his life.

But whenever he thought about his dismal financial condition these days, all those lost calves, the demands of his banker and the general bleakness of his prospects, Brock felt himself begin to stiffen and draw away from her.

Amanda had such elegant tastes. She couldn't abide anything cheap or second-rate, and Brock knew that her successful business allowed her to buy the very best for herself.

His worries and tensions about money, his own money and hers, formed a constant barrier between them, interrupted the flow of their happiness. For instance, this morning Brock was afraid to ask her how much she'd paid for that new dining room wallpaper, even though it was going to be installed in his house. What kind of man allowed a woman to buy expensive things for him and didn't ask even questions? How could he let her give him the kind of luxuries he could never afford himself?

Brock's mouth tightened. He felt a familiar unhappiness, accompanied by a wave of unreasoning anger at the position he'd been forced into. "Maybe," he said carefully, "we should just forget about the wallpaper for a little while, honey. She won't be staying forever, and we can..."

But Amanda had already risen and turned away, moving off toward the bedroom with Alvin clattering at her heels. Brock stared after her slim form with a sinking feeling of dread, watching until she vanished down the hallway.

Then he drained his coffee mug, pushed his chair back and got to his feet, waiting by the door for a moment to see if Alvin was going to come back and join him. At last he wandered alone into the sunlight and crossed the ranch yard toward the corrals, cherishing a forlorn masculine hope that the womenfolk would somehow find a way to work this problem out between them while he was gone.

"Do you know Brock Munroe?" Clint asked. "The man who owns this property."

"Not really. We've been introduced, but that's about all," Neale said, hiking along beside him. "Actually," she added, "I'm much better friends with Alvin."

Clint grinned. "The little blue heeler?"

"Is that what Alvin is? I thought he was pure mutt."

"Well, I guess he is. But there's a pretty good shot of Australian heeler in there, I'd say."

"I think he's the ugliest dog I've ever seen, but there's something lovable about him, too."

Neale paused to admire a spiky cholla cactus growing beside the trail. It was perfectly symmetrical, and its dark green spines glistened brilliantly in the morning light. She bent to examine the plant, then straightened and moved off down the trail again, conscious of her companion's eyes resting on her with lively interest.

He certainly was an attractive man, this Clint Farrell, although Marjorie was usually the one to notice such things, not her roommate. Neale tended not to be interested in men unless they were newsworthy in some way. She had no time for romance, not when it was such a struggle just to make a living....

Still, he had a nice face, with that boyish grin and sparkling hazel eyes. His eyelashes, Neale had already noticed, were as long and soft as a girl's, in pleasant contrast with his lean cheeks and firm mouth and chin.

She liked his sturdy body, too, with those broad shoulders and powerful muscles. Unlike Marjorie, Neale wasn't particularly attracted to tall men. She disliked the feeling of somebody towering way above her. But Clint Farrell was just four or five inches taller than she was, and their bodies moved compatibly as they swung along the trail with the smooth gait of practiced hikers.

"I thought you must know him," Clint was saying, "because you knew what I was doing out here. I don't think I've told anybody but Brock."

"His aunt is an old friend of my landlady's," Neale said. "She's visiting at Brock's ranch. She told us yesterday that you were looking for a cave on the property."

She glanced over at Clint, who nodded and squinted thoughtfully at the limestone cliffs above them, his boyish face looking troubled.

"You must know you can't keep anything a secret in Crystal Creek," Neale told him. "Everybody knows everything that happens around here within about ten minutes."

Clint shrugged. "I guess so," he said. "It's just that I..."

"What?" Neale prompted when he fell silent.

"I'm not anxious for a lot of publicity about what I'm doing, that's all," Clint said, turning to smile briefly at her. "I was hoping it wouldn't cause any talk and speculation in the town."

"Why? In case you don't find anything?"

"Oh, I'm pretty sure I'm going to find something. Actually, that's why I wanted to keep it quiet."

Neale looked up at him, puzzled.

"People have such a passionate interest in caves," Clint told her. "I don't know why. I mean, I've always been fascinated by cave exploration myself, but I've never understood why the general public is so interested."

"Maybe it's an ancient memory," Neale suggested with a smile. "Dating back to the time when we all lived in caves."

Clint nodded. "I think it must be something like that. Anyhow, people love caves, but they don't treat them with a lot of respect. My dream has always been to find a perfect cave and keep it pretty much a secret among speleologists. That way, it could be studied and enjoyed by professionals without the risk of being damaged by the public."

Neale felt a brief chill of alarm. She paused and reached behind her to adjust a buckle on her backpack, hiding her face from the man beside her.

Clint looked down at her with quick concern. "Is something wrong, Neale?"

"This strap has worked loose," Neale said in a muffled voice. "It's making the pack rub against my back."

He moved behind her to examine the problem. Neale could feel his fingers working against her back, making a careful adjustment to the strap. Even through the fabric of her shirt, she was conscious of the warmth and strength of his hands. She shivered unaccountably, irritated by her own responses.

I'm as bad as Marjorie, she thought with scorn. *Getting all shivery and excited just because a good-looking guy is in the area....*

Clint lingered at his task, continuing to work with the buckle, taking a lot of time resettling the pack against her shirt and adjusting the shoulder straps. Again Neale found herself enjoying the feeling of his hands, and was annoyed by her reaction to his closeness and his touch.

She pulled away abruptly, giving him a polite smile. "Thanks. That feels a lot better," she said, moving off down the trail, still brooding over his words.

So Clint Farrell wanted to find a cave and keep it secret, did he? And how would he feel if he knew that Neale was tagging along because she fully intended to publish his discovery in a national magazine? If she told him the truth, would his eyes still sparkle as brightly, and would his face light with that disconcerting glow of admiration when he looked at her?

"How did you get interested in caves, Neale?" he asked as they mounted the steep trail toward the limestone outcropping.

"Beg pardon?" Neale turned to him, still absorbed in her private worries.

"Well, as soon as you heard what I was doing, you decided to come out here and help me look. You must have some kind of interest in caves."

Neale gazed at him, her eyes wide and startled. "Oh, I... I've always loved wandering around in caves," she told him, improvising wildly. "I guess it started when I went to Carlsbad Caverns a few years ago with my family. I was so fascinated, I just couldn't seem to get that cave out of my mind. I go to see them whenever I get the chance."

What a lie, she thought grimly. The only truth in that statement was the fact that she'd visited Carlsbad as a teenager. But Neale was so claustrophobic that she'd utterly dreaded the thought of walking into the gaping cavern. She never admitted her fear, knowing how scornful her younger brothers would be, and she'd followed her family down into the cave, struggling to hide her panicky reaction in the moist darkness.

She had only a confused memory of terrifying black depths, of dripping rock walls and fathomless pits that fell away in dizzying fashion beyond the fenced trail. Mostly, though, she recalled her misery as she faltered behind her brothers along the dimly lighted tourist path, clammy and sick with fear, and then her profound relief when they finally rode the elevator back up to sunshine and open spaces.

"Carlsbad is an example of a cave that's been badly exploited," Clint was saying. "Although it's still beautiful, and they've done a lot in recent years to protect it. Most of the damage was done back in the days when it was first discovered, before there were any real environmental controls. Hundreds of people climbed in there and broke off stalactites for souvenirs. It was criminal, the way they behaved."

Neale shuddered, thinking once more about the black dripping cavern with all its bizarre shapes and formations, eerily silent in the cold bowels of the earth. For a moment she found herself wishing devoutly that Clint Farrell was searching for something a little more pleasant, like a rare cactus or a new species of armadillo. But Neale was a professional journalist, and she was prepared to endure any kind of discomfort to get the story she wanted.

Maybe Clint's cave would be different, she thought wistfully. Maybe it would have a lot of airy chambers and shafts that would let the sunlight filter through. Neale was fairly sure she could tolerate the interior of a cave if there was just a bit of natural light inside it somewhere....

Clint was talking again, telling her about Lecheguilla, the fabulous cave that had recently been discovered near Carlsbad and was now the subject of a pitched battle between environmentalists and petroleum interests.

"They want to drill wells in the area, just a few miles away from the cave," he said grimly. "If the interior pressure is altered significantly, the whole cave system could collapse. It would be an absolute tragedy."

Neale forced herself to abandon her dark thoughts about enclosed spaces, and pay attention to what he was saying. She listened carefully, wishing she could take out her writing pad and make some notes.

But in this case, she thought with a fleeting grin, she'd just have to trust her memory.

"How do you know where to look?" she asked. "What makes you so certain there's a big cave out here, anyhow?"

Again she paid close attention while he told her about water erosion and ancient riverbeds, about bats and floods and sedimentary limestone.

"So your reasoning is that if you follow the bats, you'll be able to find where they roost? They'll lead you to the cave entrance?"

Clint smiled down at her. "Isn't it logical?" he asked.

"Well . . . I guess so. Unless they're just roosting in an old abandoned building, or something. Come to think of it, my grandfather had hundreds of bats in the hayloft at his farm."

"The only buildings around here are on Brock Munroe's ranch. And the bats came from an entirely different direction last night."

Neale nodded, moving beside him along the trail. Suddenly he stopped, gripped her arm and bent his head to listen intently.

Neale stared at him in alarm. "Clint?" she whispered. "What is it?"

"Shhh. Listen. Can't you hear it?"

She frowned, trying to hear whatever had caught his attention. The morning was clear and still, broken only by the busy hum of insects, an occasional trill of birdsong and the sound of their boots shifting on the limestone trail.

"I don't think I . . ."

"Over there, to the east, just up that rise of ground. Listen."

She tried again, concentrating on the direction he indicated, and began to detect the merest whisper of sound. It was like a muffled sob, a low gusty sigh that was almost inaudible.

Neale looked up at him, wide-eyed. "What is it?"

He grinned, his eyes sparkling with excitement. "Come and see."

Neale followed him over the rough terrain at the edge of the trail, picking her way carefully through cactus and broken rock. She felt a brief chill of unreasoning dread as the strange sound grew louder. There was something both melancholy and menacing about that rhythmic sighing. It filled the sunny autumn morning with a dreadful sense of sorrow and foreboding.

Clint paused and stared intently at the ground. Neale stood beside him, gaping in astonishment.

There was a small opening in the rock at their feet, not much larger or more conspicuous than a prairie dog burrow. But the sound that issued from the tiny cavern seemed huge and ominous now that they were closer to it. It sighed and gusted around their heads, throbbed and died away into stillness, then rose again with an eerie rhythm.

"What is it?" Neale repeated, gazing in childlike horror at the dark burrow. "What's *in* there?"

"It's a blowhole." Clint knelt and looked intently into the darkness at his feet, running his hand over the opening. He glanced up at her over his shoulder. "Come down here, Neale."

Obediently she lowered herself next to him, still gazing in horrified fascination at the rocky ground. Clint took her arm and held it over the opening, and she felt a powerful rush of wind against her hand as the sighing noise rose and sobbed again.

Neale shivered, staring at her hand, then up at Clint. His pleasant face was pale and tense, and his eyes blazed with excitement.

"A blowhole indicates the presence of a good-sized cave directly underground," he told her in a hushed voice. "Especially one where the air is forced out at this velocity."

Neale was silent. Tentatively she held her hand over the hole as the sound rose once more, and felt the chill rush of air against the skin. She stared in horror at the tiny black opening. "Is this . . . are you saying that *this* is the cave entrance?" she asked.

I'd die, she thought in despair. *I don't care if they're willing to pay me a million dollars for the story, I can't crawl into a little dark hole like that. I just can't.*

But Clint was smiling at her and shaking his head. "It's just another sure indication of a major cave system in this area. A cave 'breathes' through these little holes in the crust. It blows air out or sucks it in to equalize the barometric pressure inside and outside the cave. Sometimes winds as strong as sixty miles an hour can howl in and out of these blowholes."

Neale looked again at the opening. "So you wouldn't try to get inside the cave by crawling through that little space?"

"Not until I'd exhausted all other possibilities. One of these blowholes can often lead down through a vertical shaft a foot in diameter and several hundred feet long. No experienced caver would risk an entry like that without a lot more information. Have you ever heard of Floyd Collins?"

Neale shook her head, following in silence as he got to his feet, helped her up and led the way back to the trail.

"In the early part of the century, caves were a big tourist attraction in Kentucky, especially after they discovered Mammoth Cave," Clint began. "The locals all tried to find them on their land so they could charge admission and make a living from their own private caves. Collins was one of those farmers, looking for a new cave, when he crawled into an air shaft in what's now known as Sand Cave, and then couldn't get out. He was trapped well down inside the shaft after a boulder shifted onto his leg.''

Neale shuddered, listening in silent horror to this story.

"It became kind of a national event," Clint went on, squinting at the horizon as he spoke. ''People traveled to Kentucky from all over to watch the rescue attempts, and set up camp in a field nearby. They were there for weeks.''

"What happened to him?" Neale asked, her journalistic curiosity overcoming her dread of enclosed spaces and her vivid mental image of the poor man trapped in the clammy darkness.

"He died in there," Clint told her briefly. "Nobody knows exactly how long it took for him to die, but it was months before they were able to recover his body."

Despite the warmth of the autumn sunlight, now high and beaming in the wide Texas sky, Neale felt another chill of fear. She hugged her arms and trudged along behind Clint's sturdy body, trying not to think about Floyd Collins and what his final hours must have been like.

Shortly after the discovery of the blowhole, they stopped for lunch. Clint chose a flat piece of rock outcropping sheltered by the nearby cliffs, with a breathtaking view of the valley beyond them and the rolling sweep of farms and ranch land.

He glanced at Neale's pack. "Did you bring something to eat? I'm getting pretty low on supplies, but I could probably..."

"It's all right. I have sandwiches and fruit, and some trail mix."

"Good," he said in relief. "I'll make tea."

"Tea?" Neale looked at him blankly. "You're going to build a fire out here, just for tea?"

Clint grinned and shook his head. He took a slim plastic case from his pack and withdrew a metal device that folded out into a tiny single-burner stove, fueled by a butane cylinder not much larger than a cigarette lighter. While Neale watched in fascination, he measured water from a plastic container into a collapsible cooking pot, and set it to boil on the little stove. He added a tea bag and put it aside to steep, then boiled more water in another container.

"For soup," he told Neale briefly. "I like hot liquids while I'm hiking."

"That's so neat!" she exclaimed in delight. "You can cook a meal on it, and yet it would fit into your shirt pocket."

"Cavers travel light," Clint told her, looking up again to smile at her. "We have to wriggle through some pretty tight places, so we try to keep our packs as small as possible, yet carry enough to spend several days underground."

"Several *days?*" Neale tensed and paused in the act of opening her pack and rummaging for her lunch case.

"Sometimes." Clint leaned back against a boulder, booted feet extended, and opened a plastic sack of dried fruit. He turned to look at Neale, his eyes lighting again with that look of masculine interest that had unsettled her earlier in the day. "Where did you grow up, Neale? Are you from Texas?"

She shook her head, munching on a cheese sandwich. "My family's in Kansas. My father was a company accountant in Wichita." She paused to chew and swallow a bite of sandwich, then went on. "I have two younger brothers. One's still at home with my mother, and the other just got married last spring."

"And your father?"

Neale felt a wave of the familiar sorrow that haunted her so much of the time these days. "He died in June," she said briefly. "Just a few days after my brother's wedding, in fact. He had pancreatic cancer."

Clint looked at her with sympathy. "If you're the oldest, he'd still have been a fairly young man, wouldn't he?"

"He was forty-nine. I'm almost twenty-five," Neale added, in response to Clint's unspoken question.

"That must have been hard on your family."

"It was hard in all kinds of ways," Neale said, taking a lot of time to fold and smooth the square of waxed paper that her sandwich had been wrapped in. "Worse than any of us could have imagined."

She felt reluctant to discuss the matter. Neale never talked about this to anybody if she could help it, not even Marjorie, who'd been her best friend for years. But there was something about the man sitting opposite her, such sympathy and genuine interest that, gradually, she found herself telling him about those dreadful months of winter and spring, the downward spiral of her father's illness and the toll it had taken on everyone.

"My mother was so exhausted, I thought she wouldn't survive," Neale murmured. "After a while, no matter how much you love someone, you start wanting it to be over, and that makes you feel guilty, too."

"But if he's suffering..."

"I know," she said briefly. "You see how he's suffering and wish it would end, and hate yourself for wishing such a thing. And then there's the—" She fell abruptly silent, her cheeks flaming, and gazed intently into her pack at the apple that remained in her lunch sack.

"What?" Clint prompted her gently. "What were you going to say?"

"The expense," Neale said flatly, looking up at him. "You can't imagine how much it costs to see a family member through a long terminal illness. After the insurance ran out, my mother mortgaged the house again, used up their savings... It was awful."

He gazed at her, appalled. "How is she managing now? You said one of your brothers was still at home, didn't you?"

Neale nodded. "Ted's a senior in high school. My mother's getting by," she added. "She took a job at the hardware store, and my other brother and I help out when we can, send her some of what we earn every month. It's really hard, though. It's hard for everybody."

"Where do you work?"

Again Neale felt a brief chill of alarm. She began to regret having confided in him so freely. "Oh," she said lightly, "I'm just kind of an amateur writer. I do press releases, articles for the local paper, some promotional stuff for the Austin tourist bureau, that kind of thing."

"And you make enough at your writing to support yourself and help your family, too?"

There was a note of admiration in his voice that made Neale feel uncomfortably guilty. "I have a lot of irons in the fire," she told him. "What about you?" she asked hastily. "Where's your family? You sound like you grew up in the north."

"I grew up all over. My father was a seismologist, and he acted as a consultant in a lot of earthquake areas. I guess," Clint added with a smile, "that's how I first got interested in exploring the bowels of the earth, except that I prefer them when they're not rumbling and shaking."

Neale stared gloomily at the little cooking pot. "I can imagine. Being inside a cave during an earthquake is just too horrible to imagine. Where are your parents now?"

His face shadowed with sudden pain. "They were killed a long time ago in an accident in Paraguay. My parents were always adventurous types, both of them. My mother went everywhere with my father. They were hiking together across a rope suspension bridge when it collapsed into a river canyon. I was seventeen at the time, taking my first year of college back in the States."

"No brothers or sisters?"

Clint grinned faintly and shook his head. "I was always surprised that my mother even took time out to have me. Although," he added in a quiet, reminiscent tone, "they were really great parents. They took me with them whenever they could, and taught me all kinds of things. I certainly wouldn't have traded my childhood for something more conventional."

"So now you do this for a living? Explore caves, I mean. Or is this just a hobby?"

"No, I make my living at it. I'm a geological engineer, actually, specializing in speleology. I do a lot of free-lance work for oil companies, state and national parks, even Hollywood, sometimes. Right now I'm operating on a research grant, but the money's just about running out."

"Is it a grant specifically to find a cave here near Crystal Creek?"

"No, it's for exploration and mapping of the Edwards Plateau. That's the limestone formation that covers this whole region, and forms the cave systems."

Again Neale found herself wishing she could make notes on all the things he was telling her. "Do you always work alone like this?" she asked.

"Only when I'm doing private research and surface exploration. Cavers don't tend to work alone. When you're exploring a cave, especially a new, unmapped one, it's imperative to have trained backup and support people. It's just too dangerous otherwise."

Neale nodded thoughtfully, trying not to think about black dripping caverns and narrow honeycombs of passageways deep within the earth.

"In fact, I usually like to do surface exploration for that very reason," Clint was saying, "because I get to be on my own. I'm surprised how much I'm enjoying this."

"Enjoying what?"

"This." He waved his hand at the little fire, their cozy campsite and Neale sitting tailor-fashion across from him. "Being part of an exploring partnership," he added with a teasing grin.

"I'm not much of a partner," she said briskly. "More of a nuisance, I'm afraid."

"Normally, that's what I'd think, too," Clint told her honestly. "I don't like having anybody along when I'm hiking. My first thought after you turned up this morning was how soon would I be able to get rid of you."

Neale glanced up at him, startled by his frankness.

"But," he went on, "this has really been fun, having you along this morning. And you keep up pretty well, too. You must have some hiking experience."

"I did quite a lot of hiking and rock climbing in college," Neale told him, feeling absurdly pleased by his praise. "And don't forget, I had two brothers to trail when I was growing up. I learned early that a girl has to be tough if she wants to be included in anything interesting.''

"Well, you sure learned it, all right. But I have to warn you..." Clint began, a sudden cautious note in his voice.

"Warn me? What about?"

He shifted uncomfortably and looked down at his makeshift soup bowl. "I don't mind your tagging along today, provided you're discreet about what I'm doing out here. But I can't take you with me into a cave if we find one.''

She looked at him sharply. "Why not?"

"Because you're not trained. It's extremely dangerous for amateurs to get involved in cave exploration without the proper experience.''

"So how do you get experience?" Neale asked bluntly. "Wandering around in root cellars, or what?"

"You get experience," Clint said gently, "by exploring known, well-mapped caves in the company of trained professionals, and learning all the skills you'll need while still in a safely controlled situation. Then you start to branch out.''

Neale felt a brief surge of panic, seeing all her hopes for a fabulous story drifting away as he issued these stern warnings. She set her jaw stubbornly and forced herself to smile at him. Clint Farrell was clearly attracted to her, and despite his obvious masculine appeal, he seemed to be a lonely kind of man. When the time came to apply some pressure, those two facts could no doubt be turned to her advantage.

"Come on," she said briskly, packing away the last of her lunch things. "Let's keep looking for this thing while the daylight's good. Maybe we should split up and cover more ground. Tell me what I should be watching for, all right?"

He folded up his little stove, washed his cooking utensils with a few drops of the precious water remaining in his canteen, then followed her up the curving trail to the limestone bluffs. As they walked, he described the kind of things that would indicate a possible cave entrance, and how carefully they had to be examined.

But when they finally made their momentous discovery, it seemed to happen almost by chance. In fact, it was Neale who found the actual entrance, and she wasn't even searching for it at the time. She was looking for a private space to use as a bathroom while Clint ranged across the cliff below her, investigating sinkholes and patterns of water erosion.

Neale climbed the face of the cliff to a stand of brush and stunted mesquite. She fought her way into the tangled thicket, slapping at the small flies that buzzed around her head and crawled down into her shirt collar. She checked to see that she was fully screened from Clint's view, reached for the button on her jeans and then stood transfixed, staring at a gaping hole in the limestone wall in front of her. Holding her breath, Neale edged closer and peered into the darkness, feeling a cold wind on her face. She stood in silence, awed by the echoing vastness that seemed to fall away into the depths of the earth.

For a long time Neale gazed at the black opening, still partially screened by dense shrubbery. Then she turned, forgetting everything in her excitement, and plunged down the cliff face, shouting for Clint to come and see what she'd found.

CHAPTER FIVE

WHILE NEALE and Clint were wandering through the limestone bluffs in search of their cave, Amanda was navigating some dangerous terrain of her own. But *her* hazards were less well-defined, and much trickier to deal with.

After their brief conflict at the breakfast table, she'd lingered in the bedroom, half-hoping Brock would follow but dreading his arrival. When she heard him leave the house, she hurried to the window, watched him vanish behind the corrals and then looked down at Alvin, who was lying on the bed in a nest of rumpled sheets and blankets, gazing up at her with an expression of bored disapproval.

"Don't you dare look at me like that," Amanda told him sharply. "I'm *right* about this, and you know I am, Alvin. They have no reason to treat me this way, either of them."

Alvin sighed, lowering his head to rest on his paws. His eyes dropped shut, and he belched with smug contentment.

Amanda dressed rapidly in her old jeans and sweatshirt, tied her runners snugly and then flipped the blankets, sending Alvin scrambling and clattering onto a braided rug that covered the hardwood floor.

He gathered himself together, cast her a bitter glance and marched from the room, his fat body swaying indignantly. Amanda made the bed, trying not to think about the hours of darkness in this room last night when Brock's sweet lovemaking had sent her soaring to the moon and back. Nobody had ever made her feel the way Brock did.

And all he had to do was touch her hand or even glance at her, to set her tingling and yearning all over again....

Amanda sighed and went down the hall to the kitchen, where Alvin was sitting impatiently by the door. She let him out and watched as he trotted across the ranch yard toward the corrals in search of Brock. Then she cleared the table and washed the dishes, wondering a little apprehensively where Millie was.

It was a disconcerting feeling, knowing that another woman was in the house and could pop up at any moment. Once more Amanda thought ruefully about all her foolish daydreams in which Millie had been a grandmotherly type, eager to take Amanda's side in this strange, unspoken struggle with Brock.

Fat chance, Amanda thought bitterly. *She'd hate to see me married to Brock. It's probably the last thing she wants, and I don't even know why.*

Amanda suspected that Millie's cold antagonism reflected something more than disapproval over the renovations to the house. But she couldn't understand the source of the older woman's anger. They'd never met, they lived almost a continent apart, and Millie had no real interest in the ranch except for childhood nostalgia. So why was she behaving this way?

Amanda finished tidying the kitchen, still brooding over the problem of Millie's belligerent attitude. She frowned, realizing that she was concentrating on their houseguest because it kept her from thinking about Brock, and all that his silence this morning had implied about his feelings and intentions.

She couldn't bear to think that Brock didn't love her enough to marry her. It was almost impossible to believe, especially when she remembered the things he whispered to her in the darkness, the way his face lighted whenever he looked at her, the tenderness in his hands....

Amanda choked back a sob and stood looking around the kitchen, feeling nervous and irresolute. She wandered across the gleaming pegged oak floor and studied the walls of the dining room. They were even more faded and ugly in the harsh morning light. Amanda thought wistfully about the luxurious rolls of dark maroon wallpaper in the trunk of her car, chosen so carefully to decorate these walls.

She took a few paces backward and squinted, visualizing how the rich paper would look, setting off the new oak paneling that Brock had installed as high as the chair rails. Amanda's plan was to cover the walls with maroon brocade between the chair and plate rails, then paper the upper portion with a plain creamy linen that would blend into the plaster cornices. She'd seen several older houses with that sort of papering design, and it always looked so striking in the high-ceilinged rooms.

And Brock, she remembered grimly, had been as enthusiastic about the plan as she was, in the weeks before Millie came. They'd been waiting so anxiously for the paper to be delivered, and it had taken months to come from the supplier in Chicago. . . .

Abruptly, before she could think about it further, Amanda hurried back to Brock's room, rummaged in a drawer for a cotton bandanna to tie over her hair, and went down the hall to gather her supply of wallpapering tools from the back porch.

She returned to the dining room, selected her favorite putty knife, took a deep, ragged breath and ran the knife up under a strip of the old paper, gratified at how easily it came away from the plastered surface beneath.

In many of the rooms, the paper had been glued fast to the walls, and removing it had been a tedious and messy task. But here in the dining room the old flocked velvet had been applied over many layers of other paper, forming a covering so thick and brittle that it seemed to fall away under Amanda's knife.

She worked with concentrated attention, almost mesmerized by the sweep of the putty knife, the brittle crackle of paper, the long strands that peeled loose and fell away onto the floor. The job was hard and repetitive, requiring many trips up and down the stepladder, but it still left her mind free to wander.

Amanda forced herself not to think about Millie's unpleasantness at breakfast, or about Brock and his refusal to make a commitment. It was better to think about Halloween costumes. Or about Moira Richter, the governor's wife, who had just discovered she was pregnant and would be needing to change her plans for her winter wardrobe. Or about theatrical costumes, and the need to find a new seamstress if Amy was leaving....

"My God!" a voice boomed behind her, making her jump. "What on *earth* do you think you're doing, girl?"

Amanda shivered and drew a deep breath, then turned on the step of the ladder and looked down at Millie, who stood in the archway dressed in jeans and a white cotton shirt.

Not many women of sixty looked that good in jeans, Amanda thought in startled admiration, forgetting their conflict for a moment. But she tensed again as Millie came slowly into the room, gaping at the bare, stained walls and the messy heaps of torn paper on the floor.

The older woman stood in silence, hands on hips, and looked around at the destruction. Finally, she turned back to Amanda, who had descended the ladder and stood nervously clutching her little flat-bladed putty knife, as if it would somehow protect her in the coming battle.

"I have to hand it to you," Millie said coldly. "You've sure got some nerve, don't you?"

"Not really," Amanda said with an awkward smile. "Actually, I'm quite a coward a lot of the time. It's just that I know when I'm right, Millie. And I'm right about this."

"About destroying a historical landmark that you'd never laid eyes on until a couple of months ago, and have no right to touch?"

Amanda felt a deep reluctance to get drawn into this kind of argument, but she couldn't help herself. "Brock and I have been together for almost a year," she said quietly.

"Together," Millie echoed with a brief, mirthless smile. "In what way are you and Brock together, pray tell?"

"We're . . . we love each other," Amanda said, her cheeks flaming with embarrassment. "We really do."

"I see. Are you engaged? I don't notice any rings on your fingers."

Amanda looked down involuntarily at her bare, ringless hands, clutching the knife handle so tightly that her knuckles gleamed white against her skin.

"Are you?" Millie asked.

"No," Amanda whispered, hating the woman for driving so relentlessly to the source of her misery. She felt her anger ebbing away in a tide of sorrow and loneliness. "No, we're not engaged."

"Why not? I thought he loved you. The man's almost forty years old. Don't you think if he was so much in love, he'd be wanting to marry you?"

Amanda's unhappiness mounted as she gazed at Millie's cold face.

Why did Brock continue to place her in these dreadful situations? It would only take a word from him, just the briefest of commitments, and then she wouldn't have to quail in front of his aunt like a child caught in some kind of wrongdoing. She could hold her head high, assume her rightful place in his life, smile at Millie with quiet confidence.

But Brock wouldn't give her that promise, no matter how much she pleaded with him. It was hopeless, all of it....

Millie was staring at her, watching her reactions closely. Amanda dreaded the woman's next words, but Millie didn't speak, just turned away and walked casually toward the archway.

"I guess maybe you just don't value yourself all that highly," she commented. "Well, it's too late to turn back now, isn't it, girl?" she said over her shoulder as she left, waving a hand at the mass of torn paper littering the floor. "But I hope you know what you're doing. I surely do."

Amanda moved forward to watch Millie's slim figure and erect silver head as she vanished through the kitchen, let herself out the back door and started across the ranch yard. Then she climbed wearily up the ladder again, thinking about Millie's words. The encounter hadn't been as bad as she'd feared, but she still felt utterly miserable. Millie hadn't made a terrible scene about the old wallpaper, but she'd succeeded ruthlessly in bringing Amanda's greatest unhappiness to the surface.

Millie was right, actually. It was shameful that a woman should allow herself to be treated like this, and spend her life chasing after a man who clearly didn't want or intend to build a future with her. Millie had every right to think that Amanda didn't value herself highly enough.

And maybe it was time to do something about it.

Amanda continued doggedly to strip the walls and make them ready for the new paper. Her movements were skilled and precise, her hands dexterous in their work, but her face was thoughtful and remote under the faded cotton bandanna.

MILLIE RODE one of the old brood mares on a narrow trail running along a length of barbed wire fence. The autumn sun was warm on her back, and the easy rhythm of the mare's plodding gait lulled her senses, setting her mind at ease for a little while.

She let the reins fall loose against the horse's neck and scrutinized the clear blue arch of the sky, the rolling sweep of hills and valleys, the scattered herds of grazing cattle. The Texas landscape was quiet and drowsy in the midday sunshine, exactly as she remembered it from her childhood almost half a century earlier.

Millie sighed, grateful that she'd decided to come back here for a while. The peace and beauty of her old home was so satisfying, especially after the dark and terror-filled days she'd been through recently. It was so good to be reminded that there were still places where things didn't change, where even the rocks and the trees looked the same as they had fifty years ago.

But, she reminded herself abruptly, things *did* change, even here. For one thing, the grazing herds of cattle weren't glossy Herefords, as they'd been in her girlhood. Brock ran mostly Brangus cattle now, dark, misshapen animals with heavy forequarters and cunning little eyes. Millie disliked them intensely.

And the fence lines weren't the picturesque split rails, covered with vines and tangled growth, that she recalled so vividly. The taut barbed wire looked coldly commercial, sharp and forbidding in its brutal efficiency. And as for the ranch house...

Millie shifted awkwardly in her saddle, thinking about the old stone house and all the conflicts that had sprung up within its comfortable walls.

She frowned absently and shook the reins, trying to raise the mare to a brisker pace. The horse quickened to a reluctant trot for a few paces, then settled back to a walk when she felt her rider's attention wandering once more.

Millie was thinking about Amanda, recalling the woman's beautiful pale face and tense manner, her tenderness whenever she looked at Brock, and the surprising determination in her eyes earlier that morning when Millie had found her stripping the dining room wallpaper.

She was right, of course, Millie thought with a private grin. The old paper was ugly as sin, and that was a fact. It was going to be a great improvement to have new wallpaper in the big, gracious room. Millie even found herself looking forward to getting back from her ride, just to see how the work was progressing.

Not that she intended to give the woman any satisfaction by admitting that she'd been wrong. Millie didn't believe that she *was* in the wrong, actually. Even though the changes in the house were probably improvements in a strictly technical sense, there was no denying that the woman was unforgivably presumptuous. She had no right to come waltzing into somebody else's house and start tearing things apart, changing everything to suit herself.

Brock certainly hadn't given her the right, no matter how passionately their eyes shone whenever they looked at each other. The two of them might have a great time in bed, Millie thought coldly, but there was still no ring on Amanda's finger when the sun came up.

Brock Munroe clearly had no intention of marrying his fancy city lady. Anybody could see that. And consequently, Amanda Walker had no right to swish around the ranch house as if she were already the mistress of the place.

Millie brushed at a horsefly buzzing against her cheek, frowning when she thought about Amanda. She wondered why Brock didn't want to marry her, when it was plain to see that the boy was crazy in love. The fire in his eyes was almost embarrassing to witness when the three of them were in a room together. And even before Amanda came to the ranch, Millie had noticed the husky softening of her nephew's voice every time he spoke the woman's name.

There was no doubt that Brock was deeply smitten, and so was his lady. She was clearly more to him than just a tasty bedtime morsel. But they'd been together a year and they weren't even engaged. Was there something in the relationship that Millie couldn't see? Did the woman from Austin have some deep personality flaw that wasn't evident on first inspection?

She seemed nice enough, Millie admitted grudgingly to herself, though she'd certainly never express this opinion to another living soul. The woman had arrived at the ranch looking like a fashion plate, but when she put on her blue jeans and played with that ugly fat dog of Brock's, she seemed as natural and winsomely appealing as a child.

Millie remembered the younger woman perched up on that ladder, facing her adversary with frightened determination as the dried shreds of old wallpaper fell to the floor all around them. Truth be known, this little scene reminded Millie of some memorable conflicts she'd had with her first husband's mother.

What an old dragon *that* woman had been! And how terrified and defiant Millie had been during their early confrontations....

Millie grinned in spite of herself at the fleeting memory, then sobered. If Brock didn't want to marry the woman, whatever his reason, then he shouldn't have to. And in the meantime, Amanda Walker shouldn't be conducting herself as if she already owned a half share in the Double Bar and had a right to make any changes that struck her fancy.

But something kept nagging at Millie's thoughts, an ingrained sense of honor and decency that made her suspect she wasn't being entirely fair with the woman from Austin.

I wasn't always like this, Millie brooded, gazing down at the rough dark mane and drooping head of the old bay mare. *I wasn't always so harsh in my judgments. I wonder if it's because...*

She shuddered and brought her thoughts up short, reaching down involuntarily to touch the lump in her abdomen. Even through the rough texture of her blue jeans it was clearly evident, silent and firm beneath her tentative fingers, as coldly heavy as the stone that seemed to have rolled over her heart these last weeks.

Millie knew that she should go to the doctor and have the lump examined. It was ridiculous to live all alone with this kind of heart-stopping, panicky terror. If she placed herself in somebody's hands, let some trained professional look at her body and pronounce judgment, then the burden would be lifted from her. Others would make the necessary decisions about Millie's future, tell her what to expect, help her to endure what was unendurable.

But that was precisely what Millie feared the most. As long as this thing remained her secret, she was able to deny its reality. Having the lump examined and talked about, acknowledged by others and dealt with, would give it a kind of horrible power and validity in her life that it presently lacked.

For instance, when she was absorbed in something interesting, like her current conflict with Amanda, Millie was still able to forget for a little while that she'd ever discovered this hideous silent invader within her body.

But once she was in a doctor's care, once the terrible word had been spoken aloud, then she would officially become an invalid. Brock and Amanda wouldn't fight with her anymore. They'd tiptoe around the house being thoughtful and considerate. She'd be an object of pity, clearly marked for death, and after that there would be no way, ever, to hide from the truth.

Millie set her mouth and slapped the reins against the mare's heavy neck, urging her placid mount to a startled and resentful gallop.

The wind sang in her ears and the landscape rushed past in bright pinwheels of light. Cactus, cedar and mesquite, sun-spangled grass and rocks and dark herds of cattle, all spun together in a whirling kaleidoscope of color and fragrance. For a few brief, sweet moments, Millie Munroe was a girl again, reckless and beautiful, flying across the rugged hills without a care in the world. But she reined in her horse abruptly near the limestone cliffs. The old mare stood by the fence, head drooping, lathered sides heaving, while Millie shaded her eyes and focused on a couple of people hiking down the fence line toward her.

One of them was a man with a sturdy, youthful body, striding along as if unaware of the bulky pack resting on his shoulders. The other person was small and slender, with a faded baseball cap pulled low over a delicate oval face.

Millie, who had seen that face recently, felt a quick stirring of interest.

"Well, hello, Neale," she said, lifting one boot free of the stirrup and stretching to rest her knee casually on the pommel. "Out for a walk, are you?"

The two young people exchanged a quick, significant glance. Millie's interest sharpened.

"This is Clint Farrell, Miss Munroe," Neale said politely, indicating the quiet young man at her side. "I don't know if you've met."

"I don't believe we have," Millie said, examining the man's square tanned face and hazel eyes, the curly dark hair beneath his cap and his level, forthright gaze.

"Hello, Miss Munroe," Clint said, stepping forward and reaching up to shake her hand. "Neale told me you were visiting at the ranch. You're Brock's aunt, aren't you?"

"I sure am," Millie said, still looking down at the two hikers thoughtfully. "I grew up on this place, Clint. Time was, I knew just about every square foot of it, or thought I did, anyhow. I understand you're looking for some kind of cave entrance out here?"

Again they exchanged one of those furtive glances, and the young man shifted awkwardly on his feet.

"Yes, I am," he said finally. "I thought it seemed to be a likely location."

"Any luck?" Millie asked casually. "You know, I've always wondered if there could be a cave system under this land somewhere."

Clint hesitated once more. Neale plunged into the conversation, giving the older woman an engaging smile. "Clint thinks there might be. We've been hiking all day, and we're just famished," she added brightly. "We're heading out for a big dinner at the Longhorn."

Millie glanced at her watch in surprise. "Is it that late? I must have been riding for hours. Poor old mare, no wonder she's getting tired and cranky. Of course, I stopped for coffee at Mary Gibson's a while ago, and that took up an hour or so. Have either of you seen those horrible ostriches?"

Neale and Clint both laughed and plunged into a discussion of the habits and appearance of Mary Gibson's ostriches, their relief clearly evident when the conversation moved away from caverns and cave entrances.

After a few minutes, they said their goodbyes and moved off down the fence line again, heading for a couple of vehicles parked out near the highway. Still resting her knee comfortably against the saddle horn, Millie turned and watched them go, thinking about

Clint Farrell's uneasy reticence when the cave entrance was mentioned.

"Strange," she murmured aloud, picking up the
reins and settling her boots in the stirrups again as she
turned her horse toward home. "Very, very strange."

CHAPTER SIX

NEALE SAT on the quilted bedspread in her bright dormer bedroom the next day, surrounded by a sea of textbooks, newspaper clippings and stapled leaflets. She frowned, thumbing through typed references and pages of messy handwriting, trying to concentrate on all the things she was learning about caves and the men who explored them.

"Stalagmites go up from the floor," she read aloud, "and stalactites come down from the ceiling. Why can't I ever remember that? I'll bet Clint..."

But it was a mistake to think about Clint. As soon as she said the man's name aloud, his image came surging into her mind, as vibrant as if he sat next to her on the bed, and all the papers blurred dangerously before her eyes.

In spite of herself, Neale pictured him sitting there with her in the welter of books and notes. She saw his brown hands moving among the papers, heard his voice serenely lecturing on his favorite topic, imagined how the shaded lamplight would glimmer on his curly hair and outline the contours of his cheek and mouth.

Clint Farrell had such a beautiful mouth....

"Hey, kid. What's up?"

Neale jumped as a voice cut through her reverie, startling her badly. A guilty flush spread over her cheeks when she remembered what she'd just been thinking. She looked up at Marjorie, who had popped her sleek dark head around the doorframe and was regarding her friend with interest.

"Oh, just doing a little work," Neale said lamely, avoiding Marjorie's bright glance. "I'm really fascinated with this cave thing, Marj."

"Do you think he'll ever find anything out there?" Marjorie came into the room, looking lush and gorgeous in a pair of blue-green lounging pyjamas.

Neale glanced enviously at her friend's pearl-tinted complexion, her shining dark hair and the big turquoise earrings that matched her outfit.

"You look great, Marj," she said, smiling. "Those pyjamas turned out really nice, didn't they? Most of my stuff just looks sort of muddy now. Especially my housecoat."

"Well, these were white to start with. Your housecoat," Marjorie pointed out sensibly, "was rust-colored before we dyed it. You could hardly expect it to turn a nice bright turquoise."

"I guess not," Neale agreed, sorting aimlessly through the scattered drifts of paper. "Now, where's that article about the..."

"Do you?" Marjorie persisted, giving her friend an inquiring glance.

"Do I what?"

"Do you think he'll find a cave?" Marjorie repeated patiently. "My goodness, Neale, where is your mind these days? Half the time you seem to be on another planet, or something."

Neale looked down nervously at the quilted spread beneath the mounds of paper, wondering what to say. She'd never told an outright lie to Marjorie, not once in all their long friendship. But Clint had been so passionately insistent about keeping their discovery a secret.

"I don't even want to tell Brock Munroe just yet," he'd told Neale earnestly. "I promised I'd let him know if I found something, and I intend to, but I want a chance to check this out first and see if the entrance is really viable."

"Viable?" Neale had asked.

"Negotiable. It looks good from the outside, but I have no idea what to expect when I get a little distance into the corridor. There could be an impassable waterfall down there, a sheer drop-off, anything. I don't want to talk about this to anybody until I've checked it out a bit. Promise you won't tell anybody, Neale."

And she'd promised, almost frightened by his intensity.

"I don't know," she said aloud to Marjorie, leafing awkwardly through a book about the exploration of Mammoth Cave. "I guess it's a possibility."

"Speaking of possibilities," Marjorie began cheerfully, moving a couple of notebooks aside to perch on the edge of bed, "what about our young engineer? Now, *there's* a definite possibility, I'd say."

Again Neale felt a treacherous warmth creeping over her cheeks. "Oh, Marj," she said with an awkward little laugh. "You're always seeing that kind of possibility. He's just a nice guy, that's all, and I'm interested in what he's doing. I'm certainly not interested in *him*. Not the way you mean, anyhow."

"Two dates in two nights," Marjorie said with a knowing grin. "Now, I'd call that a definite show of interest."

Neale glared at her. "That's not true!" she protested hotly. "Last night certainly wasn't a date. We had dinner together after hiking all day, that's all, and he was so tired that he practically fell asleep in his soup. And tonight is just another Sunday barbecue out at the dude ranch. Anybody can go. As a matter of fact, you and Virginia are coming along, too. I don't see how you can call it a *date.*"

"I can call it whatever I like," Marjorie said serenely. "He phoned this morning and made the arrangements with you, didn't he? I certainly got the impression that he was more interested in seeing you tonight than me or Virginia, hard as that may be to believe."

"He was just being courteous," Neale muttered, looking down at the papers again. "He was checking to be sure we had a ride out there, that's all. There's no big romance going on, Marj. Sorry to disappoint you, but there really isn't."

"Why are you trying so hard to convince me of that?" Marjorie asked curiously. "Neale, from all accounts this is a pretty nice guy. You told me yourself that he was nice. Why are you so opposed to having a little fun, for once? Why not admit that the guy attracts you, and relax a bit?"

Neale looked into her friend's shrewd blue eyes, wishing desperately that she could confide in Marjorie.

I can't allow myself to be attracted to Clint Farrell, she wanted to say, *because I'm already planning to betray him, Marj. I'm cheating the poor man, using him ruthlessly for my own purposes, and as soon as he finds out what I'm doing he's going to hate me. He's going to think I'm the most rotten, miserable...*

"Neale!" Virginia called from the hallway. "Telephone, dear!"

Neale muttered something and crawled off the bed, hurrying down the stairs to the hall, where Virginia stood by the telephone. Their landlady wore a blue cotton dress the same color as her eyes, and her silver hair shone brightly in the rich autumn light.

"Thanks, Virginia," Neale murmured, reaching for the phone. She paused, her heart beating crazily as she pictured Clint's face, his shy grin and the sturdy breadth of his shoulders. "Who is it, do you know?" she whispered.

Virginia shook her head. "It's a woman, dear. I don't think I recognize the voice. Not your mother, I'm fairly certain."

Neale's heart slowed to a more normal pace. She nodded her thanks and watched as Virginia disappeared into the kitchen to finish mixing the potato salad they were taking to the barbecue. Then she lifted the receiver. "Hello?"

"Neale? How are you?"

Neale tensed again. "Hillary? Is that you?"

"In the flesh. I dropped by my office and found your message on my machine."

Neale pictured Hillary's office in faraway New York City, piled with manuscripts and magazine abstracts. The office was always so frantically messy that Hillary, who was a small person, sometimes vanished beneath the mounds of paper, making the place seem deserted even on working days. Neale laughed, still feeling a little shaky. "Hillary, it's Sunday afternoon. I've often suspected that you live in that place, but now I'm sure of it. There must be a bed and a kitchen stove somewhere under all that paper."

"I wish," the editor muttered gloomily. "I do have an apartment, Neale, honestly I do. I even go there occasionally. But most days I drop by here to pick up my messages, even on weekends. Now, what's this hot new story idea of yours?"

Neale frowned and gripped the telephone cord, winding it nervously around her fingers while her mind raced. She hadn't expected to hear from the magazine editor until Monday at the earliest, and by then she'd hoped to have this conflict resolved in her mind. Again she pictured Clint's face, and recalled the clear honesty in his eyes. She'd only spent one day with the man, but Neale was already certain that Clint Farrell would never betray a confidence. And he'd die before he'd cheat someone, especially a friend. That knowledge made her even more ashamed of what she was about to do.

"Actually," she hedged, "it's not completely clear in my mind yet, Hillary. I'm just... researching the idea, sort of."

"We need a lead article for the next omnibus edition," Hillary said cheerfully. "Something really sexy, you know?"

"Sexy? In a *travel* magazine?"

"Not literally, you idiot. Something with cover appeal, a story that'll make them want to pick up the magazine and read it. So, have you got anything like that?"

"Well, maybe, but..."

"A dollar a word," Hillary announced in her flat eastern accent, cutting firmly across Neale's evasive murmurs.

"I beg your pardon?"

"A dollar a word, kid, plus expenses. And we're prepared to run longer than usual on this one if we can get what we want."

"How long?"

"Five, seven thousand words," Hillary said casually. "Even ten, if it's something super fabulous."

"But that's... Hillary... that's ten thousand dollars."

"Yeah," the editor said dryly. "I believe it is."

Ten thousand dollars.

Neale's eyes widened. She stared at the quiet foyer and the brassbound chest on which Virginia had placed a bowl of yellow chrysanthemums.

With all that money, she could clear away most of her mother's remaining personal debts. And after that, they'd be able to...

"Neale?"

Neale hesitated a moment longer. Then she took a deep breath and gripped the receiver tightly in her hand. "Caves," she said at last. "I've been doing research on caves."

"Caves?" Hillary echoed blankly.

"You know. Big, massive ones, like Carlsbad Caverns. I've met a guy out here who thinks..." Neale paused in agony, then forced herself to continue. "He thinks there's a huge new cave system hidden somewhere in the Hill Country, completely unexplored. He's been searching for an entrance."

"What is he, some kind of kook? Does he know what he's talking about?"

"Oh, I think so. He's very highly trained, with a degree in geological engineering. He...he wants to find this cave system and keep it a secret," Neale went on lamely. "He doesn't want the public to come stampeding in and spoil it."

"Secret!" Hillary echoed scornfully. "This is the information age, kid. People can't keep secrets anymore."

"I know," Neale muttered.

Especially not with traitors like me around, she added silently, her face twisting with unhappiness. *People who are willing to sell out their friends for money...*

"So, what's your take on it? How much chance is there that he'll find the entrance to this mythical cavern? We don't deal in fantasies, you know. We're not that kind of publication."

For a final time, Neale saw Clint's face as he smiled at her across the little camp stove, and told her with a shy smile how much he was enjoying her company.

And then, almost in the same picture, she saw her mother's pale worried face, the mounting piles of bills, and the bitter disappointment in her brother Ted's eyes when he learned that there wasn't enough money for the new saxophone he needed if he wanted to keep his place in the school band....

"He's already found it," she murmured. "I was there when he found it, Hillary."

"You *were?*" For the first time, Neale heard a lift of excitement in the editor's brisk tone. "And nobody else knows?"

"Not a soul. I...I promised I wouldn't tell anybody," Neale added miserably. "He's really obsessed with secrecy."

"Won't he be surprised," Hillary said with a wicked chuckle, "when he finds his big secret splashed across the front page of a national magazine?"

"Yes, I guess he will. He'll be really surprised."

"So, how much have you got so far?"

"Nothing, really. That's why I was reluctant to commit to it, Hillary. I mean, I've been doing lots of research on other caves. I can give you a whole lot on Carlsbad, and the new cave down there in New Mexico, and the systems in Kentucky, but..."

"Come on, Neale, that's all old stuff. Although it's interesting, and we haven't run anything similar for a long time, come to think of it. Your stuff might make back-page copy. But for a lead, we'll need something brand-new. Now, you say he's found an entrance to this place?"

"Yes. He doesn't know if it's any good, though. I mean, if it's going to be passable. He has to explore it some more to make sure it's safe to...to climb in there."

"But he's optimistic?"

Neale remembered Clint's reaction when they'd found the cave entrance. She saw him edging down out of her sight into the dark opening, and the excitement on his face when he'd scrambled back to the surface. He'd been so carried away that he'd forgotten himself and hugged Neale joyously, capering with her on the rugged hillside in an impromptu dance. She could still recall the feeling of his arms around her, his rough shirtfront against her cheek, his breathless laughter.

"Yes," she said grimly, "he's optimistic. He thinks it looks really promising."

"Well, great. Can you keep close to the project without making him suspicious?"

"I guess so," Neale said dully. "He seems to trust me."

"Great," Hillary repeated with enthusiasm, apparently unaware of Neale's misery. "We'll need pictures, kid. You need to get inside this thing and send us some pictures. Can you do that?"

Neale hesitated. "Hillary, he's a professional speleologist. He's really concerned about my amateur status. I don't think he's going to let me inside an unexplored cave."

"He's let you come this far," the editor said cheerfully. "You'll just have to think of a way to get inside."

"But I'm not sure if..."

"Neale, we don't require that you descend all the way to the bowels of the earth, or anything like that. It's probably enough for you to describe this place, how it was discovered and how it's never been explored, and where it is. We can toss in a few pictures of the cave interior and the surrounding countryside, and stress the 'fabulous new discovery' thing as a teaser, and then fill in the rest of the copy with some general information on other caves. You've already got that stuff, didn't you say?"

"Quite a lot of it. I'll need to go to the city archives and get some more information, but I think I can do a pretty good job with available material."

"Terrific. Just get yourself inside that cave, kiddo, and get some pictures. And tell us more about your mystery cave explorer, too. Our readers will want to know what makes this guy tick. Find out as much about him as you can, and fax me an outline within the next few days. I'll hold the space open for you."

"Thanks, Hillary. I'll . . . I'll be in touch as soon as I can."

Neale hung up the phone and stood unhappily by the little oak table, watching as Marjorie hurried down the stairs and into the kitchen to consult with Virginia about preparations for the barbecue at the dude ranch. Their laughter came drifting in from the other room, making her feel even more miserably alone in the sun-dappled hallway.

THE SUNDAY AFTERNOON barbecue at the Hole in the Wall Dude Ranch was a low-key affair, not at all like one of Scott Harris's dazzling season-openers, for which he imported caterers and music, and roasted a whole steer in the outdoor pit.

By now, all the family groups were gone and the guest list had dwindled to a hardy few, like Clint Farrell, who were willing to accept reduced amenities in exchange for a low weekly rate. The staff of the dude ranch looked exhausted after their second busy season, but quietly satisfied with their success.

Scott's face was still a little sad, as it had been ever since his brother Jeff's death, but he and Valerie were clearly making an effort to be upbeat for the sake of their guests. This late October barbecue was a small, casual affair, with just a few of the locals in attendance, and there was a family atmosphere around the fire pit. A lot of the women had brought salads and pies, giving Carla and her kitchen staff a much-needed break.

Clint relaxed on a rough wooden bench and smiled at his companions. Mary Gibson sat next to him, with her husband lounging on the other side. Bubba Gibson was teasing his wife about something, making her blush and giggle like a girl.

"Al Gibson," she choked, giving the big man a good-natured push with her hands, "I swear, if you don't stop it, I'll..."

Bubba leaned forward and put an arm around her, murmuring something in her ear that made her chuckle and turn even a brighter shade of pink.

Clint grinned and looked around at the crowd, wondering if this could be the same couple who'd been through such dreadful problems in recent years. By now, he'd heard most of the local gossip from the friendly staff at the dude ranch, but this was his first chance to put faces with a lot of the names.

Neale was right, he thought. Anything that happened in this town seemed to become general knowledge in about ten minutes. Crystal Creek was a hard place to keep a secret.

Clint frowned suddenly, then relaxed. His own secret was safe. Nobody knew about the cave entrance except himself and Neale, and she certainly didn't seem like the type to run around gossiping.

At the thought of her, he glanced restlessly out at the driveway, wondering what was keeping Virginia Parks and her two young boarders. Neale had promised that they'd be there well before the beef was served....

Clint shifted on the bench, realizing with sudden bleakness that no matter how pleasant this occasion might be, his evening would be ruined if she didn't show up. He was a little startled by how fully the woman occupied his mind, after just one day of acquaintance.

But then, Clint thought with a wry grin, she was hardly a total stranger. He'd been dreaming about her for years.

Clint recalled the passionate, elusive woman of his dreams, trying to imagine what Neale would say if he told her about those nighttime visitations.

But there was no denying that reality was a whole lot better than dreams. It had been wonderful yesterday to hold her in his arms. There was something so satisfying about her slim body, even in jeans and a bulky jacket. No woman had ever felt so utterly *right*. Clint was almost frightened by the unfamiliar emotions and hot tides of feeling that kept surging through him.

Suddenly he became conscious of a feather-light touch on his knee, and looked down to see a pair of solemn brown eyes gazing up at him from a round pink face.

An infant stood shakily next to him, clad in a pair of red plaid rompers and a white T-shirt, with an incongruous frilly bonnet pulled low over her face. The hand that rested on his knee was dimpled, like a fat starfish, and the child rocked unsteadily in a pair of sturdy white baby shoes with silver bells on the laces.

"Hello, Jennifer," Bubba Gibson crooned, reaching out for the little girl. She ignored him and continued to concentrate soberly on Clint.

Mary chuckled. "Look at that. She picks the best-looking guy in the crowd and makes a beeline for him. This one's going to be a real heartbreaker, isn't she?"

Clint glanced in surprise at the smiling woman next to him, amazed that Mary Gibson apparently considered him the best-looking man in the group. But she was bending down to hug the little girl, her sweet face full of happiness.

"This young lady is Jennifer McKinney," she told Clint. "She just started walking last week, and she's already getting to be a holy terror. Look at her poor mama."

Clint nodded at a slim blond woman across the terrace who was watching them anxiously. He grinned at the woman and reached out a cautious hand to touch the little girl's lacy bonnet, cupping his fingers gently around her head. She gave him an enchanting smile and moved closer, then leaned against his leg and began swinging her foot to make the bell tinkle on her shoe.

"Excuse me, sir. Is this woman bothering you?"

Clint looked up, startled, to see a laughing young woman whom he recognized as Tyler McKinney's wife. She was pregnant and glowing with a kind of joyous contentment that made Clint smile automatically in return. Behind her was another woman, barely more than a girl, with a cloud of dark hair and a lovely face.

"This is Lisa," Ruth McKinney said to Clint. "It's Lisa's job to keep Jennifer under control, the poor girl."

While Clint watched, still smiling, Lisa swept the baby into her arms and cuddled her, whispering something into Jennifer's plump neck so the baby chortled and kicked her legs in delight. Then she carried the child off to a set of swings and slides near the lodge where a young man waited for them, gazing at Lisa adoringly.

"That's Tony Rodriguez, the new veterinarian," Mary murmured to Clint. "He and Lisa are getting married sometime after Christmas."

Bubba Gibson leaned past his wife and grinned sociably at Clint. "Purty hard to keep all the names straight, ain't it?"

Clint nodded ruefully. "I feel like I know most of these people," he said to his companions, "because I've heard so much about them. But it's hard to put faces together with all the names."

Mary looked at him with sympathy. "Let's see," she murmured. "Who have you met already? That's J.T. and Cynthia, they're the baby's parents, and of course you know Scott and Val, and that's Beverly's mother, Carolyn Trent, and her husband Vern, and there's Brock Munroe, who ranches over at the Double Bar, neighboring Al and me...."

"I've met Brock. Who are those two women next to him? Is that his wife?"

Mary smiled and waved, then turned back to Clint. "That pretty lady in the pink dress is Brock's girlfriend, Amanda Walker, and the tall gray-haired woman is his aunt, Millie Munroe."

Clint looked with healthy male appreciation at the attractive young woman next to Brock. "Do they all live at the ranch? Somehow I had the impression that Brock lived all alone out there. Except for Alvin," he added, with a brief grin.

Mary laughed. "Isn't it funny? I think everybody in the county knows Alvin. He's famous."

"He's kind of hard to overlook," Clint said with a solemn twinkle. "There's just something about him. Is Alvin here today, by the way?"

Mary shook her head. "He came to the last barbecue and ruined a whole bowl of punch. He tried to climb up while nobody was looking and sneak a drink, and wound up tumbling right into the bowl. Brock had to leave early and take him home in disgrace."

Clint chuckled, picturing Alvin swimming frantically among the orange rind and maraschino cherries, his ears flapping in panic.

"To answer your question," Mary went on, "Brock isn't married. Not yet, anyhow," she added darkly, "and I sure don't know what's keeping him. Wouldn't any man in his right mind want to marry a girl like that if he had the chance?"

Clint studied Amanda Walker, drawn by her pearl-tinted complexion, her grace and composure. But, on closer inspection, there was a remote look of sadness in the woman's blue eyes that seemed out of place in this merry group.

"Yes," he said slowly. "Yes, Mary, I'd think a man wouldn't want to pass up a woman like that."

But then, suddenly, all thoughts of Amanda Walker were driven from his mind. He saw Neale approaching from the direction of the lodge, walking with two other women that Clint didn't even notice.

His eyes were filled with Neale, with her dark eyes and slim figure and laughing face. She wore a blue-green cotton romper suit and sandals, and her bare, tanned arms and legs gleamed in the golden evening light.

He watched as she came toward the group on the terrace, carrying a covered plastic bowl, which she deposited on one of the tables before turning to give Clint a shy smile of greeting. He smiled back, still dazzled by those long, shapely legs. He'd only seen the woman in blue jeans and a baseball cap. He'd had no idea her hair was so smooth and shining, her figure so trimly rounded.

Again he recalled those hot random dreams, all the nights when he'd held a woman like this in his arms and tasted the rich sweetness of her body. Longing stirred within him, then began to thrust at him with a powerful surge of hungry desire.

Clint shifted nervously on the bench, hoping Mary
and Bubba hadn't noticed his reaction. He struggled to
get himself under control, wondering at his behavior.
Normally he was quiet and reserved around women,
tending to a conduct so courtly and polite that he was
sometimes teased about his old-fashioned manners.
But with this particular girl, it was all Clint Farrell
could do to keep from leaping on her and clutching her
in a wild, passionate embrace. And *that,* he thought,
holding his breath as Neale approached the flagged
terrace and moved hesitantly toward him, was exactly
what he planned to do.

The first chance he got, Neale Cameron was going
to be in his arms, and he didn't intend to let her go until both of them were satisfied.

"LOOK AT that face," Millie Munroe whispered from
the side of her mouth. "Did you ever see such a hungry man as that? Like a fox looking at a plump
chicken."

Brock followed his aunt's glance and watched as
Neale Cameron seated herself on the wooden bench
between Mary Gibson and Clint Farrell.

"Who?" he asked with a grin. "Bubba, or the other
guy?"

"Bubba!" Millie echoed scornfully. "Now, that's
another story altogether. Any man who takes almost
forty years to figure out that he's in love with his wife,
he's likely too dumb to worry about. I meant the young
cave feller."

Brock looked at her in surprise. "Clint Farrell? How do you know him, Millie?"

"I met the two of them yesterday when I was out riding. They were hiking down to the highway."

"Two?" Brock asked. "Clint had somebody with him?"

Millie glared at him, clearly irritated by her nephew's denseness. "That girl. The one in blue, or green, or whatever that god-awful color is. They were hiking along together like one of those exploring teams on public television. Seemed like a pretty flighty pair, if you ask me."

Brock glanced again at the two young people, giving them a thoughtful, measuring glance. "That's strange," he said. "I never realized Clint had anybody with him when he hiked out there. But," he added decisively, "I'd hardly call him flighty, Millie. He seemed like a real steady young feller. I liked him."

"Any man gets flighty," Millie said with scorn, "when he falls in love. Just look at *you.*"

"Am I flighty?" Brock grinned at his aunt and put an arm around Amanda, cuddling her fondly, then found himself worried again by the rigid tension in her slim body.

Things had settled down a bit at home since the scene at the breakfast table yesterday. Amanda had gone quietly about her work, stripping off the old wallpaper and cleaning up the mess. She'd even had time to mount a few sheets of the new paper, which looked beautiful, exactly as she'd said it would.

Millie had come back from her ride, inspected the dining room in grim silence and tramped up the stairs to her room. Brock knew that she couldn't find any fault with what Amanda was doing, because she'd certainly have voiced a criticism if she could. He wished his aunt could have been gracious enough to give the younger woman a few words of praise, but that didn't seem possible these days.

Brock frowned when he thought about Millie, wondering again just what could have happened to the colorful person he remembered from his boyhood. This bitter, sharp-tongued woman was a stranger to him, but still he felt bound to his aunt by powerful ties of family and tradition, and miserably torn between her and Amanda.

"Who are you talking about?" Amanda asked quietly from his other side. "Who's this moonstruck, flighty person?"

"Clint Farrell," Brock told her, gesturing at the young people sitting with the Gibsons. "That's the young guy I told you about who's looking for a cave entrance on my property."

Amanda glanced thoughtfully at the people across the terrace. "The one sitting with Neale Cameron?"

"Is that her name? She's one of Virginia's boarders, isn't she?"

Amanda nodded. "I met those two girls at Lynn's baby shower last week. I really liked them." She was silent a moment, studying Clint Farrell, who seemed to have brightened up considerably since the young woman's arrival. "I wonder if he'll find his cave."

"Well, he sounded pretty confident," Brock said. "I guess there's a good chance. This whole region is like a big honeycomb under the surface, you know."

"But a cave...Brock, if he found a big cave out there, would it add to the value of the property, do you think?"

Millie snorted. "For someone with no claim on the property, she sure takes a mighty strong interest in its value, doesn't she?"

Brock glared briefly at Millie, shocked by her dreadful rudeness. But his thoughts turned immediately back to Amanda, whose face had drained of color. Her lips trembled and her hands shook with emotion as she struggled to get herself under control.

"I think I'll just...go for a little walk," she whispered abruptly, getting up and fleeing across the freshly mown grass toward a heavy wire fence down near the stables.

"Sorry," Millie murmured to her nephew after Amanda was gone. Despite her words, the older woman looked bright-eyed and distinctly unrepentant. "I guess that wasn't real nice of me, was it?"

"For God's sake, Millie..."

But there was no time to get into an argument with his aunt. Brock watched Amanda in wretched concern as she made a show of peering inside the fence, gripping the wire in her shaking hands. From this distance she looked fragile and vulnerable in the delicate pink dress, and Brock felt a surge of that familiar longing to protect her from anything that would ever threaten to harm her.

Some protection he was, Brock thought bitterly as he got to his feet and started walking across the grass toward her. He couldn't even keep her from being hurt within the confines of his own household. How could he hope to shield her from all the other dangers that life might hold?

He reached the fence and moved toward her awkwardly, longing to take her in his arms and comfort her. But they were still in full view of the group up on the terrace, and Brock knew that she would be even more humiliated if anybody was aware of her distress. So he stood quietly beside her, looking through the fence at part of Scott's herd of exotic animals. A zebra grazed quietly near them, its beautiful striped hide glistening. It cropped grass steadily, ignoring the antics of a pair of wildebeests who capered nearby, prancing on their hind legs and making sudden passes at each other with their horns.

"I've always thought," Brock ventured nervously, smiling down at the woman beside him, "that a wildebeest looks like an animal put together by a committee. They're uglier than Alvin, aren't they?"

But no answering smile came from Amanda. She stared at the playful animals, her eyes wide and dark in her pale face.

"Mandy?" Brock whispered, agonized by her pain. "Sweetheart, I'm sorry about Millie. I can't bear to see you hurting like this. Should I ask her to leave? I will if you want me to."

She glanced up at him, her expression still unfathomable in the mellow twilight. "Leave? Of course not. The ranch is her home, after all. Besides, she's right, Brock. She's absolutely right."

He stared at her with mounting anxiety. There was something in Amanda's voice that he'd never heard before . . . a dead, cold tone that terrified him.

"She's not right!" he protested. "She's wrong to talk like that. It was completely out of line, and I mean to—"

"She's right," Amanda repeated in that same lifeless voice. "I have no interest in the land, and no claim on you. None at all. It's wrong for me to keep pretending that I do."

"That's not true! Sweetheart, you have a claim on everything I own. I love you, and I always will. I'd do anything for you."

"Then marry me!" Amanda whirled to face him. "Marry me, Brock," she whispered in a low, passionate tone. "Tell me right now that we'll be married before Christmas. Don't keep talking about how much you love me. Show me some proof of it for a change! Give me a decent, honest place in your life."

Brock stared down at her, his mind spinning crazily. Here it was at last, out in the open, throbbing between them on the evening air. There was no ignoring the issue any longer.

He looked at her tense face, wondering what to say. The easiest thing, of course, would be simply to yield and give her what she wanted, and everything within him longed to do that very thing.

Brock wanted Amanda to be happy, and he wanted nothing more for himself than to have this woman securely tied to him for life, anchored firmly at the center of his world, where nothing could ever take her away. Wistfully, he thought of waking up every morning to find her next to him in bed, imagined the way their lives would grow and blossom, and children would run happily through the big old house. . . .

Brock shivered with yearning, then took himself sternly in hand and forced himself to deal with the cold facts of his situation.

If he proposed to her this evening, he'd have to borrow the money to buy her an engagement ring. He couldn't even afford a new suit to get married in. Maybe, he thought bitterly, he could ask Amanda for a loan, since she appeared to be the most prosperous person of his acquaintance right at the moment.

Sure, honey, I'd love to marry you. By the way, do you think you could slip me a couple thousand bucks? I'll need it to cover my wedding expenses. . . .

Amanda was staring at him with a fathomless gaze, waiting for his reply. The silence lengthened between them, grew miserable and finally unbearable while Brock continued to hesitate.

At last she put her hand on his arm, nodding as if a private opinion had just been confirmed. "Never mind, Brock," she said quietly. "I understand. I'll talk to you later in the week, all right? Beverly's leaving soon, I think, and she'll give me a ride out to the ranch to pick up my car."

"Amanda, sweetheart, please don't—"

"If you start an argument," Amanda told him softly, forcing a smile as Val Harris and Lynn Russell walked past them on their way down to the stables, "then I'll start crying and disgrace both of us. Please, Brock, if you're going to do this to me, at least let me go with a little dignity. It's all I have left, after all."

She turned on her heel and walked quickly away, heading for the lodge in the fading twilight while Brock watched her in miserable silence.

CHAPTER SEVEN

ON WEDNESDAY AFTERNOON, Amanda sat at her desk, paging listlessly through fashion catalogs. Finally, she pushed the heavy books aside, took off her glasses and rubbed her temples, then got up and wandered through the office into the big workroom at the back. They'd moved the shop in the spring, when the success of Amanda's business had caused her original shopping service, called Spree, to overflow that first little cubbyhole at the end of the mall. They were still in the Arboretum, but they'd taken over a much larger facility, recently vacated by a manufacturer of printed T-shirts and customized exercise wear.

Now Amanda had an elegant reception and display area, a couple of consultation rooms for private discussions with clients, an entire office for herself, another smaller one for the bookkeeper and a huge workroom at the back with banks of cutting tables, sewing machines and storage shelves.

The workroom hummed with activity, heaped with a wildly colorful variety of fabrics and trimmings as the seamstresses worked on last-minute Halloween costumes and the first of the theatrical outfits. The girls chattered merrily as they worked, filling the room with a pleasant singsong rhythm of soft voices, laughter, the thrum of sewing machines and the muted swish of scissors cutting through silk and velvet.

Amanda paused and looked around, smiling automatically as one of the seamstresses looked up and waved a greeting. Normally she loved coming back here. Everything about the workroom was appealing to her. She liked the promising scent of fresh-cut fabric, the skill of the women's dancing fingers, the teasing give-and-take of their conversations as the creations grew and took shape beneath their hands.

But today nothing seemed able to lift her mood, not even the colorful racks of completed costumes that hung along one wall, awaiting her inspection.

"I'll look at them later, Conchita," she murmured to the head seamstress, who had noticed Amanda's arrival and was moving forward with an inquiring look. "Maybe this evening or tomorrow, all right?"

Conchita nodded, then exchanged a troubled glance with the two women at the front table as Amanda turned and wandered back out to her office.

She'd caught the glance, and it didn't surprise her. She knew the girls were worried about her. This silence and lack of interest were certainly not her usual style. The seamstresses had all seemed to catch her mood lately, and even the merry laughter and occasional bursts of song from the big workroom were more subdued these days.

Amanda sighed wearily, put her glasses back on and forced herself to concentrate on the book of winter garments in front of her.

But the pictures blurred before her eyes until all she could see was Brock's tense face when she'd issued that ultimatum. He'd actually turned pale beneath the tan, and his jawline had tightened visibly....

Poor Brock, Amanda thought involuntarily. *I've caused him so much misery.*

They hadn't spoken since that night. Amanda worked late at the shop most weeknights, and there'd been no messages from him on her machine when she went home. Amanda was reluctant to call him, knowing she had every right to be resentful of his refusal to make a commitment to her. Any woman would be angry and unforgiving, justifiably furious with a man who'd used and humiliated her in such a fashion.

But Amanda understood Brock Munroe so well. It was difficult to stay angry with him when she knew how honest and sincere he was, how tenderhearted and loving, how utterly reliable. Besides, she loved him so much. And she needed him so desperately, every moment of the day, that it was torture to be out of touch with him.

Amanda sighed, fighting back a miserable flood of tears and forcing herself to think about the situation calmly.

He wasn't being deliberately cruel, after all. There were probably all kinds of good reasons why Brock was reluctant to commit himself to marriage. He'd lived such a solitary life, with a drunken and undependable father. His only vivid memories of his mother were times when she'd cried from the sheer hopelessness of her life. And now his aunt, one of the most stable figures from his childhood, had turned out to be a bitter and unhappy woman as well.

No wonder the man feared an intimate relationship of any kind. Nothing in his life had taught him how to be close to another person, and he certainly had no reason to trust that a woman, any woman, would be careful of his feelings as the years went by.

No doubt he truly believed he was better off alone, safer and less likely to be hurt. Amanda wasn't going to convince him otherwise if she kept railing at him for his inability to commit to marriage. But even with all the love and understanding she could possibly summon, her patience was wearing dangerously thin.

And Millie's harsh frankness certainly didn't help matters.

"Hi, Angel. Why the long face? It's so unbecoming."

Amanda looked up blankly, then smiled in delight when she recognized her visitor.

"Edward! Where did you come from?"

"Manhattan." Edward Price sauntered into the room and cleared a pile of fabric samples from one of the gilt-backed chairs, then seated himself and crossed his legs with casual elegance.

Amanda smiled at him again, pleased by his unexpected arrival. All the old feelings for Edward, the stormy passion she'd felt during their long-term relationship, seemed to have vanished completely as soon as she met Brock. Now she felt only a friendship, and a pleasure in Edward's company that she hadn't been aware of during the turbulent days when they'd been lovers.

"You flew in this morning?"

"By fits and starts," Edward said with a grimace, then looked with sudden attention at one of the fabric samples in his hand. "For some unexplained reason, we had two stops along the way. Angel, what are all these gorgeous fabrics? Are you expanding into the drapery market?"

"We're doing costumes for *The Phantom of the Opera*. Those are the court dresses for the masquerade."

Edward chuckled. "I thought perhaps you'd taken on Marie Antoinette as a client. You've got everybody else, after all. How's the cowboy?"

"He's . . . he's fine. You're looking well, Edward."

Edward wore corduroy slacks and a tweed jacket with leather elbow patches, a rustic look that he liked to cultivate when he came to Texas. But, Amanda noted with amusement, he still couldn't resist a washed-silk shirt of dark rust that brought out the ruddy highlights in his auburn hair. He would have been a striking figure even back home in Manhattan. Down here in blue-jeans country, he was a real knockout.

Edward grinned, comfortably aware of her admiration. "So, 'why so pale and wan, fond lover?' " he quoted. "You can't fool me, Angel. I knew you when you were a poor struggling salesgirl, after all. Is the cowboy giving you problems? Do I have to call him out at high noon with six-guns drawn?"

Amanda smiled briefly at this engaging picture, then sobered. "Actually, we're having some problems over the commitment issue. Brock loves me, but he doesn't want to get married," she said, a little startled by her frankness.

Still, it felt good to talk to somebody she could trust, and there were some things she couldn't tell her friend Beverly, no matter how long they'd known each other.

Edward looked at her with sympathy. "The man has got to be crazy," he said firmly.

Amanda gave him another bleak smile. "Thanks for the vote of confidence, Edward. I can use a little praise these days. But," she added, "I really don't think he's crazy. He could have all kinds of good reasons for being afraid of commitment, you know, none of them necessarily related to me. I keep telling myself that," she added gloomily, "but it hurts so much."

Edward was silent a moment. "I came by to invite you to dinner," he said at last. "Do you have something really smashing to wear? Something that'll set this old cow town on its ear?"

Amanda shifted uncomfortably. "Edward, I don't know if..."

"Never fear. We'll be a foursome," he went on serenely. "Salome will be my date. She has a friend who's at loose ends tonight, and we thought you might be able to fill in. Think of it as a small courtesy on your part."

"Who did you say was with you?"

"Salome Maroc. Remember, Angel, the designer from Dallas who's joined me recently as head buyer? She flew down with me this morning."

Amanda nodded, feeling awkward. "I didn't realize you two were . . . traveling together," she said lamely.

"She wanted to pay a visit to her hometown and do a little business. Anyhow," Edward went on, crossing his legs again and leaning back, "Salome's friend is here in Austin, quite a presentable young oilman, I believe, who just happens to be going out to dinner with us tonight. We both hoped you might be able to come along."

Amanda studied him, her eyes narrowed suspiciously. "Edward," she asked, "are you by any chance trying to fix me up?"

"Certainly not," Edward said with a look of hurt innocence. "Must everything be reduced to this vulgar level of sex and mating? Although Salome assures me that the man is quite an acceptable specimen. Name of Judd Hinshaw."

"Judd *Hinshaw!*" Amanda echoed, astounded by this casual announcement. "But Edward, the Hinshaws are . . ." She floundered, momentarily at a loss for words.

"One of the Lone Star State's leading families," Edward said jovially. "I know. And Salome tells me that Judd is not only rich, powerful and handsome, he's really quite nice. So, are you coming? We thought we'd start at Kickers, just for atmosphere, but please don't wear your jeans and boots, Angel, because later we'll be moving on to something more civilized.''

Amanda stared at the urbane man in the opposite chair, her mind reeling. She was a little surprised to realize how much Edward's suggestion tempted her. The chance to dress up and enjoy an evening out, have a lot of fun with some witty and cultivated people, be flattered and admired...

And, she thought with a sigh, there'd be none of the tension that had clouded her relationship with Brock in recent months. No doubts and silent accusations, no sidelong glances and awkward silences. Best of all, no Millie watching sharply and passing judgment on Amanda's every move.

"You should meet Brock's aunt," she told Edward with a little grimace. "Actually," she added after a moment's thought, "you'd probably *like* her, Edward. Neither of you would win any prizes for tact and gentleness, that's for sure."

Edward grinned, not at all disturbed by her words. "Wear white," he advised. "You've always looked so marvelous in white, my dear. Virginal, but just a little bit naughty."

Amanda chuckled. "You're hopeless, you know that?" she said. "Just hopeless."

But her heart was pounding pleasantly, her cheeks were warm, and she knew that she was, indeed, going to accept Edward's surprising offer.

BROCK SETTLED BACK in his chair and listened to the empty ringing of the telephone at the other end. When Amanda's recording came on, asking him to leave a message, he hung up and frowned at his watch.

It was past midnight. She must be at home, still refusing to answer the phone. He hated to keep bothering her, but his need to hear her voice was so overwhelming that it drowned out all reason and caution.

Besides, he was haunted by the irrational conviction that she wasn't home, after all. Brock loved this woman so deeply that he felt a mystical, inexplicable bond with her, even when she was angry with him. If Amanda was sitting at home, listening to the same telephone that was ringing in his ear, he was sure that he would sense some kind of connection. Tonight, though, he had the hollow, aching feeling that the phone was jangling in an empty room, and she was somewhere far away. But where could she be after midnight? She never worked this late at the shop.

Brock had a sudden mental image, painfully vivid, of Amanda's little car smashed against a freeway overpass, her body broken and racked with pain, and nobody around to help her.

He groaned aloud, passed a shaking hand over his face and reached for the phone again, then hesitated.

If she really *was* at home and determined to ignore him, then he was keeping her from sleeping by calling her constantly. He hated to be so inconsiderate, especially when he knew how hard she was working.

Brock's face hardened.

Dammit, he thought, *she's kept me from sleeping all week! She can damn well answer the phone, just to let me know she's all right.*

Again he dialed and waited. Until now he hadn't left a message, just hung up each time her recording began. But this time he prepared himself to speak to the emptiness, to swallow his pride and plead with his love to talk with him.

"Hello, this is Amanda. I can't come to the phone just now..." her cool voice said on the other end of the line. Brock shuddered in the grip of a hot surge of desire, then composed himself to wait for the beep.

"Hi, sweetheart," he began at last, his voice low and husky. "I'm sorry to keep bothering you, but I think I'll die if I can't hear your voice. It's just after midnight, and I sure hope you're safely home." He paused, feeling foolish, wondering what he could say that might induce her to pick up the receiver and talk to him.

"Matter of fact," he went on with sudden inspiration, "I'm a little worried about Alvin, too. He ran off early this morning, and he hasn't come home yet. I don't know what to—"

"Brock?" she said, startling him. She sounded so close that he could almost feel the sweetness of her breath against his cheek. He fell abruptly silent, weak with tenderness. "Brock, what did you say?"

"Hi, honey. I was just telling you how lonely I am. How've you been?"

"I'm fine. What were you saying about Alvin? Is he lost?"

Brock smiled sadly. She wasn't concerned with his pain at all, just Alvin's whereabouts.

"He ran off this morning right after I finished the chores, and didn't come home for supper. There's no sign of him anywhere."

"Oh, *Brock* ..."

"No need to get too alarmed, sweetheart," Brock told her, worried by the anguish in her voice. "It isn't the first time he's done this."

"I've never known Alvin to miss a meal. Not once since I've known him."

"It's something he does in the fall, for some reason. He goes through a little spell of wandering every year around this time. It seems to last a week or two, then he goes back to being lazy as ever."

"But has he ever stayed away overnight?"

"Once or twice. I guess Mary Gibson's tomcat had him cornered in their barn one night, and wouldn't let him out till morning. Come to think of it, the trauma of that experience probably scarred him for life."

"You're laughing," Amanda said accusingly. "Brock, that's really mean. Poor little Alvin."

"Sorry," Brock said with instant repentance. "How are you, darling? I've been calling all evening, but I guess you were down at the shop. You must be pretty busy," he added wistfully, hoping that maybe she wasn't angry with him after all, that she'd just been too busy to call him, and now things between them would get back to normal without a lot of fighting.

But her next words dashed his hopes. "I wasn't at the shop," she said, sounding a little awkward. "I was . . . I went out for the evening. In fact, I just came in the door when the phone rang."

Brock tensed, but kept his voice deliberately casual. "You were out? Who with?"

"Just some people. Actually," she went on, "Edward's in town with his new lady. You should see her, Brock. She's so gorgeous."

Brock sagged with relief. "So the three of you went out for dinner? That was real nice, honey."

"Well . . ." she began, sounding evasive once again. She murmured something Brock didn't catch.

"Beg pardon, sweetheart? What did you say?"

"I said, there were four of us for dinner. Salome brought along a friend of hers."

"Girlfriend?"

"No, it was a fellow she went to college with, at Baylor. His name is . . . is Judd Hinshaw."

Brock gave a low whistle. "Wow. Pretty fancy company for a friend of Alvin's," he commented, trying to keep his voice calm and free of emotion.

He imagined Amanda sweeping into a classy restaurant on the arm of Judd Hinshaw, whose picture he remembered from *Texas Monthly*. Jealousy gripped him, raw and savage, accompanied by a fear that was more powerful than any he'd ever known.

If Brock lost this woman, then he would die. He couldn't live without her. He needed her face and her smile, needed her in his life, required the sweetness of her as much as the air he breathed.

"It was a nice evening," Amanda was saying, her voice deliberately casual. "But then, I suppose you and Millie are having a good time at the ranch, too, aren't you?"

"Millie's away."

"She is? Where?"

"She and Virginia are in Austin for a couple of days, visiting old school friends. Maybe you'll run into her, honey."

"Good Lord," Amanda murmured fervently. "I hope not."

Brock chuckled, relieved that she seemed able to joke again, although he could still sense some strain in her voice.

"Guess what, Brock?" she went on. "Tonight Edward took us to this little out-of-way restaurant that costs a fortune, and you know who we met while we were there?"

"I can't imagine," Brock said dryly.

"The governor and his wife! You remember, I told you she's a client of mine?"

"She's pregnant, right?"

"That's right. And guess what else?"

For the first time she was beginning to sound natural again, full of excitement and animation. "What?" Brock asked, smiling in spite of himself.

"She invited us to a party, Brock. This weekend, at the governor's mansion. Isn't that exciting?"

"Who did she invite?" Brock asked, his pleasure giving way to another dull wave of pain. "You and Judd?"

"Oh, Brock, don't be like that! She invited all of us, and any escorts we'd care to bring. And I'm asking you if you'd like to come."

"Wouldn't you rather go with your friend Judd?"

"For goodness sake, don't keep saying his name like that," Amanda said impatiently. "You have no reason to be jealous. I didn't do anything tonight that you could possibly be angry about. Besides," she added with pointed emphasis, "it's not as if you and I are engaged or anything, Brock, as your aunt is always so quick to point out. I guess I'm free to go out with friends for the evening if I choose to."

Brock realized that they were edging back onto dangerous ground, and beat a hasty retreat. "You really want me to go with you to this party, sweetheart? At the *governor's mansion?*"

"Please, Brock, would you? It's such a great opportunity for me. I'll meet all kinds of people, and make valuable contacts..."

Brock hesitated, grappling with a familiar discomfort. He recognized Amanda's invitation as a peace offering, a small olive branch that she was extending in an attempt to put their quarrel behind them. It would be petty of him to refuse, when she so seldom asked him for anything like this.

The problem with the whole plan, he thought bitterly, was really quite simple. He just didn't have a thing to wear.

Brock pictured himself wandering around the governor's mansion in the shabby black suit he'd bought eighteen years ago for his high school graduation. It wasn't a pleasant thought. Particularly when his vivid imagination supplied him with an image of Judd Hinshaw standing at Amanda's other side, immaculately attired in black tie and tux.

"Honey," he said, trying to keep his voice casual, "I'm not really up on these things, you know. How much does a good tuxedo cost these days?"

"I'm not sure," she said. "Let me think... One of my clients' husbands just bought a tux a couple of months ago, and I think she said it was..."

Brock gripped the telephone, picturing her beautiful face and the little frown between her eyebrows that always deepened when she was concentrating. He felt shaky with longing, so hungry for her that his throat was tight, and his heart pounded noisily against his denim shirt.

"I think you can probably get a pretty good tux for about five or six hundred dollars," she said finally. "Nothing fancy, but serviceable."

Five or six hundred dollars.

Brock's grip tightened on the receiver. At the moment, he was fully occupied by the effort to come up with four hundred dollars for a final payment on the new bull he'd purchased in the spring. He had no idea how he was going to find that amount, let alone the cash for a tuxedo, of all things. But there was no way on earth he was going to let Amanda know the real extent of his money troubles.

"Is that right? Well, I guess I'm way behind the times," he confessed. "I thought seventy dollars would about cover it. I think that's what I paid for my graduation suit."

"That was a few years ago, Brock."

"Yeah, I guess it was."

They were both silent for a moment, while Brock ran his mind frantically over his miserable financial situation. "Seems like a whole lot of money for just one night. Maybe I could rent one," he ventured at last. "How much would it cost to rent a tux, do you know?"

"Oh, Brock," Amanda said with a touch of impatience, "you don't have to *rent* a suit for this party. After all, I'm in the clothing business, you know. Why don't you just come into town tomorrow and we'll go shopping for something nice that fits you properly?"

"And you'll pay for it?" Brock asked softly.

"Brock, really, it's no big deal. I spend that much on my own clothes all the time. Besides, I can get a terrific bargain, especially if I . . ."

His hand shook and the room blurred around him as he struggled to control himself. "Look, sweetheart," he said at last, "I may be a bad manager and a real sorry excuse for a man, but I still haven't stooped to letting a woman buy my clothes. I'm sorry that you think so little of me."

"Brock!"

"Goodbye, honey. I think I hear Alvin at the door. I'd better go let him in."

Brock hung up hastily, before his hurt pride and outrage caused him to say something really damaging. He hurried to the kitchen door, but Alvin wasn't there after all. The autumn night was dark and moonless, silent except for the chirp of crickets and the occasional sad cries of a nighthawk in the tree by the barn.

"Alvin? Are you out here?"

Brock stared unseeing into the starry blackness, feeling lonely and chilled, trying not to think about the hurt bewilderment in Amanda's voice just before their conversation ended.

"LOOK, CLINT. Isn't that Alvin over there?"

"Where? I don't see anything."

"Just coming up the hill. See, over behind that clump of mesquite?"

Clint peered in the direction Neale was pointing, then grinned. "Damn, I think you're right. What's he doing out here all by himself, I wonder?"

Neale bent to greet the ragged little dog, who was running in their direction, ears flapping wildly. Gravel and dust spurted from under his paws as he scrambled up the hillside. His sides were heaving, pink tongue lolling from his open mouth.

"Poor thing," Neale murmured, patting him and turning to look up at Clint. "You know, I think he's hungry."

"He's always hungry."

"No, I mean he's really starving. Look, he even seems a bit skinnier than usual, doesn't he?"

"Skinnier!" Clint echoed in disbelief, watching as Alvin broke away from Neale's grip to nose frantically among their supplies. She took a package of dried beef from one of the packs and offered it to him, and the dog fell on the morsel as if he hadn't eaten for weeks.

"I wonder if he's been fed lately," Neale murmured, her concern growing. "Look, Clint, he acts like he's practically starving. Doesn't he?"

Clint knelt beside her, studying the dog as Alvin wolfed the pieces of meat. "Maybe he hasn't been home for a while," he suggested at last. "This is pretty far from the ranch, Neale. He might have been wandering and spent the night out here. Better give him a drink, too."

She poured some water from Clint's canteen into a shallow dish, touched by the look of slavish adoration in Alvin's dark eyes as he pressed close to her and began to lap frantically at the water.

Finally, much refreshed, the little dog settled back on his haunches and looked up at them with mild inquiry, his tail beating softly against the dusty ground.

"Go home, Alvin," Neale murmured. "You have to go home now. You can't come with us."

Alvin gazed at her, looking puzzled and hurt.

"You can't," Neale repeated firmly, and gave his collar a gentle tug. "You have to go home. Brock is probably really worried about you."

"Home!" Clint echoed, glaring at the dog with mock fierceness as he pointed in the direction of the ranch buildings. "Home, Alvin!"

Alvin tensed, then sighed and began to trudge wearily down the hill, pausing occasionally to give them a bitter glance over his shoulder.

Clint chuckled and lowered himself to the ground beside Neale, watching as the dog trotted off into the hazy distance. "What a character," he observed, dropping a friendly arm around her shoulder.

Neale shivered at his touch. The man was becoming so attractive to her that she could hardly contain herself when she was close to him. She found herself thinking about him all the time, wondering how it would feel to be in his arms, loving him. . . .

As if reading her thoughts, he bent close to her and stroked her cheek. "Hey, Neale," he whispered. "Are you in a real hurry to get back to town tonight?"

"I sure am," she said, keeping her voice light and casual, as if her face wasn't still tingling from the brush of his fingertips.

"A real big hurry?" He pulled her into his arms. "Can't stay out here with me for a while and watch the moon come up?"

He kissed her forehead and cheeks, then found her mouth, his lips warm and tender but insistent.

This was a different matter altogether from the few casual kisses he'd given her since they met. Neale gasped at the sweetness of his caress, and the fiery response that stirred within her as he leaned closer, powerful and intent, pressing her body down into the sun-warmed grass.

"Hey," she protested, wriggling beneath him, still trying to sound offhand and amused. "What's all this? We hardly know each other."

"That's what you think. I feel like I've known you all my life," he whispered against her throat, his breath uneven. "I've been wanting you as long as I can remember."

The amazing thing was, Neale felt just the same. She couldn't imagine a time when she hadn't known this man, with his sunny smile and good-humored face, his powerful body and his quirky, passionate absorption in his job.

But she could hardly tell him something like that. It was bad enough to be taking advantage of Clint Farrell the way she was. It would be far worse to let herself fall in love with him, no matter how inviting his mouth was, and how she hungered to explore his body and yield to his urgent caresses.

"Well, maybe I could stay a little later," she muttered at last, pulling away and struggling to compose herself. "But first, you have to get inside the cave and look around, right? Let's get it over with while there's still some...some daylight. Okay?" she faltered, feeling hot and foolish.

"Yeah, sure. As if daylight matters inside a cave," he teased. But he obeyed, giving her another fierce hug before he got to his feet. "Later? You promise?"

"I said maybe. No promises."

He gave her a keen glance. "You feel it too, don't you? You want this as much as I do. I can tell by the way you kiss me."

"Hey, don't flatter yourself, Casanova. *I'll* decide what I want, and if it involves you, I'll let you know," Neale said, with considerably more bravado than she felt at the moment.

She didn't want to give in to him, because she knew she'd be lost if she did. But it was important not to discourage him too severely, either. Not if she was going to get what she needed from him.

Clint seemed pleased by her response. He lifted his pack and smiled at her. "Okay. I'd better get going, Neale. I'll be back in an hour or two. Will you get bored out here, waiting for me?"

"No, I won't," she said in a tone of deliberate calm, though her body was suddenly sick with tension. At least, all the disturbing thoughts of warmth and intimacy had vanished completely from her mind. "Because I'm going with you."

Clint paused and stared at her as she scrambled to her feet and stood facing him. "No, you're not," he said mildly. "No way, girl."

"There's no point in arguing about it," Neale told him. "I'm going in there with you, and that's final. You can't stop me. Besides, I'm the one who found the entrance in the first place, remember? I have every right to see the inside of the cave."

"Neale, I have no idea what's inside that cave. There could be all kinds of—"

"Oh, nonsense," she interrupted briskly. "You've been inside twice since we found the entrance, and you told me that it's a good roomy passageway all the way in."

"As far as I went," Clint argued. "But that's just a few hundred feet down to the first chamber. After that, God knows what I might run into."

"So," Neale said cheerfully, "I'll just go as far as the first chamber, and wait for you there. At least I'll get to see a bit of the cave."

Clint was silent, still regarding her with deep reluctance.

"Why did you even bring me along today," she went on, pressing her advantage, "if you weren't going to let me go inside?"

"Because I want your body. Because you threatened to hitchhike out here and explore the cave on your own if I didn't."

She grinned amiably. "Well, maybe I did say something like that. And I'd do it, Clint, I swear I would. So you might as well take me along now, when you can protect me and be sure I don't fall into any underground rivers, or anything."

He glared down at her, his face suddenly ashen. "Don't joke about something like that, Neale! God, just the thought of you . . ." He fell abruptly silent and turned away, adjusting the strap on his pack, while Neale looked at him curiously.

"What, Clint?" she prompted. "What were you going to say?"

"Nothing," he told her briefly. "You'd better come along if you're going to insist on this. We'll leave most of the equipment out here and just take our backpacks."

"Okay." Having gotten her own way, Neale gave him a sweet smile and lifted her pack into position. As it settled against her shoulder blades, she felt the small weight of her camera and tripod, and wondered again whether Clint would be so protective of her safety if he knew the truth.

More likely, she thought with a sad grimace, he'd be tempted to push her into one of those bottomless underground chambers and leave her there.

She shuddered at the thought and followed him up the hillside toward the cave entrance, trying hard to control her sudden terror.

With grim concentration, Neale forced her mind to dwell on pleasant things, like the bells on little Jennifer McKinney's baby shoes, and Virginia's oatmeal cookies, and the cloud patterns that massed and billowed in the autumn sky above their heads.

Pretty soon, there'd be no sky overhead at all, just dense blackness and a million tons of rock....

A little involuntary moan escaped her, and Clint glanced back over his shoulder with a look of concern. "Something wrong?"

"I slipped on a loose rock and almost turned my ankle," Neale lied. "It's okay," she assured him hastily when he seemed on the verge of stopping. "Really, Clint. Nothing happened. It just startled me a bit, that's all. Hurry up. Let's get in there before the bats start waking up."

He nodded and started climbing again. Neale followed him, thinking gloomily that it had probably been a mistake to mention the bats. Now she couldn't get them out of her mind.

Thousands of furry little fanged creatures massed somewhere in the darkness, waiting...

"Here we are," Clint said, pausing by the cave entrance and reaching inside his pack for a white plastic helmet with a spotlight fixed to the front. He fitted the contraption on his head and strapped it in place, then turned to her. "Neale, I sure wish you'd reconsider. Please don't insist on doing this."

Neale ignored his plea. "Do I get one of them?" she asked, indicating the helmet.

"I wish I had a spare, but I don't." Clint sighed and moved reluctantly toward the entrance. "You'll have to stay close behind me all the time. Don't take a step in any direction unless I've stepped there first, all right? Not even a single step."

Neale quelled her fears and gave him a jaunty smile. "Count on it," she said dryly. "Lead on, MacDuff."

She watched as he stooped to enter the gaping cavern, then she pressed close behind him, her heart pounding so wildly that she felt on the verge of suffocation.

The trail sloped steeply downward, a rounded tunnel about four feet wide and just high enough for them to stand erect. Soon it opened into a lofty chamber that seemed to fall away underfoot, wide and echoing, illuminated by an eerie kind of muted daylight. There was a stale, musty smell of earth and water, and a troubling animal scent that was sharp and pungent.

"Probably thousands of different animals have sheltered in here over the years," Clint murmured below her, kicking with his hiking boot at some bones scattered on the dusty floor. "This area is called the entrance zone. Farther in, there'll be almost no evidence of animal life, unless you know where to look."

Neale climbed down behind him into the chamber, glad to escape the narrow path. "Is this where the bats are?" she whispered.

"Some of them. They're hanging on the ceiling above us."

Neale followed him through the dim, musty chamber, trying not to think about bats on the ceiling. "Well, this isn't so bad," she murmured. "I didn't know there'd be this much daylight inside."

"The entrance zone is still partially illuminated by the cave opening." He paused and grinned down at her, switching on the lamp at the peak of his helmet. "Now we'll enter the twilight zone."

She gazed up at him blankly, then looked around at the glistening rock walls, lost in eerie shadows. "You mean this isn't the chamber you were talking about?"

"This? Hell, no. This is just entrance level, Neale. There's no decorations or cave formations at all up here. The first chamber is about a hundred yards farther down, along that passageway."

He gestured with his helmet. Neale's eyes widened as she saw the narrow fissure in the rock that he was heading toward.

"Through *there?*" she whispered. "*A hundred yards?*"

"Maybe you should go back up to the entrance and wait for me. I'll only be down here an hour or so."

She lifted her chin and glared at him. "You're not getting rid of me that easily, Clint Farrell. Come on, let's go."

He hesitated, shook his head in resignation and prepared to enter the narrow opening in the cave wall.

"This is pretty straightforward, all the way down to the first chamber," he told her over his shoulder. "There's one muddy section where you'll have to watch your footing or you could take a tumble. I'll warn you when we get close to it. And there's a bit of open water, too, along a stretch of flowstone where I haven't been able to gauge the depth. We'll hug the wall real tight when we get to it."

Neale felt herself beginning to waver.

Maybe it *would* be better, after all, to go back up to the surface and wait for him. She could take a few pictures of this entrance chamber and send them to Hillary, along with a description of the cave's location and Clint's search. That would probably be enough to secure the assignment and get an advance. Then later, she could...

"Neale? Are you ready?"

She glanced around at the musty chamber, then back at the man who stood by the dark passageway, his face full of concern. Her temptation faded, giving way to the stubborn determination that had always been a central part of Neale Cameron's personality.

"Hey, quit wasting so much time," she told him with a shaky grin. "I'll have to take over as the leader if you're not more decisive."

He smiled back at her, his eyes admiring, and shouldered his way into the dark crevice, waiting to be sure that Neale was close behind him before he edged forward. The trail began to slope downward again, so steep in places that Neale had to grip the clammy walls to keep from tumbling onto Clint in front of her.

"That's why we can't carry our flashlights," he told her. "You'll need both hands in some places."

The passageway was really nothing more than a broad horizontal crack in the limestone. In one section the opening lowered until they had to crouch and waddle along on their haunches, breathless and panting with effort in the musty stillness.

Then it lifted again, and Neale felt almost dizzy with relief when they were able to stand erect.

"Here's the mud," Clint muttered. "Careful where you place your boots, Neale. Be sure you've got solid footing before you commit your weight."

She nodded, edging cautiously downward through the sticky mass, thinking that this was similar, after all, to rock climbing, just in a different kind of dimension. And Neale was fearless when she was on the face of a cliff, no matter how sheer the wall or how dizzying the drop-off beneath her feet.

But there was one major difference. On a cliff face, you weren't all closed in like this, lost in clammy darkness. You were out in the open with the heavens soaring above you, and there was none of this breathless, heart-stopping terror of the unknown....

"Careful," Clint told her softly. "Keep to the left wall, Neale. It's going to open out a bit here."

As he spoke, she glanced over his shoulder and saw the path fall sharply away on one side. His helmet light glimmered on murky depths, a wide pool of water so dark and ancient that she almost expected some hideous dinosaur creature to come swimming to the surface and regard them with hooded, sightless eyes.

"God," Neale whispered, staring in horrified fascination at the silent water. "How deep is that pool, did you say?"

Clint shrugged. "No way of knowing until I run some tests. It could be two feet, or two hundred. Isn't the flowstone beautiful?"

But Neale couldn't even spare a glance for the smooth wall of glistening white limestone above the water's edge. She shivered and looked down involuntarily at the path. If their footing gave way...

"It's safe," Clint assured her, following her glance. "The trail is really good here. If there was any danger, I wouldn't have brought you this far, believe me."

She nodded, then looked at the pool of water again. "What exactly would constitute danger in your mind, I wonder?" she asked him.

Clint paused on the narrow path to consider her question seriously. "I've been in situations in caves where I had to make a portage across an unknown body of water, or do some rock climbing up a chimney, or work my way through a tunnel that was partly filled with water, or follow a ledge across a deep crevasse.... All kinds of possibilities. That's the fun of this, Neale. You never know what you're going to encounter next."

"Fun," she echoed dryly. "I see."

"I thought you were fascinated by caves. You said you'd been to lots of them."

Neale looked up at him quickly, alarmed by the sudden doubt in his eyes, and decided that honesty was probably safest in this situation. Insofar as it was possible for such a terrible liar to tell the truth for once....

"I've never been inside an unexplored cave like this one, Clint. It's a little bit different when there are no handrails and lights on the path, you know."

To her relief, he seemed to accept this. "That's for sure," he agreed with boyish enthusiasm. "It's really an awesome feeling, isn't it, knowing that you're probably standing in a place where no human being has ever stood before?"

Neale nodded. "It's the same feeling I have when I'm rock climbing."

"I know. That's why I want to keep this place a secret as long as I can. The public would come pouring in and ruin it as soon as they heard about it. Wait till you see the first chamber, Neale. You'll be amazed."

She nodded and followed him down into the darkness again, trying not to look at the glittering water beside them. She stared instead at Clint's broad shoulders, wondering how anyone could actually enjoy wandering around in these treacherous depths.

But when he stepped out into another cavernous opening and shone his light on the walls, Neale stood behind him, gasping in awe, stunned by the incredible loveliness that surrounded them.

CHAPTER EIGHT

"OH," SHE WHISPERED, gazing around at the echoing cavern. "Oh, Clint, I've never seen anything so marvelous."

The chamber was about fifty or sixty feet in diameter, deeply shadowed and filled with amazing shapes and eerie designs. With a jubilant laugh Clint dropped an arm around Neale's shoulders, giving her another impulsive hug. He moved to direct his helmet beam onto a massive central column that was almost two feet thick.

"See this, Neale? This is a perfect column, one of the biggest I've ever seen. And look at the colors!"

"What makes it?" she murmured, following close behind him to stare at the fluted structure. "Where did it come from?"

The column was about eighteen feet tall, extending all the way to the jagged ceiling. It glistened in the light like golden marble, streaked and whirled with red, turquoise and green throughout its gleaming length.

Smaller rock forms of varying heights were grouped around the tall column, reaching toward it like sharp inverted icicles, giving Neale the dizzying sensation that the floor was somehow dripping upward.

"Stalagmites," Clint said, gesturing at the sharp eruptions from the floor. "Those are formed over the centuries by water dripping through the ceiling, carrying deposits of minerals. The more mineral content, the richer the colors. Every decoration inside the cave is formed by those little trickles of water. Look up there."

Neale glanced up and saw another mass of delicate icicles hanging above their heads.

"Those are stalactites," Clint told her. "Each one is matched to one on the floor, you see. The dripping water forms a decoration up there, and then trickles down from it and makes the one on the floor as well."

Neale suddenly understood. "And a column like this... that's what happens when the two formations finally meet?"

"Yes, but they're very rare. This one is actually a composite of a lot of smaller elements fused together. Usually some kind of earth shift or disruption of the cave system happens long before they can all meet and form a column."

Awestruck, Neale studied the tall, golden swirl of rock. "How long would it take?" she breathed.

"Nobody knows. Thousands of years, that's for sure. Probably many, many thousands."

Neale was silent, examining the column with its circle of silent attendants. For a moment she forgot her claustrophobia, her anxiety over her plans to betray Clint, everything but the wonder of this place they'd discovered.

Clint watched her, his eyes darkly shadowed beneath the glowing light on his helmet.

"Neale," he murmured softly.

"Yes?" she asked in a distracted fashion, still staring in amazement at the bizarre rock forms in front of her.

"You weren't telling me the truth, were you? You've never done any cave exploring. This is the first time you've seen a real column, isn't it?"

She tore her eyes away from the golden surface and turned to him, suddenly tense and cautious.

"Yes, I was lying," she said at last. "I'm sorry, Clint. I just..." She faltered, wondering what to say that would ease his suspicions. "I really wanted to see this," she told him. "I wanted it so much, and I was afraid you wouldn't bring me inside if you knew I had no experience at all. So I made all that stuff up, about having gone to visit lots of caves. But," she added with an apologetic grin, "I *am* an experienced rock climber. I really am."

He nodded. "I was pretty sure you were exaggerating, at least, about all the caves you'd seen."

She gave him another nervous smile. "Am I that transparent?"

"This is my job, Neale. It's not that hard for me to tell if somebody's experienced at it."

She felt a surge of relief when she realized that he wasn't angry. In fact, he seemed almost amused by her courage and initiative.

But the man was no fool, Neale reminded herself grimly. From now on, she'd have to be very careful how she conducted herself if she wanted to make a success of her plans.

"I can never remember which are which," she murmured aloud, gazing up at the ceiling.

"Beg pardon?"

"Stalactites and stalagmites. Which is it that hangs from the ceiling?"

"Stalactites on the ceiling, stalagmites on the floor. An easy way to remember is to think of ants in the pants."

"Ants in the pants?"

"The mites go up, and the tites come down," he told her with a grin.

Neale chuckled, and stifled a sudden distressing urge to stand on tiptoe and kiss him. He looked so adorable, alone with her in these blackened depths, with his dirt-smeared boyish face and shining eyes.

She turned away quickly and reached into her pack for her flashlight, shining it on walls covered with eerie formations, and riddled by smaller caves and grottos in the rock.

"Is it safe?" she asked Clint over her shoulder. "Can I look around without falling into some cavern or something?"

He nodded. "This whole chamber is flat-bottomed and secure. Just don't go into any of the passageways unless I'm around, Neale. I'll be back in a little while."

She glanced at him, suddenly nervous. "Where are you going?"

"I want to check that corridor running down on the left. It looks like the best way to get to the next level."

Neale peered anxiously at the sloping passageway opening into one of the rock walls. "You'll be really careful, won't you?"

"Yeah," he drawled, smiling down at her. "I'll be really careful."

He stood watching her intently, his smile fading. Then, with calm deliberation, he gathered her into his arms and kissed her, his hands moving hungrily over her hips and thighs and sliding up under her jacket to touch her breasts.

Neale pressed close to him, breathing hard. She felt powerless to resist, mesmerized by the savage beauty and strangeness all around her.

"Damned equipment," Clint muttered, tugging at the straps on her backpack.

At his words, the memory of what she carried in her pack brought Neale abruptly to her senses. She pulled away from him and pretended to be deeply interested in the walls of the cave.

"Clint, what are all those spiky things?"

"Soda straw formations," he said briefly, adjusting his helmet. "If anything should come up," he added casually, "and I'm not back in an hour or so, you could climb out by yourself, couldn't you, Neale? It's pretty straightforward to get back to the main entrance. You just have to be a little careful on the path by that water."

She shivered with dread, then forced herself to smile. "Don't be silly. Nothing's going to happen to you, Clint Farrell. Just hurry up and get back here."

"I will," he promised, edging into the darkened passage. "You don't mind waiting here for me?"

"Not at all," she told him, anxious for him to be gone so she could get busy with what she had to do. "After all, there's lots to look at it in here."

"There's some beautiful drapery stone over above that grotto," he said, waving a hand at the wall behind her.

"Drapery stone?"

"It's a thin, flat rock formation, just like a drape or a piece of fabric. Some of it's really exquisite. You'll see."

Neale nodded and watched while he edged into the narrow passage and disappeared. She counted slowly up to a hundred, holding her breath and listening to the receding noise of his boots as he scrambled down the rocky corridor.

At last she reached into her pack with trembling hands, removed a small, collapsible tripod and set it up on the damp floor of the cavern. She mounted a wide-angle lens on her compact SLR camera and took out a battery-operated flash.

She might be stone broke, but at least she had good equipment. All these things had been purchased a few years ago, back in the days when Neale felt no qualms about spending her hard-earned money on herself and the equipment she needed for her job.

But that was before her father's devastating illness.

Nowadays, Neale felt guilty if she bought a tube of lipstick, as if she were somehow taking food from the mouths of her mother and her brother....

Thinking about her family's desperate financial plight helped to strengthen her resolve. Neale moved quickly and efficiently, keeping her mind concentrated on the task at hand, as she positioned the tripod and aimed her camera slightly upward to get a good shot of the central column and the fantastic shapes on the walls behind.

Then, taking a deep breath, she switched off her flashlight and crouched in total darkness, an absence of light so profound that it was almost palpable, like a dense, clammy shroud of black velvet.

"This is going to be great," she murmured aloud, trying to comfort herself in the fearful blackness by the sound of her own voice. "Just great." She clenched her fists to keep them from shaking. At last, operating solely by touch, she locked open the shutter on her camera, aimed the flash off to her right and squeezed the control button. The cave sprang into sharp illumination, then vanished abruptly when she switched off the flash.

Neale continued this maneuver as she aimed the flash in different directions. With the shutter locked open, the camera's wide-angle lens would give her a single image of the cave's interior, fully lighted in all directions.

Everything was going exactly as she'd planned. She closed the shutter and switched her flashlight on again to move the tripod. After she'd taken a number of the multiple exposure shots, she got about two dozen close-ups of some of the more fantastic rock formations, so absorbed in her work that she was hardly bothered by her claustrophobic terrors.

By the time she heard Clint crawling back up the narrow passage, Neale had all her camera equipment safely packed away and was concentrating innocently on a close examination of the drapery stone.

"It's a great trail," he told her with enthusiasm as he hauled himself back up into the chamber.

"Did you climb all the way down to the next level?"

"Not yet, but I got far enough that I could see right into the chamber. There's some flowstone across the path farther down that I didn't cross because I didn't want to take the time to put my bootees on."

"Bootees?"

He dropped his pack from his shoulders and rummaged inside to show her a pair of tight-fitting cloth and plastic slippers, heavily corded and ribbed for traction.

Neale examined the strange footwear, and glanced up at him with a puzzled frown.

"We wear these to cross flowstone, so it doesn't get marked," Clint explained. "The bootees are soft enough to grip on the surface without leaving any tracks."

"But... but why would you bother? Why not just wear your boots?"

"To keep the cave interior in a natural state. Glossy flowstone is so smooth and beautiful, and it's really quite delicate. If everybody who explored the cave went tramping across it with their hiking boots, the surface would show signs of wear before long. Cavers try really hard to keep a cave looking as if it's never been entered."

Neale pondered this information in gloomy silence.

"In fact," Clint went on cheerfully, his eyes sparkling, "if we have to swim across a shallow pool anywhere, we usually strip naked before we go into the water."

"Naked! Why on earth would you do that?"

"So the water doesn't get contaminated by dyes and chemicals in the clothing fabric."

Neale stared at his face, trying to decide if he was teasing her. "I see," she said dryly. "And are there any pools like that farther down in this cave?"

"I sure hope so," he said with a meaningful grin.

Neale's cheeks turned warm in the shadows. She watched as he shouldered the pack again, then prepared to follow him up the trail to the main entrance, still brooding over his story of the cave bootees. At last, despite his teasing smile when he'd told her about swimming naked through the underground pools, she was convinced that Clint was absolutely sincere in his desire to keep this cave pristine and undamaged by the public.

And, traitor that she was, Neale was about to announce its existence to the whole world.

"SO I JUST PUNCH the numbers in like I'm making a regular phone call?"

Neale looked over at Marjorie, who frowned in concentration as she made notes on a legal form. "Yes," Marjorie said, glancing up briefly. "It's all set. Go ahead and send it."

Neale hesitated a moment longer, then activated the fax machine with a sense of grim finality.

No turning back now, she told herself. *It's all out of my hands, the whole thing.*

"So what's this big urgent story?" Marjorie asked idly, still squinting at the sheet of paper in front of her. "You don't usually run around using couriers and fax machines, kiddo."

"I sent the photographs by courier," Neale told her friend, shifting uncomfortably on her feet as she watched the pages of typed paper slide out into the tray on the machine. "And I'm faxing the story outline because they wanted it by tonight."

"Is this the cave story?"

"Of course. You know I haven't been working on anything else lately, Marj."

"So he really has found something? You're always so secretive about this cave, Neale."

Neale put the outline back into her briefcase and crossed the room to sink into a chair opposite Marjorie's desk. The two young women were in the reception room at Martin Avery's law office, where Marjorie was finishing her day's work before walking home to the cottage for supper.

"Did he?" Marjorie persisted. "You were out hiking with him all day, Neale. Did the two of you really find a cave entrance?"

Neale felt another wave of the miserable unhappiness that had been dogging her all week. "He doesn't want me to talk about it, Marj. He made me promise I wouldn't tell anybody, not even you."

Marjorie lowered her pen and stared at her friend in disbelief. "If I'm not mistaken, you just sent all the pertinent details to a national magazine. Doesn't that sort of fall under the category of 'telling somebody,' Neale?"

"They're paying me so much money," Neale murmured in anguish. "It's a dollar a word, Marj! But Clint's going to hate me when he finds out what I've done. Oh, God, I could just die. . . ."

Suddenly alert, Marjorie put her pen down and regarded her friend with thoughtful sympathy. "Why don't you tell him?" she suggested sensibly. "Tell him about the money, and why you need it so badly. Maybe he won't be as upset as you think."

"If I tell him what I'm doing," Neale said, staring out the window at the tree-shaded main street of Crystal Creek, "he won't take me back into the cave again.

I need some more information to be able to write a good story, Marj. I have to keep lying to him for a couple more days until I've sucked him dry. Then I can throw him away."

She fell silent, appalled by the sad bitterness of her own voice.

"Look, Marj, let's not talk about it anymore, okay? People do what they have to do to make a living, and I guess I'm no different. Let's talk about something more pleasant."

"Okay," Marjorie said slowly, still looking at her friend in concern. "Like what?"

"I don't know. Like the Halloween party at Zack's on Saturday night. Is everybody going?"

Marjorie's pretty face brightened. "They sure are. Even Martin and Billie Jo are dressing up, but he wouldn't tell me what they're going to be. He says Billie Jo designed the costumes, and he thinks it's a lot of damn fool nonsense. But you know what, Neale?"

"What?"

"Martin was trying not to grin the whole time we were talking. I think he's really tickled about the idea of dressing up."

Neale nodded, briefly diverted from her own misery by the thought of Marjorie's dapper employer and his fascinating May-September marriage. "Love is such a mystery, isn't it, Marj?" she commented, thinking about the way Clint had smiled at her down in the cave, his eyes sparkling beneath the brim of his helmet.

"It sure is," Marjorie said with another shrewd glance at her friend. "In fact," she went on casually, "speaking of love affairs, guess who's having some problems these days?"

Neale shrugged. "How would I know? You're the one who keeps up on the local news, not me."

Marjorie leaned across the desk. "Brock Munroe and Amanda Walker," she whispered.

Neale looked at her blankly. "They're having problems? Come on, Marj. They're the most loving couple in the world. They adore each other."

"But didn't you see them at the barbecue last week? Remember how she left with Beverly, and he stayed behind? There seemed to be a lot of tension between them that night."

"Every couple has tension sometimes. Maybe it's not that easy for them, having his aunt Millie staying out there at the ranch. It seems to me she could be a pretty formidable houseguest."

"I think it's more than that," Marjorie persisted. "I saw Brock in the bank this morning, and he said they aren't going to the Halloween party."

"So? Not everybody is as crazy about costume parties as you are, Marjorie Perez. Amanda works all week in the city. Maybe they just want to spend a quiet evening alone together."

"But she's not coming out to the ranch at all this weekend. Brock says she's going to a party at the governor's mansion in Austin on Saturday night, so he decided not to come to Zack's by himself. He looked really unhappy, Neale.''

Neale absorbed this information in silence.

"If I had a man like Brock Munroe," Marjorie went on with passionate emphasis, "I wouldn't trade him for a *dozen* parties with the governor. I wonder what on earth Amanda Walker can be thinking of.''

AMANDA CRUMBLED a piece of garlic toast nervously in her hands, listening to the man across the table as he reminisced about his college years and his long friendship with Salome Maroc, who was Edward's new love.

She felt awkward, and almost wished she hadn't accepted this invitation for a casual dinner before going back to work at the shop. But Judd Hinshaw had dropped in unexpectedly while she was working, and she'd been so lonely.

Amanda wasn't accustomed to the prospect of a solitary weekend in the city. It was already Thursday evening. Usually by this time on Friday night she was out at the ranch, sitting placidly with Brock and Alvin on the veranda, watching the sun go down beyond the misty hills.

Amanda smiled automatically when Judd paused, thinking that he really was a very nice man, and incredibly handsome. He had a square-jawed, sun-browned look, like a cowboy in a magazine advertisement, but there was no doubt that he was warm and sincere. And there was certainly no denying the fact that Amanda was the envy of every other woman in the restaurant.

Still, there was something about the man that bothered her, not a visible flaw so much as an absence of some essential ingredient. When she looked at Judd's pleasant face she found herself craving Brock, with his cheerful, disheveled look, his sparkling eyes and wicked grin, his disconcerting wit.

Judd Hinshaw simply lacked spice, she decided. He was white bread and butter, and Brock was chili with jalapeño peppers. There was nothing bland about Brock Munroe. The man might be irritating, obstinate, baffling and infuriating, but he was never boring.

She felt a sudden flood of longing for him, hot and urgent. In her mind's eye Amanda could see her lover sitting across from her, see the hard, tanned line of his jaw, the dark graying hair that fell onto his denim shirt collar, the flat, powerful line of his shoulders and the surprising gracefulness of his big, well-shaped hands.

She remembered those hands moving across her naked skin with infinite tenderness—caressing, touching, stroking—until she was helplessly lost in desire and passion....

Amanda stifled a moan of anguish and forced herself to pay attention to her dinner companion. "Will you?" he was asking, draining his coffee cup as he kept his eyes fixed on her.

She blushed and floundered briefly. "I...I'm sorry, Judd," she murmured. "I didn't catch what you said."

"I was asking if you'll be going to Moira's party on Saturday."

Amanda thought about her recent argument with Brock on the telephone, and his cold anger when she offered to buy him a tuxedo. "Yes," she said listlessly. "I'll be there."

"With a date, or on your own?"

"On my own, I think." Amanda picked miserably at her food, wondering if Brock would be going to the costume party at Zack's along with all his Crystal Creek neighbors.

"At least it's not a costume party," Judd said with a grimace. "I sure hate dressing up in those silly rigs, don't you?"

Amanda stared at him in brief confusion, then realized that he was still talking about the party at the governor's mansion. She had a sudden, regretful image of the merry group at Zack's on Saturday, the laughter and teasing as they crowded into the bar in their bright array of Halloween outfits.

"Yes," she agreed, pushing her plate away and taking a sip of the lukewarm coffee. "I'm glad it won't be a costume party. I'm getting a bit tired of costumes."

"Would you like me to pick you up, Amanda? I'll be on my own, too. We might as well go together."

Amanda hesitated, tempted by his offer. It would be nice to have an escort at the party, especially someone who knew everybody and moved so comfortably in those well-heeled circles. But if Judd picked her up, he'd also be taking her home, and she wasn't ready to deal with that particular set of complications.

Not yet, anyway, Amanda told herself unhappily.

If it was really over between her and Brock, then she'd eventually have to start learning how to live on her own again and relate to other men. She couldn't keep running after a man who didn't want to marry her. But the thought of being touched by anybody else was so distasteful that she had to stifle a frown as she sat across the table from her handsome companion.

"Thank you, Judd," she murmured, "but I don't know what time I'll be able to get away from the shop. Maybe it's best if I just see you there, all right?"

He nodded with quiet courtesy, and handed his credit card to the waiter. "Sure thing. I'll get there early, and be watching the door until you arrive," he told her with a smile.

Amanda smiled back uncertainly, relieved when he finally escorted her outside and tucked her into her little car. She'd insisted on bringing her own vehicle to the restaurant because, she told him, she wanted to stop off at her apartment before going back to work at the shop. This was partly true, but a lot of her reluctance stemmed from the simple fact that she didn't want to be alone with Judd Hinshaw if she could help it.

It was really strange, Amanda mused, waving at him as she pulled out of the parking lot and headed downtown to her apartment. She was being pursued, surprisingly enough, by one of the most eligible bachelors in Texas. Judd had even made it clear in a couple of casual remarks that he'd reached the stage in his life when he was ready to find a wife and settle down on his ranch near Houston. Yet Amanda spent all her time longing for a man who didn't want to commit to marriage.

There was no explaining the vagaries of love and attraction between men and women. The man who refused to marry her was the only one whose touch she hungered for, whose smile could make her dizzy with longing, whose thoughts touched hers with a gentle understanding and intimacy she'd never known....

But thinking about Brock was too painful. Amanda forced herself instead to concentrate on the fashion show she'd attended that afternoon, and whether the current trend toward shorter skirts was really going to take hold or if it was just a passing thing. She was still thinking about skirt lengths when she parked at her building, hurried through the lobby and paused by the elevators.

"Miss Walker?"

Amanda turned around to see the young doorman approaching her, bouncing across the thick carpet.

"Yes, Jay?"

"I wanted to let you know that your aunt's up in your apartment. She came by about an hour ago, and looked really tired, so I let her into your place instead of making her wait down in the lobby. Is that all right?" he added.

"My aunt? I didn't know my aunt was in town, Jay. What does this woman look like?"

The young man shrugged and grinned. "Like an aunt. Gray hair and stuff. She gave me a nice tip," he added ingenuously. "I liked her."

Amanda nodded thoughtfully. Lacey, her mother's sister, lived west of Abilene. She came to Austin several times a year to visit and shop, usually staying a couple of days with Amanda.

But Lacey was the perfect houseguest, good-natured and unobtrusive, going her own way and requiring no entertainment from her hostess. Amanda brightened when she realized that she wouldn't have to spend a solitary weekend in the city after all. It would be nice to have a long, cozy chat with Lacey, who'd always been one of her favorite relatives.

She stood impatiently in the elevator as it climbed to her floor, then rushed down the hall and fumbled for her key. "Lacey?" she called as she let herself into the apartment foyer. "Lacey, I didn't know you were coming! You should have called. When did you decide to..."

A shadow fell across the entry to the living room. Amanda fell abruptly silent, tense with shock and astonishment. Millie Munroe stood framed in the doorway, looking watchful and cold.

CHAPTER NINE

"SO YOU FINALLY DECIDED to come home, did you? Your phone's been ringing off the hook for the past half hour."

"My phone?" Amanda said blankly, tugging her coat collar up around her throat with a nervous gesture.

Millie studied the young woman in the hallway, struck by her beauty.

She really was lovely, this girl that Brock had chosen. Millie was a little surprised by how happy she was to see Amanda again. She'd actually found herself missing the girl since Amanda left the ranch on the weekend, and regretting her own uncharitable behavior. She really would have liked to be more friendly, to settle back and laugh with this charming young woman, take Amanda out somewhere nice for dinner and have a good time.

But the stone that had rolled over Millie's heart a month ago still rested there, cold and heavy, keeping her from showing any of her feelings. All she seemed able to express was a kind of sour harshness that made her feel worse than ever.

"I finally got tired of all that noise and decided to answer your phone. It was the older Hinshaw boy, who's been calling you every ten minutes. He seemed real anxious to talk with you," Millie went on, wincing at the sardonic note in her own voice. "Said he forgot to tell you something when you all were having dinner together. Does Brock know you're such cozy friends with Judd Hinshaw?"

Amanda had obviously regained her composure by now, and her face was set and cold. She hung her coat away in the closet, then moved past Millie into the living room. "Do you know the Hinshaws?" she asked, ignoring Millie's pointed question about Brock.

"Percy and I used to stay at their place whenever we went to Houston, but Judd was just a little fellow in those days. His mother is a charming woman. She's been busy for years restoring that old family mansion of theirs, with tastes a lot like yours, come to think of it. Of course," Millie added thoughtfully, "looking at *this* place, it's not easy to tell what your tastes are really like, is it?"

"What do you mean?" Amanda said warily.

Millie waved a hand at the sparse chrome and leather furnishings. "This is hardly the look you've tried to achieve out there at the ranch, is it? I wonder which is really you, and which is just playacting."

The girl's cheeks flamed, and Millie could see that her shot had struck home. She felt no satisfaction, though, just a kind of bleak dismay at all these cruel things she couldn't seem to keep herself from saying.

She was actually on the verge of trying to apologize, standing awkwardly in the entry to the living room and staring at the younger woman, when the telephone jangled noisily in the tense silence. Amanda moved over to pick up the receiver.

"Hello?" she murmured. "Oh, Judd, it's you. No," she said after a moment, "that was my aunt. Well," she added with a brief glance at Millie, "not my aunt, exactly. She's the aunt of a . . . a friend of mine."

Again her cheeks warmed, and Millie felt another tug of treacherous sympathy. She was causing the poor girl so much embarrassment, just by being here.

"They'll all be going with you? Oh, I see. No, it's nice of you to offer, but I still think I'd . . . I'd prefer to go on my own. All right, I'll see you there. Thanks, Judd."

Amanda hung up and turned to face her visitor. Millie studied her in silence for a moment. "Brock tells me you're not coming out to the ranch this weekend," she said, her voice sharp with a challenge that she didn't really feel.

"No," Amanda said quietly. "I'm not. There's a function in town that I have to go to, and Brock doesn't want to come with me."

"So you're going with Judd Hinshaw instead? No wonder Brock isn't ready to get married. You seem to be having some difficulty making up your mind about things, don't you?"

"Judd's going to the same party with a group of other people, not me," Amanda said wearily. "What business is it of yours, anyhow?'' she added with a sudden flash of anger. "What do you care if I go out with Judd Hinshaw? You'd be happy to see me fighting with Brock, wouldn't you? After all, that's what you've been trying to accomplish ever since you got here.''

''Me?'' Millie asked with an air of lofty innocence, though she felt tense and chilled by the accusation. "What does any of this have to do with me?''

''I don't know,'' Amanda said in despair. "I don't know why you don't like me, and I don't know why you've gone out of your way to be cruel to me and cause trouble. Most of all, I don't understand why you've bothered to come here and look me up. I would have thought I'd be the last person in this city you'd want to visit.''

''Virginia's going to a concert tonight with one of her nieces,'' Millie said, keeping her tone deliberately mild, "and her niece is a most unpleasant young woman. I thought I'd just come over here for the evening to escape from them. You flatter yourself, my girl, if you think I've got any deep feelings about you, one way or the other.''

''I see,'' Amanda said, her voice tight and shaking. "So you just like to be cruel for the fun of it, is that right? It amuses you to hurt people and destroy things, even though you don't have any strong feelings about them? What a way to live,'' she added bitterly. "I think I'd rather be dead.''

Fear rose in Millie's throat, heavy and choking. She glared at the younger woman. "What do you know about life and death, you silly girl?" she said angrily. "What do you know about anything? You're young and beautiful, and you have your whole life ahead of you. You have your health and your successful business and a man who adores you. Wait till you're old and alone and...and sick..."

Millie's voice broke. She turned away in grim silence and moved toward the closet to get her coat.

"Not so fast," Amanda said sharply. "You can't say something like that and then just go away. What do you mean, 'old and sick'? Are you sick? Is that what's making you act this way?"

Millie grabbed her coat from the closet and shrugged into it. Amanda moved toward her and grasped one of her sleeves.

"Is it?" she persisted. "Is something the matter? Brock said you're a lot different than you used to be. He couldn't understand why you were behaving like this. Is there something wrong with your health, Millie?"

"What do you care? What does anybody care if I live or die?"

"Maybe if you gave people half a chance, you'd be surprised how much they care."

Millie tried to pull away from her. "I can manage very well without your pity, thank you. I don't need anybody," she said coldly.

But she found herself battling an urgent desire to throw herself into Amanda's arms and cry on her shoulder. The longing to tell somebody was so overwhelming that Millie didn't think she could control it much longer.

Despite the harsh words, Amanda, too, seemed to sense her guest's moment of weakness. "Tell me," she urged, still clinging to the soft tweed of Millie's coat sleeve and giving it a little shake. "Tell me what's the matter."

"I have cancer," Millie said abruptly, shocking both of them into silence.

The words echoed in the stillness of the autumn night, dark and menacing. But there was an enormous relief, too, in having voiced the unspeakable for the first time. Millie drew a deep breath and repeated it.

"I have cancer in one of my ovaries. I'll probably be dead in six months. So don't talk to me about life and death, and how I should behave."

Amanda was studying her, pale and tense, her eyes almost black with emotion. "How...how do you know that?" she whispered. "Have you had tests? Did the doctor say..."

"I haven't seen a doctor," Millie said coldly. "I'm not letting anybody poke and prod at me."

"But then how do you know if..."

"I can feel the lump," Millie said. "I don't need anybody to tell me what it means. I've read some books about it, and I know."

Amanda stared at her. "But that's...that's crazy! A lump could be any number of things. It could be completely benign."

"I know what it is," Millie repeated stubbornly. "It's my body, after all. You think I wouldn't know?"

To her surprise, the young woman in front of her was no longer looking shocked and sympathetic. In fact, Amanda's delicate face had hardened into an expression of angry impatience.

"Well," she said finally, her voice calm and measured, "if that isn't the most ridiculous thing I ever heard. And you call yourself an intelligent woman."

Millie gaped at her, stunned into silence.

"Making your own diagnosis, and thinking that it gives you some kind of right to go around behaving like a monster," Amanda went on, glaring up at the taller woman. "What an absurd thing to do. Anyone with an ounce of sense would go to a doctor and learn the truth before she decided her life was over. You know what you are, Millie Munroe?"

Millie bit her lip, still too shocked to respond.

"You're a coward," Amanda went on relentlessly. "Just a coward, hiding under a lot of bluff and bluster. And I think you should be ashamed."

She fell silent and let the coat sleeve drop, but kept her eyes fixed on Millie's.

Millie glared back at her, gradually beginning to recover her shattered composure. "Are you finished?"

"Yes," Amanda said quietly. Her burst of emotion had clearly subsided. "I guess I am."

"Good. Then I never have to listen to you again, do I? Goodbye, Amanda Walker. And good riddance!"

Millie flung her scarf around her neck and snatched her handbag from the console table. She stormed out of the apartment and down the hall, frantic to escape from the young woman's steadfast air and the blunt honesty of her words.

A *coward!* she thought furiously, quickening her steps. The little hussy actually had the nerve to call her a coward!

She was still conscious of Amanda's eyes resting on her back. Millie had to fight the urge to break into a run as she hurried toward the elevators.

"ARE YOU OKAY? Can you manage?" Clint asked, pausing in the narrow passage and looking over his shoulder at Neale, who was struggling along behind him. They'd made several trips into the cave over the past few days and she was getting more competent all the time in the cramped spaces, but he still worried about her.

"Of course I can," she said with some annoyance. "Quit fussing about me, okay? I'm probably as athletic as you are, and I'm a lot smaller, too. If you can do this, *I* certainly can."

He grinned and reached back with a mud-smeared hand to pat her shoulder. She looked so pretty in the glow of his helmet lamp, even in those damp, stained clothes and with her face covered in dirt.

"You're one hell of a woman, Neale Cameron," he murmured. "Did anybody ever tell you that?"

"Not nearly often enough," she said, trying to smile. "Come on, let's get going," she added, giving him a push. "I want to find another nice big chamber. I hate these cramped spaces where I can touch the ceiling."

But he was rooted to the spot, suddenly overcome with emotion. There was something about her nearness, the intimacy of this narrow rocky place, the jubilation of being inside his own cave and alone with the woman of his dreams, that was too much for Clint to bear.

With a husky murmur, he pulled her toward him and bent to kiss her. Neale's body was supple in his arms, and her lips were warm against his, soft and intensely sweet. He found himself drowning in hot sexual desire.

Despite Clint's best efforts, Neale had continued to elude him, holding him just at arm's length over the past few days while they hiked together and explored the cave. Far from discouraging him, her resistance had served to fire his passion, until by now he was almost crazy with hunger for her slim body.

But there was a new emotion, too, a sweet, tentative feeling that he recognized with surprise and wonder.

"Hey, guess what? I'm in love with you," he whispered against her mouth. "Did you know that, Neale Cameron? I've fallen in love. You've got me thinking about things like vine-covered cottages and backyard barbecues."

"Well, that's the silliest thing I ever heard. Who could haul a barbecue down into a cave like this?" she said, obviously trying to joke away his intensity. But he could feel her trembling in his arms, and he knew that she was feeling the same kind of emotion.

"We've shared a lot in these past few days, haven't we?" he murmured.

"Once you finally lightened up and decided to let me come down here with you," she replied. "Oh, Clint," she whispered, dropping the teasing note all at once. "Kiss me again. It feels so good."

He obeyed, kissing her with rising passion. His hands roamed hungrily over her body, stroking her hips and cupping the small, rounded breasts that he'd never seen, but had already fallen in love with. At last she pulled away and gave him a shaky smile.

"Enough," she muttered. "Let's wait till we get out of here and we can drop these big packs, okay?"

"Tonight's the night, kid. You can't hold me off any longer. Tonight I get to see all of this little body, not just learn it by Braille."

She gave him a questioning glance, looking startled and wary.

"Did you forget that we're spending the night down here?" Clint asked her. "Once we get settled in our campsite, and you've curled up in that sleeping bag," he said with a meaningful grin, "I'm probably not going to be able to leave you alone, sweetheart. You'll be too tempting to resist."

"Oh, go on. By the end of the day, we'll both be too worn-out for any of that stuff."

"Speak for yourself, girl."

She chuckled and gave him another gentle shove. "Quit thinking about things like that," she told him. "Concentrate on the job at hand. The first thing is to find a campsite that's warm and dry, and preferably has enough room to stand upright. Do you think you can manage that, you fearless cave explorer?"

"I think I can," he told her soberly. "Especially if you'll kiss me one more time."

She smiled and reached up to give him a lingering kiss, then straightened her pack and fell into step behind him again as they moved down the passage.

It was Friday afternoon, the day before Halloween and almost a week after their initial discovery of the cave. Over the intervening days, Neale had worn away at Clint's resistance until he'd finally agreed to take her farther down into the cave with him for an extended exploration. He had been deeply reluctant to do this, but she was so persuasive, and he was falling more deeply in love with her all the time as they spent long hours together, talking and laughing about everything under the sun, sharing their dreams and plans.

Besides, he told himself, edging up through the passage, she was right about her physical abilities. He'd never met a girl like Neale Cameron. She was strong and graceful, surefooted and agile in her movements, and obviously fearless. She was the perfect mate for a man like Clint, able to follow him anywhere, just as

Clint's mother had accompanied his father and shared fully in his life.

He couldn't believe his luck, finding two treasures at the same time. First this fabulous unexplored cave, and then the woman he'd always wanted. . . .

While Clint was rejoicing, the narrow passage ended abruptly and fell away underfoot. He caught himself just in time, and huddled at the brink of a dark precipice with Neale close behind him.

"What?" she asked. "What is it?"

"It's a big cavern, I think. And we've entered it from somewhere high up. I'm not even sure where the floor is."

"So you're just in a sort of hole in the wall?" Neale said. "Is there any kind of a ledge, or is the wall sheer?"

"It looks like there's a narrow ledge formed by run-off from the passageway," Clint muttered, peering down into the darkness. "But if I can't work my way down, we're at a dead end. We'll have to backtrack all the way up to the column chamber and try a different passage."

"Oh, damn," she muttered. "It took us all day to get this far."

"Maybe I can find some footing on this ledge. Stay right where you are, and I'll try to see how far down the chamber extends."

Clint edged his way cautiously out of the opening and onto the wall of the cavern, directing the beam of his helmet down into the chamber. To his relief, he could see the floor about twenty feet below them, and a dim view of a cave interior decorated with fantastic shapes and designs.

"It looks great," he said to Neale over his shoulder, lifting his body cautiously out onto the ledge. "It's a big, dry chamber, and the decorations are terrific. Wait'll you see it."

"Do we need ropes for the wall?" Neale asked behind him. "Clint, don't try it till you know the footing is safe!"

"All right," he said. "I'll just go out a few feet to test the rock, then move on down the wall and wait for you if it's passable. Don't try the ledge until I call you, Neale."

"Okay," she said. "You take it really slow and careful."

He grinned and reached back to touch her knee as she crouched behind him. Then he turned to face the wall and started to work his way down the narrow ledge, setting his boots carefully on the rocky outcropping and gripping the rough limestone wall with his hands.

These were the moments Clint loved, the times of high adventure, when there was nothing between him and disaster but his own skill and daring. And below him, a cavern full of unimaginable wonders, never before seen by human eyes...

It happened so fast he was hardly aware of changing position. One moment he was creeping like a fly down the face of the rock wall, and the next he was hurtling through space, falling into blackness. He landed with a thud on the rough floor of the cavern and felt a sharp pain thrusting along his back and into his abdomen.

Clint shifted awkwardly in the blackness, then tested his legs and arms to make sure nothing was broken. Finally, he checked his helmet light and nodded in relief. Everything seemed fine except for that pain in his back, and it was probably just bruised from contact with a ragged outcrop on the limestone floor.

"Clint!" Neale shouted frantically, her voice dropping and echoing into the vast cavern. "Clint, what's happened? Are you all right?"

"I'm fine," he called back. "Don't try to come down, Neale. The ledge isn't safe. It just crumbled away under my boots and I slipped. Stay where you are and I'll climb back up to you."

He directed his helmet beam into the darkness toward her, then shone it on himself to show her that he was still in one piece.

Finally, he gathered himself together and started to get up, pulling himself awkwardly to his feet. The pain ripped through his body, so intense that he felt a wave of nausea. Clammy sweat broke out on his forehead, and his hands shook.

"God," he muttered, sinking to his knees and waiting for the agony to subside.

"Clint?" she called again. "What is it? What's the matter?"

He turned and stared up into the blackness above him. "I don't know," he said. "Just a little pain in my midsection. Maybe I tore a muscle when I fell."

"I'm coming down."

"No!" he shouted. "Neale, it isn't safe. Don't try to..."

But the pain stabbed at him again, so agonizing that he couldn't speak. Clint fell onto his side and doubled up on the cold floor, clutching at his abdomen, moaning softly to himself. Neale crouched at the lip of the dark abyss, staring anxiously down at the pool of light on the rocky floor around Clint's helmet. She could see him writhing in pain, hear his soft moans as he doubled up and drew his knees toward his chest.

Without taking time to think, she backed out onto the ledge and began to work her way downward, clinging to the rock wall with all her strength as she reached blindly for footholds.

"No!" Clint shouted when he saw what she was doing. "Neale, don't try it! Go back up to the passage and wait for me. I'll be all right in a minute."

She ignored him, continuing to edge her way downward, testing each foothold with infinite care. Some of the intense blackness lifted, and she realized that Clint was directing his light up toward her, shining it on the wall at her feet.

Before long she reached the place, more than fifteen feet above the floor, where the ledge crumbled away to nothing. Neale paused, drew a deep breath and let herself fall, trying to keep her body limp as she slid down the cliff face. She landed in a heap a few feet away from Clint, stunned and breathless from the force of her impact. After a moment she picked herself up and hurried over to him.

"Clint," she murmured, kneeling beside him. "Clint, what is it? What's the matter?"

He turned to her, his face ghastly pale in the shadows. "I've got a terrible pain right here," he said, indicating his jacket front. "Maybe a cracked rib, but it feels as if something might be hurt inside, too. I'm not sure."

"Can you walk?"

"Sure. Just give me a few minutes. I'll rest a bit, then we'll see, okay?"

"Of course. Here, let me help you...."

She bent to remove his pack, then took out the sleeping bag and pillow and tried to make him comfortable, terrified when she saw how much pain he was in. Clint tried to hide it from her, but there was no way he could disguise the flare of agony in his eyes, or the grim tightening of his jaw whenever he moved.

"Just rest a bit," Neale murmured. "I'm going to look around, all right?"

He rolled his head on the pillow, biting his lip and grimacing.

Neale strapped Clint's helmet onto her head, then moved away to examine the wall they'd descended. She tried to remain calm and look on the whole situation as a straightforward problem in rock climbing, like many others she'd encountered over the years.

Still, she couldn't help being terrified by the blackness, the oppressive mystery of their surroundings and her frantic concern about Clint and his condition. Besides, the wall above her was no simple matter. The ledge that had brought them partly down was now almost out of sight, high up and indistinct in the darkness. Below it, the wall was smooth and damp, with no visible footholds of any kind. There was no way they could climb that wall, not without a lot more sophisticated equipment than they'd brought with them.

But the passage up there on the cliff face was the only way back to the entrance.

Clint had been mapping their route on a hand-held computer, and his printout recorded every twist and turn in the complex system of passageways. He'd assured Neale that he never got lost when he had mapped his route back to the surface. Neale had no idea, though, how they'd possibly get out if they couldn't make their way back up to that mapped area. She studied the rest of the smooth rock face, feeling increasingly hopeless.

At last she faltered across the rocky floor to where Clint lay, hoping he had some kind of plan. But he seemed worse than when she'd left him. He was sweating profusely, and his teeth chattered as his body shook in harsh spasms.

Instinctively, Neale threw off the helmet and lay down beside him, trying to avoid his injured side. She cuddled into him, covering him with her own warmth. After a moment she felt his arms close gratefully around her. For a long time they lay with their bodies wrapped closely, and Neale had to fight to keep herself from crying. She thought about all the times she'd fantasized this very thing, dreamed about the first time she and Clint would lie together in each other's arms, and how wonderful it would feel. But she'd never expected their first real embrace to be under these bleak and terrifying circumstances.

"Sweetheart, you feel so good," he whispered against her hair, letting her know that he was thinking the same thing. "Wish I could . . . do justice to the occasion."

Neale lifted herself on one elbow and kissed his cheek, trying to smile. "I'm probably lucky," she said, keeping her voice deliberately light, "that you're a little bit incapacitated. Otherwise I'd be fighting to preserve my virtue."

He chuckled, then gasped with pain and clutched his abdomen again.

"Oh, Clint," she whispered. "It must feel so awful. . . ."

"It's pretty awful," he murmured when he was able to talk again. "Doesn't seem . . . to be getting any better."

"At least you look warmer now. I was afraid you were going into shock."

"I guess that's a danger, isn't it? Where's the other sleeping bag? Maybe we should . . . cover up for a bit, just to be safe."

Neale shook out her own lightweight bag and spread it over him, then sat back on her heels to examine him, relieved to see that he looked somewhat better. His color had improved, and his teeth weren't chattering anymore.

"Clint..." she ventured.

"Yeah?" He turned his head on the pillow and tried to smile at her.

"We'll never be able to climb that wall. Even if I could improvise some foot pegs and find a way to pound them into the rock face, you wouldn't be able to get up there safely. Not with this kind of pain."

He considered for a moment, regarding her with fixed concentration. "You're probably right," he muttered. "Have to find ... some other route."

"But where?" Neale held up the helmet light and looked around. The cavern wall was smooth and impassable behind them. Across the room, the chamber seemed to open into a myriad of small passageways, honeycombed into the limestone. But all of those tunnels led away from the route they'd traveled, deeper into the bowels of the earth.

Clint followed her eyes, studying the mass of dark openings in the opposite wall. "Could be ... a way out over there," he whispered, his face clouding with pain once more.

"I don't see how. That's not the way we came, Clint. It's entirely the wrong direction."

He shivered and groaned, caught in another spasm. After a moment he composed himself, gripping the sleeping bag tightly with his hands before he turned back to her. "Contour of the landform," he whispered. "It's on the map."

Neale took the topographical map and computer printout from his pack, staring blankly at the mass of symbols and drawings. She looked back at him with a questioning glance.

"We came in at the top of the ridge," he explained, pointing to the upper part of the diagram with a shaking finger. "See? Up here?"

She nodded tightly, forcing herself to concentrate.

"We've been traveling down in a northeasterly direction for most of the day. We could be near the lower side of the hill, out here."

She studied the chart, beginning to understand what he was telling her. "So we might actually not be too far from the surface, is that what you're saying? We could possibly find our way out down here on the opposite slope somewhere?"

He nodded and lay back on the pillow, exhausted by the effort.

Neale felt a brief surge of hope, but it faded as abruptly as it came. "Even if there's another entrance out there somewhere, how would we ever find it?" she asked, looking again the shadowy mass of darkened passageways that dripped with stalactites and graceful drapery stone. "It took us days to find the way in, Clint. It sure wouldn't be any easier from down here, would it?"

But Clint was no longer able to hear. He was breathing harshly, and his face was once again bathed with sweat.

Neale moaned briefly in terror, then took herself firmly in hand. She brewed a pot of tea, laced it heavily with sugar and fed it to him in little sips. After the tea was gone she covered him with the blanket again, watching as he drifted off into an uneasy sleep.

When Clint was resting more comfortably, she strapped on the helmet, shouldered her pack into position and set off to explore the warren of passages, shuddering with reluctance as she ventured into the black depths of the cavern.

The opposite wall was riddled with openings. There were grottos recessed into the stone, filled with shadowy formations like bizarre nativity scenes, and passages ranging from small tunnels to large, airy hallways. Neale slipped into one of the larger passages and moved along it for a few dozen feet until she rounded a turn and lost sight of the entrance to the central cavern.

Alone in the dim pool of light from the helmet, she clenched her hands into fists, taking deep breaths to calm her racing heart. Then she turned and hurried back into the cavern and across the rough floor to where Clint lay on the folded sleeping bag. His eyelids fluttered and his chest rose and fell unevenly as he slept. Occasionally he groaned aloud in pain, a sound that wrenched her heart.

Neale took a spool of thin nylon cord from his pack and knelt to tie one end of it firmly around his ankle. He opened his eyes while she was working and gave her a sleepy, questioning glance.

"No matter what happens," she told him, "I don't intend to lose you, Clint Farrell. I want to be able to find my way back here."

"That sounds good to me," he whispered huskily, with a smile so tender that it brought a lump to her throat. "I sure don't want to lose you, either, girl. Not ever."

She bent to kiss him and pulled the blanket up closer around his shoulders, then moved back across the cavern and into one of the larger passageways.

Neale edged her way along the tunnel in the rock, playing out the spool of cord as she went, moving through the winding labyrinth with a growing sense of hopelessness. She couldn't tell what direction she was heading, or where she might be on Clint's topographical map. The terrain varied so much that she didn't even know whether she was working her way up or down within the hill. In places the path tilted until it was almost a sheer climb, and in others it sloped downward so that she found herself sliding and bumping over the rock.

She clung desperately to the spool of cord in her hands, knowing that it was her lifeline, the only thing that connected her to Clint and the tenuous safety of the cavern.

But there was no real protection back there, either, and Neale realized it all too well. She was grimly aware that Clint was far more seriously injured than he pretended to be, and that he needed immediate medical attention. Their only hope was for her to somehow find a way back to the surface so she could go for help. The urgency and danger of their position was terrifying to Neale.

But there was a kind of bitter justice in all this, too. In a sad, horrible way, she'd brought all this on herself. It was a fitting punishment, Neale thought, for betraying and deceiving such a good man. It served her right to be in a position where his safety, possibly even his life, rested on her shoulders, and nobody else could help. If she couldn't find a way out, both of them would die in this silent grave.

She had to fight constantly against a rising panic, and a paralyzing feeling of claustrophobia. As she moved farther and farther away from the cavern, deeper into the winding maze of passages, she found herself almost overwhelmed by terror, and a choking urge to fight her way free of this musty blackness. If she couldn't see the sky and breathe fresh air, she was certain that the darkness would suffocate her.

Neale fought down the panic attack, forcing herself to stay calm and keep walking. She couldn't give in to her own weakness. She owed it to Clint to maintain a level head and do what she could to help him.

Suddenly, faraway and indistinct, she heard a sound that was magnified by the intense silence of the cave's interior. She paused and strained to listen, then moved cautiously in the direction of the sound until she recognized it and stood rigid with horror, flattening herself against the rock wall.

What she heard was the unmistakable noise of a waterfall, of a river tumbling and breaking over rocks. Neale stood wide-eyed with fear, picturing the underground cataract somewhere in this black maze, perhaps only a few steps away. One careless move and she could tumble into it, just as Clint had fallen into the cavern, and be washed away into the cold depths of the earth.

"Oh, God..." she whimpered, pressing her fist against her mouth. "Please, God, help me...."

For a long time she stood against the wall, afraid to take another step into the clammy black depths of the cave. And then, gradually, she became aware of another sound that was faint and faraway, but still discernible over the roar of the waterfall.

It was the sound of a dog barking.

Neale jerked herself erect and listened in tense silence, her thoughts whirling rapidly. There were no animals in the cave at this depth, not even the swarms of bats, the sightless cave insects and the blind, colorless lizards that had evolved at some of the upper levels. Down here, the only living things were the bits of algae and lichen that stained the dripping stalagmites.

But still, faint and insistent, Neale could hear a dog barking.

It had to be coming from somewhere on the surface, she thought, wild with excitement. Clint was right. They'd climbed all the way down through the limestone ridge, and they were close to the other side, possibly just a few hundred feet away from the blessed light and air.

Maybe it was Alvin barking out there. After all, the whole cave system was on Brock Munroe's land. Maybe Brock himself was out there somewhere in his truck. Neale pictured the man's big, capable body and his engaging smile. She sagged against the wall, dizzy with relief and happiness.

"Alvin!" she shouted, so loud that her voice rang and echoed in the stillness. "Alvin, is that you? Is anybody up there? Help! Help us! We're trapped in here and Clint is hurt!"

She continued to yell, stopping at times to listen to the far-off barking, trying to gauge where it was coming from. But the maze of passages tended to deflect and amplify sounds, making them seem to come from all around her. And the rumbling of the underground waterfall continued, muffling everything else in its distant roar.

At last Neale stopped shouting, aware that she could no longer hear the faint barking. Sick with disappointment, she sank down and huddled on the cold floor of the passage, pressing her face against her knees and trying not to give way to tears.

Suddenly she felt something wet and cold slithering against her cheek. She screamed in terror and scrambled backward on the rock, directing her helmet beam wildly into the black tunnel. A pair of yellow eyes glittered and moved toward her, bright and feral in the darkness.

Her numbing horror faded abruptly and she laughed aloud. "Alvin," she whispered, as the little dog flung himself against her and licked her face again. "Alvin, you sweet, wonderful dog. How did you find your way in here? Can you show me how to get out? Alvin, I'm so happy to see you...."

But Alvin clearly wasn't interested in her feelings. He pressed against Neale in the darkness, nosing insistently at her pack. She slipped it from her shoulders and opened the nylon flap to rummage inside, offering Alvin a piece of the beef jerky that he loved and resting one hand on his ragged back as he wolfed it down.

"Alvin, you're really hungry, aren't you?" she murmured. "Have you been out wandering again? What time is it, Alvin? It must be getting dark out there. How did you ever find your way in here, sweetie? Where's the cave entrance?"

She laughed again, delighted by the sound of her own voice in the musty darkness, and of Alvin's greedy presence. He finished the beef and looked up at her hopefully, waiting as she poured a little water from her canteen into a metal bowl and set it down carefully on the floor.

Alvin gulped the water, then sat back on his haunches, licking his muzzle while Neale shouldered her pack again and turned to gather up the spool of nylon cord.

"Now," she said cheerfully, "you can lead me out of here, Alvin, and we'll go for help. Just wait till I..."

But when she stood erect and turned around, the cold stillness hit her like a blow in the stomach. Alvin was gone, vanished without a trace, and the dark passage was empty once again.

CHAPTER TEN

MILLIE MUNROE SAT in the quiet waiting room, observing Crystal Creek's tree-shaded main street. In the stores and offices across the way, she could see grinning skeletons and livid orange pumpkins taped to the windows. A couple of young girls hurried past on the sidewalk beyond the window, carrying costumes and masks and giggling together with excitement.

Of course, Millie thought, turning away from her contemplation of the street, and leafing aimlessly through a dog-eared magazine in her lap. She'd just remembered that it was Saturday morning.

Today was Halloween.

She smiled grimly at the irony of the situation. How fitting that it should be Halloween. And this morning, Millie Munroe was disguised as a normal, grown-up woman while her heart beat crazily and her soul curled up in terror. In fact, beneath her fine tweed suit and silk blouse, she felt younger than one of those ten-year-olds outside the window. She felt lost and bewildered and on the verge of tears.

After she'd left Amanda's apartment on Thursday afternoon, Millie had wandered for a long time through the streets of downtown Austin, barely noticing where she went. Finally she'd taken a cab back to the hotel and waited tensely for Virginia to return, startling her friend as soon as she stepped through the door by insisting without explanation that they drive back to Crystal Creek that very night. And early the next morning, still haunted by Amanda's accusation of cowardice, she'd gone into town and visited Nate Purdy. The old family doctor had been grave and quiet as he examined her, performing a lot of tests but not saying much.

Now it was a day later. After a sleepless night in her old room at the ranch house, Millie waited to hear Nate's verdict.

Again she looked out at the quiet autumn streets of her hometown, wishing that she'd chosen to see a doctor in the city instead of coming here to Nate. Somehow it would seem more impersonal and easier to bear, hearing her death sentence from a stranger in a place she didn't know.

But then again, this familiarity was the very reason Millie had decided to come to Nate Purdy, an old school friend she'd known all her life. She simply couldn't bear to place herself in the hands of a stranger. Not for the most intimate crisis of her life...

"Millie?" the nurse said quietly. "The doctor will see you now."

Millie's throat tightened and her hands began to tremble. She kept her face impassive, laid the magazine aside and got up, pausing to smooth her tweed skirt with an unconscious gesture. Taking a deep breath, she followed the nurse into Nate's comfortable, book-lined office.

He sat behind the desk, regarding her thoughtfully as she seated herself.

"Well, Millie," he said, putting on his glasses and studying the file in front of him. "How are you this fine morning?"

"How do you think I am?" she asked tightly. "I didn't sleep a wink all night. In fact, I've hardly slept for the past month. I'm waiting to hear what you've got to say, Nathan Purdy, so just cut the professional bedside garbage and get to it, all right?"

Nate shook his head sadly. "You always were a firebrand, you know that? All the boys were scared of you, Millie. You were the prettiest girl in six counties, and nobody dared to ask you out for fear you'd bite his head off."

"Please, Nate," she whispered, dropping her hostile tone and appealing to him. "Please, just *tell* me."

"Well, you seem to have a real fast-growing tumour in there, Millie. A bit of a nuisance, but nothing lifethreatening."

Millie stared at him in stunned disbelief. "Not...not life-threatening?"

Nate shook his head. "Completely benign. It'll have to come out, of course, because the thing's not going to go away, and if it gets any bigger it could start causing some nerve damage. But that's the worst it can do."

Millie felt herself drowning in confusion, struggling with her shock and disbelief. "But...how can you tell that it's benign? You just...sort of poked at me, Nate."

"I did a needle biopsy. Don't you remember when I aspirated some fluid from that mass in your abdomen?"

Millie shook her head. "I just remember being poked at a whole lot," she confessed, "and feeling a general haze of terror."

Nate chuckled. "First time Millie Munroe's ever admitted to being afraid of anything in her life, I reckon. You're a whole lot easier to like nowadays than you used to be, Millie, you know that?"

Millie ignored this comment, as she'd ignored all of the boys' teasing since she was ten years old. "So you poked a needle in there..."

"It's a very efficient form of nonsurgical diagnosis. Fluid is aspirated from the mass and tested for cancerous cells. I sent your sample in right away yesterday, and called the lab just a few minutes ago for the results. The fluid was clear. No sign of malignancy at all."

"Just a benign tumor," Millie whispered, still feeling dazed and light-headed.

"That's right," Nate agreed. "Lord's sake, Millie, why didn't you have the thing tested when you first noticed it? You must've been going through pure hell this past month or two."

"I have," she confessed, looking up at him with a bleak smile. "I surely have, Nate. But, you know, it took someone calling me a coward before I'd actually do something about it.''

"Is that so? Now, who on God's earth would have the nerve to call *you* a coward?" Nate asked, shaking his head in awe.

"Somebody who deserves a whole lot better than she's had from me, and that's a fact.'' Millie got to her feet and stood a little unsteadily by her chair, looking at the doctor. "Is that all, Nate? Did you want to tell me anything else?"

"Not really. You need to have that tumor removed pretty soon, Millie. We can do it here, or you can make arrangements with your own doctor in Oregon if you're going back before too long."

"You know, I think I will be,'' Millie said slowly, again studying the street beyond the window. She turned back to the doctor and smiled with sudden radiance. "I came home because I thought I was dying, Nate. Now that I'm not, I find that I'd like to get back to Oregon and see my house and friends again. I'm feeling real homesick, but not for Texas anymore. I think I'll head back right away."

He nodded. "That's likely a good idea, to have your surgery in your home state. Give me a call before you leave and we'll send along these test results."

"I'll give the address to your nurse. I think I'll probably leave for Austin this afternoon, and fly home from there."

He raised his eyebrows. "That soon?"

"I hope so, if I can book a flight tomorrow and wangle a ride into town. I'm real anxious to get home, Nate. The world seems different all of a sudden, and I want to see my house again. But," Millie added thoughtfully, "there are a few things I need to do before I leave."

The doctor nodded and took off his glasses, watching with a smile as Millie Munroe turned and walked out of his office. Her white head was joyously erect, her stride as firm and graceful as it had always been in her girlhood.

ALVIN LAY on the veranda under the porch swing, resting his muzzle on his folded paws. He watched listlessly as Brock moved back and forth in the sunlight, carrying pails of feed from the chophouse into the pen where the bulls lazed in the autumn warmth.

Normally Alvin would be down there as well, trotting at Brock's heels as he went about his chores. Alvin liked being close to Brock, liked the feeling of security that came from having his master always within sight and smell.

But these days it was different. Every fall there was something about the crispness of the morning air, the slanting light in the afternoon and the distant scent of wood smoke on the evening breeze, that upset all of Alvin's comfortable routines. For a couple of weeks the little dog was driven by a nameless urge, some deep primitive longing that troubled him and set him wandering far from home, searching for something he never seemed able to find.

Alvin didn't really enjoy these lonely, nocturnal travels of his. He was frightened most of the time, weary and footsore, missing his regular meals and cozy bed. But until the autumn deepened and the nights grew colder, he seemed helpless to fight the restless spirit that drove him.

He perked up his ears briefly when Brock's truck pulled into the yard and parked near the house. But he tensed and edged farther under the porch swing when he saw Millie get out and start up the walk toward the veranda.

Alvin and Millie hadn't managed to establish a cordial relationship. The ragged dog was painfully conscious of this strange woman's disapproval, and frightened by the harsh note in her voice when she spoke to him.

Today, though, she seemed different. Alvin sensed a change in the aura that surrounded her, a kind of lightness and shining happiness that he hadn't seen before. She even smelled different, more pleasant and easy, like the sweetness of the autumn day. He lifted his ears in disbelief at an unfamiliar sound, and realized that Millie was singing as she walked.

She paused by the porch swing. Alvin stared out nervously at her fine leather shoes and cowered back under the swing, but she bent to peer into the shadows at him.

"Well, hello there, Alvin," she said gently. "How are you? Have you been out wandering all night again, you poor little fellow?"

Her voice was different, too, softened by warmth and kindness. She sounded almost like Amanda, whom Alvin adored nearly as much as he loved brock. He stiffened in amazement as Millie rummaged in her handbag, then reached under the swing to offer him part of a chocolate bar before going into the house.

Alvin huddled under the swing and gobbled the rich tidbit, his weary body craving the sugar. He finished all of the bar, ate a few nuts that had fallen from it, and licked the floorboards, where a trace of chocolate still lingered. Then he settled back in a heap, rested his chin on his paws and resumed his mournful study of the sunlit ranch yard.

Something was bothering Alvin. Deep in the recesses of his mind he knew there was a living thing dangerously out of place somewhere on the ranch, and he didn't like the feeling.

Despite his questionable pedigree, Alvin was descended from a race of keenly intelligent herd dogs. Herding and protecting were born in him, stamped indelibly on his genetic makeup and his brain cells. With proper training, and a personality less clouded by laziness and timidity, Alvin would probably have been a talented addition to any working ranch.

As it was, he tried hard to avoid physical effort and hazardous situations. Still, his conscience occasionally troubled him because of this behavior, and it was troubling him a great deal right now.

Alvin sighed and cocked a hind leg to gnaw furiously at his dusty flank, then settled back again and dropped his eyes shut. He thought about the young woman he'd encountered yesterday in the darkness, and salivated briefly at the memory of the beef jerky that she'd given him.

But his recollection of the treat was overshadowed by Alvin's gloomy knowledge that the woman was in the wrong place. She shouldn't be off all alone like that, deep in a hole under the ground. It wasn't the right place for her to be, and Alvin ached with the herd dog's instinct to get her moved back into position, safely included in the general mass of humanity once more.

He shuddered when he remembered the hole in the ground. It had been terrifying for him to make his way through the clammy tunnel, echoing with the roar of distant water. But he'd heard her calling and been powerless to resist.

Actually, when the woman first started yelling, Alvin had been ranging happily in the valley overhead, barking at the flights of bobwhite quail that burst upward from the grass and shrubbery, their wings beating noisily on the autumn air. He'd been planning to spend the last few daylight hours hunting for a small rodent or some carrion to eat so he wouldn't have to go all the way back to the ranch, and he hoped to pass the night in the safety of the cave that opened beneath a dense thicket nearby.

Alvin had discovered this cavern in the valley floor a couple of years ago, when he'd first started his restless autumn wanderings. He liked the cavern because it was clean and dry, sheltered from the elements and not frequented by other, bigger animals that might be frightening to a cowardly ranch dog.

He knew that a tunnel ran downward from the wall of his secret cavern, deep into the earth where it opened onto a twisting labyrinth of underground passages. But Alvin had never ventured very far along the narrow opening until yesterday, when he heard the strange, displaced sound of the woman's voice, calling him frantically from somewhere beneath his feet.

Alvin thought again about the woman, still bothered by the fact that she seemed badly out of place, not part of the herd that she belonged in. A good dog would have nipped firmly at her heels and insisted that she come up to the surface and resume her rightful position. Alvin knew that he shouldn't have left her down in that hole, so far away from everything. Especially when she smelled so potently of loneliness and terror....

He crept from the shelter of the porch swing and hesitated at the edge of the steps, looking toward the east with an indecisive air. But the autumn sun was warm on his body, and he was so tired. He dropped back onto his stomach and his eyes closed again. All thoughts of the lost woman drifted from his mind, and he fell heavily asleep in the morning warmth.

BROCK SMILED briefly as he glanced over at the veranda where Alvin lay sprawled at the top of the steps.

Poor little devil, Brock thought. Alvin had just about run himself ragged these past few days, roaming the countryside under the harvest moon. His wanderlust seemed even more pronounced this year than it had been in the past. Some days the dog didn't come home at all, just stayed in the rough country until he was worn out and half-starved.

Maybe the urge was starting to wear down, Brock thought hopefully, looking again at the furry lump on the veranda. To tell the truth, he missed the ugly little sucker trotting at his heels as he went about his daily chores.

At least when Alvin was around, Brock knew that someone cared for him with an unconditional love, not a wayward emotion that could apparently vary with the season and the circumstance. . . .

Brock's face darkened with misery. He tossed the empty pails into the chophouse and latched the door, trying not to think about Amanda. But it was impossible not to think about her. She was so intimately lodged in his heart and soul that he couldn't draw breath without feeling her presence deep within him.

She should be here right now, working happily at some project inside the house, or following him around as he did his chores. It was Saturday, and Brock was accustomed to having her close by on weekends. The ranch seemed unbearably lonely without her, as if all the coziness and brightness had been washed away.

Even the sun looked cold and pallid this morning, leaving Brock bereft.

He thought about the Halloween party tonight at Zack's, and how little fun it would be to go by himself. Nothing was much fun without Amanda. But it was far more galling to visualize her attending some fancy party in Austin, at the governor's mansion, no less, with a lot of stuffed-shirt types that she couldn't possibly be interested in.

Brock still cherished a forlorn hope that Amanda wouldn't go the party in Austin after all, that she'd reconsider and come out to the ranch instead. Maybe she'd been planning all along to surprise him by dropping in at Zack's in some kind of wonderful costume, as she'd done last year at the McKinneys' Halloween party. Brock couldn't forget the way she'd looked in that low-cut gown of velvet and Spanish lace, with her hair pulled back under a lacy mantilla and her bosom gleaming in the moonlight.

His throat went dry, and his body ached with frustrated sexual desire. He got into his truck, pulled it around to the feed stack and started to toss bales of hay into the back, his mind still surging with random images of the woman he loved, of her eyes and smile and laughter, her curving body and the sweetness of her kisses. . . .

"Nice day, isn't it?" he heard a voice say below him, interrupting his fantasies.

Brock looked down to see Millie standing nearby in a pair of well-cut tan slacks and a taupe silk blouse, open at the throat. She wore a heavy gold necklace with matching earrings, and looked well groomed and surprisingly happy.

"Well, you sure look nice, Millie," Brock said with startled admiration. "What's the occasion?"

"I'm leaving you," Millie told him breezily. "That's what the occasion is."

"Leaving?" Brock asked. "Why? Where are you going?"

"I'm going home, son. I've bothered you long enough. Bubba and Mary are driving into Austin this afternoon," Millie added. "They're stopping by to pick me up in an hour or so, and I've got a flight booked to Oregon at six o'clock tomorrow morning."

Still stunned by this information, Brock looked down at his aunt cautiously, trying to judge whether she seemed offended about something. But her dark eyes glowed with happiness, and her whole being was animated with that keen, restless energy, uniquely hers, that he recalled from his childhood.

"There's no need for you to go so soon, Millie. You're welcome to stay as long as you like." Brock heaved another bale into the back of the truck and paused to wipe a shirtsleeve across his forehead. "Even my dog's more or less deserted me. If you go away, too," he added mournfully, "I'll just be real lonely."

"I know." Millie gave him a measuring glance. "And that's not right, Brock. Your lady should be here with you."

Brock stared down at his aunt. "Well, I never thought I'd hear you say that, Millie. I thought you didn't like Amanda."

Millie smiled up at him ruefully and shook her head. "This past while, I haven't liked anybody very much, son. Especially not myself. But I feel a whole lot different about things now, and I want you to know that your Amanda is too good a woman to throw away. You're being real foolish."

"I'm being foolish?" he asked in outrage. "What am I doing? My life and my feelings are just the same as always, Millie. If things are changing, it's Amanda who's doing it, not me."

"That's pure bullcrap!" Millie said rudely, glaring at him. "And you know it as well as I do!"

Brock grinned at her blunt speech and jumped lightly down from the haystack. He strolled forward and leaned against the side of the truck, chewing on a straw and smiling at his aunt. "Bullcrap, Millie?" he asked in a teasing voice.

"Damn right it is," she said furiously. "And don't stand there grinning at me like an idiot, Brock Munroe. I changed your diapers when you were a baby, and don't you forget it. I guess I know you pretty well."

"So you think it's my fault that she isn't here? What have I done to drive her away?"

"It's what you *haven't* done, you fool."

"Millie, if we're going to have a productive discussion here, you've really got to quit calling me names. It isn't nice."

"I'm sorry," she said automatically, but there was no apology in her voice.

Brock chuckled. "Yeah, I'll just bet you are. Now, what should I be doing that I'm not doing, in your gentle opinion?"

"You should be *marrying* the girl, that's what you should be doing. Can't you see how frustrating and humiliating this whole situation is for her?"

Brock tensed at her words, and felt a familiar stiffening of opposition. "I don't see why it's so terrible for her. I couldn't be any more committed than I am, Millie. I'm loving and faithful, and I always will be. A piece of paper isn't going to make any difference. Why is marriage so damned important?"

"Because without it, she can't make any plans for the future. That piece of paper, Brock Munroe, is your promise to her that you're going to be around for the long haul, and she can go ahead safely and put her life in your hands. Without the paper, a woman just doesn't feel safe."

"Why not? If a man gives his word and intends to stand by it, why doesn't it have any meaning for a woman until he signs on the dotted line? I've never understood why women have to keep pushing so hard for a legal commitment."

Millie snorted in impatience and gave him a pitying glance. "Men," she commented. "You're all so big and strong, and so *dumb.*"

"I want to know," Brock persisted. "I want to know why a marriage license makes such a big difference."

"I told you. A woman doesn't feel safe without it. Until you marry her, she'll spend all her time wondering why you're so reluctant to commit yourself, and when you're going to run off and disappear."

Brock turned away and stared gloomily into the hazy morning sky. "I'm not the one who'd be likely to disappear," he muttered. "Where would I go? I'm tied to this goddamn place."

Millie watched his face in disbelief. "I've never heard you talk like that before. You love this place, Brock. You always have."

He moved restlessly and gripped the edge of the truck box. "Sure I have. But it's frustrating as hell, Millie, trying to make a living these days. You talk about Amanda's frustrations. Did you ever spend a minute thinking about mine?"

She looked up at him, her face quiet and thoughtful. "I can't say I have. How about if you tell me what they are, son?"

Brock tossed the straw aside and watched as it drifted into the dusty soil at the base of the feed stack. "It's not easy to be a rancher these days," he said. "All your plans have to be long term, and in the short term you never have enough money. Something always seems to go wrong. I just feel so broke all the time, Millie."

"I can't understand that. This ranch is prime land, after all. It's got to be worth a small fortune."

"Sure it is, if I wanted to sell. But what would I have then? A whole lot of cash, and nothing to live for. I lost half my calves to sickness last year, Millie. It almost wiped me out. Sometimes I get so tired of being land-poor, but I can't see any alternative."

Millie listened in silence, her fine-drawn face softening with concern.

"But it's different for Amanda," Brock went on, surprised by the relief of talking about their problems after all his months of suffering and indecision. "She's got no emotional stake in this place. She wasn't raised on the land the way I was. How much is she going to enjoy spending her life sacrificing and doing without to keep my ranch going?"

"If she loves you the way I think she does," Millie told him calmly, "then she'll be happy working with you to make your dreams come true, no matter how hard it is at first."

Brock stared at the horizon again, feeling an aching flood of unhappiness. "That's easy to say, Millie. It sounds good in the books and movies. But in real life, a woman like Amanda could get pretty tired of life here on the ranch."

He turned back to his aunt, wanting passionately to make her understand. Millie listened in silence, her face impassive.

"Amanda likes beautiful things," Brock went on. "She never wants anything cheap or second-rate. And on her own, she can afford to buy what she likes. She can have whatever she wants. What will she have if she teams up with me?"

"Maybe she'll have what she really wants."

Brock shook his head stubbornly. "Sure, but what if it's too hard for her after a while? What if she gets tired of the struggle and wants to leave? I'd die, Millie. I love her too much to have her for a while and then let her go. I'd rather not start a marriage than have it break up after a couple of years."

"A few days ago, your lady called me a coward, Brock. Did you know that?"

Brock stared at his aunt in astonishment. "*Amanda* called you a coward? Why? When did this happen?"

Millie smiled. "Never mind. I stopped in to visit her apartment on Thursday, and we had an interesting talk. Maybe she'll tell you about it sometime. But the truth is, Brock, she was absolutely right. I was acting like a pitiful coward, and if Amanda hadn't told me so, I probably wouldn't have forced myself to come to terms with my problem. So now I'm returning the favor. I'm telling you that *you're* the one being cowardly, creeping around here being afraid of life and not trusting enough in the quality of the woman you care about. You might keep yourself from being hurt, but you'll never be happy."

Millie paused for breath after this remarkable speech, her eyes flashing, and waited for his response.

Brock shifted and looked away, unable to look at her.

He wanted so much to believe what she said. He wanted to go to Amanda, bring her home and keep her with him forever. But when he thought about the party at the governor's mansion, and pictured Amanda in an elegant gown on the arm of a man like Judd Hinshaw, he knew that there were some things he could never offer. He had no right to tie Amanda to a life that might be bitterly unfulfilling after the novelty faded. And, as he'd told Millie, he couldn't bear the anguish of having her and then losing her.

While Millie stood watching in silence, he shrugged and turned away, crossing the ranch yard with a listless stride and disappearing behind the corrals.

CHAPTER ELEVEN

NEALE SHIFTED on the hard floor and pressed closer to Clint, frowning when she felt him begin to stir. He whispered something against her cheek. She leaned up on her elbow and switched on the battery-operated lamp, then looked down at him in surprise. His eyes were open and he was regarding her with a steady smile.

"Clint," she whispered.

"Hi, kid. You're sure a pretty sight to wake up to," he murmured huskily. He bent to kiss her, wrapping his arms around her and holding her close.

Neale sighed and nestled against him, so deep in love that for a moment the horrible reality of their situation faded and she felt a rush of happiness.

It was good to see him smiling and alert. For most of the past day he'd been slipping in and out of consciousness, weakened by raging attacks of fever that seemed to strike without warning. They sent his temperature soaring and then left him limp and sweating, muttering incoherently in pain.

Neale had tried to help him, scouring the meager contents of their first-aid kit for something, anything, to ease his suffering. But the only medication they had

was a small jar of aspirin, and that was completely in-
effective against whatever internal damage Clint had
suffered in his fall.

Neale was frightened by his growing weakness and
even more alarmed by his occasional bouts of delir-
ium. Somehow she had to find a way out of the cave
and get help for him, but she was tormented by fear
and indecisiveness. After Alvin had run off and left her
alone in the clammy corridor, she'd been too afraid of
the distant waterfall to venture any farther. And for the
first time in her life, Neale's fear wasn't for herself.
Suddenly, under the strangest and most terrifying of
circumstances, Neale Cameron had fallen in love.

Now her thoughts and fears were all for Clint. When
she pictured herself falling into that raging cataract and
being swept away, her mind supplied her with a horri-
fying image of the man she loved, all alone and helpless in the hidden cavern, growing weaker and weaker,
with nobody to look after him or even know where he
was....

Neale shuddered and turned away quickly so Clint
couldn't see her face. She scrambled to her feet and
moved around the cavern to stretch her cramped body,
then knelt and rummaged in Clint's pack, examining
their dwindling food supply.

"What time is it?" he asked.

Neale looked at her watch. "About three o'clock."

"Day or night?"

Neale frowned, trying to remember. "Isn't it weird
how time all runs together down here when you can't
see the sun? I think it must be afternoon," she said at

last. "Saturday afternoon. We've been sleeping for almost twelve hours, Clint."

"That's the way it is when you're deep inside a cave. You tend to begin sleeping for longer periods of time."

"Well, you're looking a lot more chipper this afternoon," Neale said, trying to keep her voice light. "Is the pain any better?"

"Maybe. Let me see if..."

He lifted himself with one hand and tried to pull his body into a sitting position, then fell back heavily onto the sleeping bag, gray with agony.

Neale moaned softly and hurried to kneel beside him, taking his hand in both of hers. "Don't try to get up anymore," she whispered. "Please, Clint, don't keep trying. I can't bear to see you in pain like this."

"I have to get up," he said. "I have to find a way out of here, Neale. We're going to run out of food before long, and I need some kind of medical attention. You know it as well as I do."

Neale looked down at him helplessly. "I feel so useless," she muttered. "Look at me, strong and healthy, nothing wrong with me at all, and yet I'm such a baby. I can't find my way out and go for help, even though I know there's probably an entrance nearby."

"How do you know that?" he asked, suddenly alert.

Neale bit her lip, instantly regretting her careless words.

She hadn't told him about Alvin's visit, fearful that if Clint knew they were close to the lower surface of the ridge, he'd force himself to get up and try to find the passage when he could barely creep a few feet across the cavern on his hands and knees. Neale knew that he shouldn't be trying to move. He'd just do more internal damage....

"Neale? What makes you think there's an entrance nearby?"

"Yesterday," she began reluctantly, "while you were sleeping, I went into one of those bigger passages over there to see if I could find a way out." She waved her hand at the dark openings that honeycombed the opposite wall. "After a while I could hear the sound of running water, like the noise a river makes when it goes over rocks?"

She cast him a questioning glance. Clint nodded, his face beginning to lose a little of the grayish pallor as he rested against the pillow.

"Not a good idea to go any farther on your own if there's a waterfall nearby," he told her. "That can be really dangerous stuff, kiddo."

"I know. I was terrified. Especially because I couldn't tell where it was. You know how the sound seems to come from all over when you're down here?"

"I know. Promise me you won't try to crawl any farther in there on your own."

"But, Clint, we have to—"

"Promise me."

"I promise." Neale hesitated, trying to smile at him. "Actually, there's not much chance of me being reckless. I'm brave about most things, but I'm a pretty big coward inside this cave."

"Good. I'm glad to hear it, because cowards tend to live longer, sweetheart. Now, tell me the rest of your story."

"Well," Neale went on, "after a while I heard another sound, really faint and faraway, but still recognizable. It was a dog barking."

Clint's eyes widened with excitement. He struggled to lift himself on his elbow, then fell back again, clutching at his stomach.

"Clint, *please*..."

"Sorry. I won't...do it anymore. What happened after you heard the dog barking?"

"I started yelling as loud as I could. After a while the barking stopped and I sat down to rest in the tunnel. When I looked up, Alvin was right there beside me."

"Alvin! My God..."

"I was so happy, Clint. I was sure we were saved, that I could just follow him outside. I gave him some beef jerky and water, and then bent down to pick up my stuff. When I turned around, he'd vanished. I tried to find where he might have gone, but there were a dozen passages branching in all directions. I had no idea which one he'd taken, and I was so afraid of falling into that river. The water noise seemed to be all around me when I went farther into the cave."

Clint nodded thoughtfully, considering her words. "What chance do you think there is that he'll come back, Neale?"

"I don't know. He really loves that beef jerky, and he seemed happy to see me. But he's such a coward,

Clint. Everybody knows what Alvin's like. Down in that dark tunnel, he looked as scared as I was.''

"Poor girl," Clint said softly, reaching up to touch her face.

When she looked down at him, she was surprised to see tears sparkling in his eyes. "Clint," she whispered. "What is it? What's wrong?''

"Oh, God, sweetheart, I feel like such a bastard, bringing you down here and getting you stuck in this mess. It was completely irresponsible of me, Neale. I knew better, but I just loved having you close to me, and I was excited about spending the night with you down here in my cave. Now I can't lift a finger to help you get out.''

She sat hugging her knees and looked away from him, her heart wrung with emotion. "Don't talk like that," she murmured. "Clint, I'm the one who should feel guilty, not you. At least you were honest with me.''

"What do you mean?''

Neale drew a deep breath and bit her lip as she stared into the cavernous depths.

Stalactites dripped from the ceiling above, like icy fingers reaching toward her. The lamp at Clint's side cast eerie shadows onto the walls, wavering shapes that shimmered in the blackness. The air was cold and musty, with an ancient, untouched feeling, as if they were caught in some bizarre time capsule.

Maybe sometime in the distant future, untold centuries from now, archaeologists would find the mummified bodies of a man and a woman deep in the earth, and be intrigued by their strange appearance. They'd be carried up to the light and air, unwrapped and displayed before curious multitudes who would file past and study them with wide, exotic eyes. . . .

"Neale? What are you talking about?"

Neale shuddered and drew herself erect. "I lied to you, Clint. I'm so sorry."

"About being an experienced caver? I know that, honey. We already talked about it."

"Not that." Neale looked down at him sadly. "I'm not a very nice person, Clint. Here we are stuck together down here, and you're really going to hate me when I tell you what I've done. It's going to be hell for you," she added with a bleak smile, "being stranded in a cave with a woman you hate."

"It's hard to imagine hating you, Neale. I've never met a girl as wonderful as you. You're the woman I've always dreamed of finding."

"Don't say that!" Neale whispered. "Please, Clint, don't say that. Wait till you hear what I've done."

"Okay. Tell me."

Neale moved closer to him and took his hand again, staring down at his fingers. Absently she ran her hands over each of them in turn, pressing and releasing them with a gentle motion. She loved the feel of his hands, and their manly, capable look.

"First," she said in a low voice, dropping her head so she wouldn't have to look at him, "I want you to know that I'm so sorry. If I had it to do over, I'd never make the same mistake again. I didn't know," she added, looking into his eyes for a moment. "I didn't know how...how it would feel to be in love with a man this way. I've never loved anybody before.''

''Neale...''

''I betrayed you,'' she went on, squeezing his hand to silence him. ''I went behind your back and sold the story about this cave to a national magazine, Clint. It's called *American Travel*.''

She glanced up and saw him nodding calmly. ''I know the magazine,'' he said. ''A real glossy publication, isn't it? I once contributed to an article they were doing about caves in Mexico.''

Neale hesitated, astonished by his matter-of-fact tone. ''You don't understand,'' she said at last. ''I knew that you wanted to keep this a secret, but I went ahead and told my editor about it, sent them a description of the cave and some information about you and what you were looking for, and even...'' Neale paused in agony, then forced herself to continue. ''Even some pictures,'' she finished in a halting voice. ''I sent them all by courier and fax machine. They're in New York already.''

Clint grinned. ''No kidding. How did you manage to get pictures without letting me know?''

Neale shifted uneasily on the hard floor. ''When you left me in the column chamber that first day, I...I took a lot of pictures while you were exploring the passage. I had my camera and flash and a small folding tripod in my pack.''

''What an enterprising girl,'' he commented, his eyes teasing.

"Clint, you don't understand! All the time that I was pretending to be your friend, I was just tagging along so I could get the story. I knew that you didn't want the public to know about this cave, but I sold you out anyway. I betrayed your trust. Don't you see how terrible it was?"

He reached up and drew her down beside him, pulling her into a gentle embrace and kissing her cheek. "Okay, Neale," he whispered. "If it was such a terrible thing, why did you do it?"

"I needed the money."

"What for?"

"My family. I told you about how my father died, and his illness cleaned us out. I've been . . . trying to help. They need so much, my mother and my younger brother. And the magazine offered almost ten thousand dollars for this story. Oh, Clint," she said, her voice breaking, "I sold you out for ten thousand dollars. If I could do it over, I wouldn't take a million dollars for that story. I hope you believe me."

"Of course I believe you. Now, stop crying and give me a kiss."

"You're not angry?" she asked, sitting up and contemplating his face in wonder. "You don't hate me?"

"I love you," he told her simply. "I really love you, Neale. More than I ever thought I could love anybody in this world."

"Oh, Clint . . ."

"I was the one who was wrong about this, not you," he went on, staring at the shadowed walls with their fantastic, unearthly decorations. "I had no right to keep all this to myself, Neale. Everybody should be able to share in something as wonderful as this cave. You were right to blow me out of the water. We wouldn't be in this mess if I'd been more open about what I was doing. Then somebody besides us would know the cave location and have the preliminary maps. How could I possibly be angry with you, sweetheart, when I've caused all this misery by my own selfishness?''

"Clint, please...don't say things like that. It breaks my heart."

"When we get out of here," he went on quietly, "maybe I can help with some of those debts your family has. I've got a lot of money from my parents that I've never touched, Neale. I've been waiting for a good reason to spend it. And I think this sounds like a pretty good reason."

"Clint, I couldn't take your money!"

"Sure you can. After all, I'll owe you my life."

"Your life?"

"You bet. When I finally crawl out of this cave, it's going to be thanks to you. I'll owe you for everything. I hate to admit it, Neale, but I'm not going to make it on my own. I've got some kind of internal injury, and I'll need your help. Now, let's discuss our options, shall we, honey?" he added in a more businesslike tone.

Neale looked at him, still dizzy with the relief of having confessed her crime and been forgiven. She didn't share Clint's optimism about the possibility of escaping from their clammy tomb. But no matter what happened to them, it felt so wonderful to know that there were no secrets between them anymore, and that he didn't hate her for what she'd done.

"Our options," she echoed, pulling herself back with difficulty to the matter at hand. "Do we have options, Clint?"

"I sure hope so. Look, you said you sent a description of the cave to this magazine, and it's in their office by now?"

Neale nodded.

"Okay. And how soon is somebody going to miss you if you don't come home?"

Neale hesitated, frowning. "I'm sure that I told Marj we were spending the night down here. Yes," she added, her cheeks warming, "I remember telling her. In fact, she had a comment about how romantic it was going to be, sleeping in a cave with a hunk like you."

Clint laughed.

"Marj is a wonderful friend," Neale said wistfully, suddenly wondering if she was ever going to see Marjorie's smiling face again. Tears burned behind her eyes. She swallowed hard, and forced herself to continue. "I think I might have told her we'd be down here a couple of nights, Clint. I didn't want Marj waiting up to grill me as soon as I got home. I doubt that anybody's going to miss me until early in the week. A couple more days, anyway."

He nodded again, and Neale could tell by the troubled expression on his face that he was afraid a few days might be too late. He must really be suffering, she thought. Maybe he knew something about his condition that he wasn't telling her. Maybe he was . . .

But before Neale could voice her concern, Clint held up his hand, touched her lips gently and continued. "When somebody does start to miss us, do you think you've given the magazine enough information that a search party could find the entrance where we came in?"

Neale grasped his train of thought and felt a surge of hope, but it faded as quickly as it came. "I doubt it. I just said the cave was in this area of exposed limestone on Brock Munroe's ranch. But you knew that long ago, Clint, and it still took you weeks to find the opening. There's no reason to think anybody looking for us up there would be able to find it any sooner."

"Unless Alvin could lead them to it. Alvin probably knows several entrances to this cave system. He saw us going in at the top of the ridge the other day, and he came into a lower opening just yesterday."

Neale sat back on her heels and gave Clint a sad smile. "Somehow I can't see Alvin being one of those hero dogs like Lassie, bravely leading his master to the poor people trapped inside the cave. More likely he's at home stuffing himself with dog food and sleeping in the sun. I think he's probably forgotten all about us."

"He might come back, though. If he wanders anywhere near, it's possible he could remember you're down here, and that you have food and water."

"But, Clint, if he does come inside, what good will it do? He'll just run away again."

"Maybe you could catch him and use the cord to tie him up, then get him to lead you out."

"I thought about that," Neale said. "I really kicked myself for not doing it while he was here. But you should have seen how dusty he was, Clint. And some of those passages narrow to openings just a few inches across. I think it's possible that he squeezed through a tunnel so small that only a little dog like Alvin could get into it. Even if I had him on a leash, I'd have to try to dig my way out behind him, and you know that most of this cave is solid rock. Besides, I'm so afraid of that waterfall...."

Clint was silent a long time, staring at the dripping ceiling, his brows contracted in thought. Finally he turned back to Neale. "Tell you what, honey," he said, reaching up to stroke her cheek with an awkward hand. "I've got a plan. It's a pretty long shot, but I think it just might work. I'll have to talk fast, though, because I might not be lucid for very much longer."

"Oh, Clint..." Neale leaned forward to study his face, and saw that the dangerous flush was creeping up his cheeks again. His eyes were unnaturally bright, and his breathing was getting rapid and shallow. "Clint, I don't know what to do about this fever! It's so scary, sweetie. What can I do to help you?"

"I don't think...I don't think there's much...you can do. I need to be in a hospital, Neale. It's not your fault. It's just...the luck of the draw."

"I wish I had some kind of antibiotic, or at least more aspirin...."

"You've got to listen to me, Neale. We don't have...have much time. Are you listening, honey?"

She nodded and forced herself to concentrate, biting her lip and leaning forward to hear Clint's harsh whispers as he struggled with another attack of pain and fever, trying to outline his plan.

THE SUN DIPPED lower in the sky, and the afternoon breeze freshened as the light began to fade. Alvin opened one eye, yawned hugely and scratched at his ear before he dragged himself out from under the porch swing. He stared at the misty, rolling hills, then looked wistfully back at the ranch house, where a light had just begun to shine from the kitchen window. Brock moved around inside the room, briefly silhouetted against the ruffled paisley curtains. He was all alone. Millie had left hours earlier, and Alvin had a hopeful feeling that she wouldn't be coming back. He longed to go and whine at the kitchen door, be admitted to the brightness and warmth and curl up safely under Brock's chair.

But the hills were calling him, sending a restless stirring through his blood, and he couldn't resist. He wandered to the top of the steps and clattered down onto the grass, looked back at the lighted window one more time, then sighed and started off toward the hills, heading into the pale twilight.

After a while his pace quickened to a brisk trot and his ears perked up. The cool evening air was rich with seductive fragrances, traces of animal scents and other fleeting, mysterious odors that hinted darkly of nighttime and a world of dangerous excitement.

Alvin moved on through the fields and pastures until he began to approach rough country, where he had to be cautious about loose rock underfoot, and cactus spines that were long and sharp enough to pierce his soft pads and make them bleed. After a couple of hours he was back at the edge of the sheltered valley that he especially liked, where the autumn flocks of quail roosted everywhere in tangled thickets, drowsing in the twilight.

Alvin sat on the hillside for a few moments, outlined against the shimmering golden bowl of the sky. Then he trotted down the hill, barking joyously as the quail came bursting out of the thickets and beat their way off into the glowing sunset. Soon he'd forgotten his homesickness, his fear of the dark and even his hunger and laziness. He was caught up in a frenzied enjoyment of the chase, running wildly in circles and snapping at the air as the fat little birds flew overhead.

The sky faded from gold to bronze to liquid silver, and a full moon drifted across the hills, spilling a radiant pool of light into the hidden valley. Alvin sat back to recover his breath and stared up at the moon. Primitive urges throbbed in his blood, hot and strong. He lifted his ragged muzzle and began to howl, long, wild cascades of sound that left him feeling limp and drained.

After a while he fell silent and dropped onto the grass, panting heavily. As his breath returned, he lifted his ears, surprised by an unfamiliar noise in the deepening stillness. It was a human voice, strangely muffled and faraway.

Alvin cocked his head to listen. Memory stirred within his mind. He saw the woman down in the dark hole, recalled her terror and her distressing solitude. Along with that image Alvin remembered the taste of spicy beef and the bowl of water, and his eyes brightened with interest.

He got up and hurried down toward the thicket at the base of the hill, startling another flock of quail. But this time Alvin paid no attention to their noisy flight. He trotted along a rabbit path that led deep into the thicket, smelling the cold darkness of the cavern as he approached.

Soon he was at the edge of a narrow opening that yawned under the tangled brush. A rounded shaft sloped down vertically for several feet, then opened out into a small cave in the hillside where Alvin paused, tongue lolling, head cocked, and sniffed alertly in the musty darkness. Several passages branched from the first cavern, opening downward into the earth.

Without hesitation Alvin chose the widest of the passages, trotting through the rocky tunnel toward the sound of the woman's voice. The tunnel branched in places, opening onto other passages that led deep into the cave. But Alvin's keen nose led him on toward the promise of the woman and the contents of her pack. His pace slowed and he hesitated briefly as the crashing noise of the waterfall grew louder, but his longing for food and water was even stronger than his caution.

The path began to slope sharply downward, making him scramble and tumble for footholds, and in one place a deep pool of standing water lurked by the path, invisible in the darkness but smelling strongly to Alvin's sensitive nose of cold and chemicals. He pressed his body against the wall and picked his way gingerly through the tunnel until he couldn't smell the water any longer.

At last he reached the opening just above the woman. Her scent was strong, and so was the enticing smell of the rich beef. Alvin barked joyously and tumbled down through another narrow vertical shaft into the lighted tunnel where she waited.

He wagged his tail happily, enjoying the woman's caresses and whispered endearments. But he was hungry, and he let her know it, whining and sniffing impatiently at her pack until she fed him a generous portion of the beef and poured him a bowl of water.

"Alvin," she whispered as he drank, tears running down her dirty face. "Alvin, you're just the most wonderful dog, aren't you? You're so brave and smart. Here, sweetie, let me..."

She began to fumble at his collar. Alvin endured her touch for a moment, then nervously tried to pull away. He didn't want to be tied up and kept down here in this dark, frightening place. He wanted to smell the night breezes and the silver moonlight.

He wanted to get away.

She held him, whispering frantically as she worked at his collar. But he tugged more forcefully, twisting and clawing until he broke free of her grasp. Then he turned and scrambled back up the tunnel, pausing once to look over his shoulder before he rounded the wall of rock.

The last Alvin knew of the woman was her tear-streaked face and soiled clothes, weirdly illuminated by the lantern at her feet, and her cry of loneliness and terror as he vanished into the darkness and began to struggle up through the twisting, sloping maze of passages toward the welcoming moonlight.

AMANDA STOOD in front of the tall mirror on her dressing table, cocking her head to one side as she fastened an earring. The earrings were her favorite pair, although she hadn't worn them for more than a year. They were fashioned of white gold, a rich, glittering cascade of finely woven chains that winked softly in the shaded light. Perfect with this dress, she decided, smoothing the black silk over her hips with a critical frown as she turned to examine herself in the mirror.

The dress wasn't hers, actually. She'd borrowed it from shop inventory, and one of the seamstresses had worked all day to make the necessary alterations so it would fit Amanda's slender figure. It was deceptively simple, a graceful fall of silk that left one shoulder bare and skimmed down her body to flare just above her dainty high-heeled sandals. Apart from the earrings, she wore no other jewelry or adornment of any kind, and the stark simplicity of the outfit gave her a satisfying air of elegance.

At least, it should have satisfied her. This was precisely the look that she always strove to attain, and instructed her clients to work for as well.

"Less is more," Amanda told them earnestly. "If you can possibly get along without it, don't use it. Too many women smother the look and spoil the line with too much jewelry, too much makeup, too much accessorizing, too much of everything. That kind of over-decoration just shows a lack of confidence. Go for simplicity whenever you can.''

And the way Amanda looked tonight was clear proof that her advice was well founded. She should have been feeling happy and excited about the evening ahead, the prospect of mingling with important people and advancing her career, moving confidently among such an impressive group.

So why was she constantly fighting this empty feeling of misery and sadness?

''I won't think about him,'' she said firmly to her troubled reflection in the mirror. ''I refuse to think about him. If he doesn't want me, why should I run after him? I'm going to go this party and I'm damned well going to—''

But her brave words were interrupted by the sudden ringing of the doorbell. Amanda frowned and glanced at her watch.

Whoever was outside the door had to be someone the young doorman had allowed upstairs without announcement. Amanda knew that the boy was deeply impressed by Judd Hinshaw, and would no doubt have admitted him to the building.

But Amanda didn't want to go to the party with Judd. She thought he'd understood that, and he was such a gentleman. Surely he wouldn't . . .

She smoothed the dress over her hips with a brief, nervous gesture and hurried to open the door, then gaped with astonishment. Millie Munroe stood in the hallway, her eyes sparkling as she looked down at Amanda in her sophisticated black silk.

"Wow!" Millie said, stepping past the younger woman and into the apartment. "That's a great dress, honey. You look like a million dollars."

Amanda felt a surge of weary frustration. It just didn't seem fair that she should have to deal with Millie's rudeness and sarcasm again. Especially not on a night like this, when she was trying so hard to forget all about Brock and the ranch, and have a good time on her own.

"Millie, why are you here?" she asked in despair. "What more could you possibly have to say to me?"

Millie walked a few steps away from her and paused near the entry to the living room. Amanda looked at her visitor's slim back, appalled by her own harshness. After all, the woman was sick. She was frightened and suffering.

"I'm sorry," Amanda murmured. "I didn't mean to be so...abrupt."

Millie turned, and Amanda was surprised to see that she was grinning broadly. "Well, honey, I guess I've been a little abrupt myself from time to time, haven't I now?"

Amanda hesitated.

"Haven't I?" Millie urged.

"Maybe you have," Amanda said. "But you're under a lot of pressure, too. I...understand that better now, and I didn't mean to be rude to you."

"You're a real nice girl, you know that?" Millie commented, bending to pick up a porcelain model of a spaniel that sat on the console table. She studied the china dog with sudden interest.

"Millie...you're so different today," Amanda said. "What's happened to you?"

"I went to see Nate Purdy yesterday," Millie said, holding the dog in both hands as she spoke. "As soon as I could make an appointment after you called me a coward. It's about time," Millie added with a smile, "that somebody talked to me that way, girl. I sure needed a good tongue-lashing."

"What...what did the doctor say?" Amanda whispered.

"He said it was a completely benign tumor, nothing to worry about."

Amanda sagged against the doorframe. "Millie, that's wonderful! I'm so glad."

Millie looked at her curiously. "You really are, aren't you?" she said. "You're really, truly happy for me. What a nice girl you are," she repeated. "And Brock's a fool," she added without emotion. "He's just a damn fool."

Amanda stood quietly, unsure how to respond to this, while Millie squinted at the dog in her hands. "You know where a row of these porcelain dogs would look nice?" she asked.

"Where?"

"On that shelf above the kitchen table at the ranch house. Wouldn't that be pretty?"

Amanda felt a growing sense of unreality. "That's what I bought him for," she said. "And there's a beagle that's so adorable, and a Pomeranian and a dalmatian that I'd like to buy, too, but..."

She fell silent, looking nervously down at her feet.

"But what?"

"But I can't," Amanda murmured.

"Why not?"

Amanda looked up to meet the older woman's keen, dark eyes. "They're too expensive," she said miserably. "Far too expensive for me to contribute when I..." Again she stopped abruptly, finding it hard to believe that they were having this conversation at all.

"When you have no assurance that the situation will be permanent," Millie finished calmly. "I know. And you're absolutely right."

She set the china dog carefully back on the table and looked at her watch while Amanda waited in silence. "I have a cab down there with the meter running," Millie said. "I can only stay a minute. I won't keep you from your party," she added with another admiring glance at the sleek black dress. "I just wanted to apologize for being such a nasty bitch this past week, and tell you why Brock's so reluctant to get married. Maybe you'll be interested to hear it."

Amanda tensed and gripped the doorframe. Her throat went dry and her heart began to pound with fear. She wanted to put her hands over her ears and run away, but she knew that no power on earth could keep her from asking. "Yes," she whispered. "Please tell me. Why won't he marry me?"

"Because you've got more money than he does," Millie said.

Amanda gaped at her, too stunned to absorb this information. Of all the dreadful revelations she could have heard from Millie's lips, this was probably the last thing she'd expected. "Money?" she said blankly. "It's... it's about *money?*"

"Damn right it is. Funny thing about money," Millie added thoughtfully. "It's always a whole lot more important to the folks who don't have it than the folks who do. Did you ever notice that?"

But Amanda wasn't interested in Millie's philosophical observations. "I can't...Millie, he owns that whole big ranch. The land alone is worth—"

"Not a red cent unless you sell it, honey. A lot of ranchers are land-poor these days. They're sitting on a million dollars worth of real estate and wondering how to pay the grocery bills."

"Brock never told me he was in any kind of financial difficulty. I know things are a little tight these days, but he's always got money to spend on the house renovations, and on..."

She paused, frowning as she tried to think about anything else Brock might have spent money on recently.

Millie gave her a shrewd glance. "He didn't want you to be disappointed," she said. "He knows you like to do things up right, and buy quality fixings."

Amanda put both hands to her face, trying to cool the painful flush that warmed her cheeks. "I feel so...so awful," she whispered. "You mean that all the time we've been doing this, he's been ..."

"Pretty badly strapped for cash," Millie said cheerfully. "Don't worry, Amanda. It's not going to be permanent, you know. Brock's a smart man and a real hard worker, and he's got a good property there. He'll get over this rough patch and be prosperous again before long. But in the meantime, he loves you too much to ask you to give up all your comfort and security for his sake."

"He ... you think he loves me?"

"He sure does. He loves you so much that he's just sick at heart over all this, but he's too stubborn to admit the problem to you and talk about it."

"But I'd be so happy to help. And I don't need fancy expensive things, Millie. I just need him!"

Millie smiled gently and moved closer to touch Amanda's bare arm. "I know," she murmured. "You think I can't tell how much you love him? It shines in your eyes every time you say his name. Problem is, he needs to know, too."

Amanda shook her head in despair. "But if he doesn't know by now, how can I ever convince him? If he still thinks, after all we've been through, that it matters one scrap to me how much money he's got, then it's probably hopeless."

Millie looked at her thoughtfully. "Men are a real strange breed, girl. They act so tough and strong, and inside they're just little boys, terrified of being hurt. I think if you really love that man, you need to talk about what scares him. He wants you more than anything, but he's afraid of being selfish, marrying you to make himself happy and stealing your security from you in the process.''

''But my security has nothing to do with my money or my business success! My security is all tied up with him. Millie, I can't imagine living without him.''

''Maybe you should tell him that,'' Millie suggested gently.

Amanda stared up at her. ''Maybe I should,'' she whispered.

Suddenly she wanted Millie to be gone. She wanted to tear off the black silk dress and high-heeled sandals, throw on a pair of jeans and drive to Crystal Creek. The urge was so strong that it was all she could do to keep from taking hold of Millie's sleeve and pulling her toward the door.

Millie chuckled, obviously reading her expression. ''All right, I'm going,'' she said mildly. ''Right away. I'm staying downtown near the airport tonight, and catching a flight back to Oregon at six in the morning.''

Amanda forgot her eagerness to change her clothes and hurry away. She looked at Millie with a childlike flood of disappointment.

''So soon?'' she asked. ''Can't you stay a while now that we're...finally getting to know each other? Millie, I don't want you to leave. Cancel your flight and stay here at my apartment tonight.''

Millie patted her cheek. ''That's sweet of you, honey, but you and Brock have things to work out.

Better if you're on your own for a while. How about if I come back for a visit at Christmas?''

Amanda smiled and felt tears beginning to gather on her eyelashes. ''I think that would be lovely.''

''So would a Christmas wedding,'' Millie said with another of her irrepressible grins. ''A Christmas wedding would be real pretty, don't you think? And I'd sure love to be a guest.''

''You'll be the guest of honor, Millie.''

''That's a promise?''

''That's a promise,'' Amanda said recklessly, her heart singing with happiness. ''It may not be a big fancy social event, but there's going to be a Christmas wedding, and you're going to be my maid of honor. You'd just better plan to be there.''

Millie took Amanda into her arms and hugged her tightly. ''I never had a daughter,'' she whispered. ''But if I did, you know what? I'd want her to be just like you.''

''Oh, Millie...''

The tall woman pulled away and gave Amanda a gentle push. ''All right,'' she said gruffly. ''Enough of this sickening mushy stuff. You get out to that ranch and talk to your man, and call me when you have some good news to tell. Brock's got my number.''

Then she was gone, whirling off down the apartment hallway with her long, swinging stride.

Amanda leaned in the doorway and watched. Millie paused near the elevators, turning to smile at her.

''Amanda?'' she called.

''Yes?''

"You were right about the wallpaper, too."

Then she was gone. Amanda stood in her doorway with tears running down her cheeks until at last, galvanized by sudden excitement, she ran back into her apartment and pulled off her dress. Tossing it unheeded onto a chair, she slipped into jeans and casual shoes, packed some things hastily in a suitcase, called her hostess to give her apologies and then hurried down through the lobby to the parking lot.

The night was mellow and the harvest moon rode high above the trees, shining like a blessing on her car while Amanda skimmed along the highway that took her westward into the night.

CHAPTER TWELVE

BY THE TIME Amanda entered the ranch yard it was getting close to eleven o'clock, and the Halloween moon was no longer a shimmering orange balloon caught in the tree branches. It had risen and condensed until it glistened far above the hills like a single pearl on dark blue silk, spilling a white radiance over the countryside.

The light was clear enough to cast shadows, pools of darkness that lay starkly on the silvered expanse of the lawn and the bare earth near the corrals. Amanda parked under the cedar trees near the ranch house, looking hopefully up at the windows.

Maybe Brock hadn't gone to the Halloween party at Zack's, after all. Maybe he was in his old chair right now, watching a late movie on television with Alvin curled at his feet. Visualizing this, Amanda felt a surge of longing so intense that it left her feeling weak and frightened. She caught her breath and hurried up the stairs to the veranda, rang the doorbell and listened to its distant echo in the silence of the night.

But there was no answer. Eventually she opened her handbag and rummaged for the key, then let herself inside, switching on the hall light and looking around expectantly.

The house was silent and empty. There was no sign of Brock or his dog as Amanda walked through the lower rooms. She paused at the entry to Brock's bedroom, almost faint with yearning and sadness as she looked at his neatly made bed under the bright patchwork quilt. Amanda stood quietly in the doorway, remembering the hours of blissful happiness that they'd spent together in this room.

Haltingly she crossed the floor, opened the closet and gathered an armful of his clothes to press her face into the clean, familiar scent of him.

"Brock," she whispered, tears stinging in her eyes. "Oh, Brock, my sweet darling, I love you. I love you so much."

Amanda rocked slowly back and forth, still clutching the armful of clothes while she marveled that it was possible to love anyone so deeply, and wondered how she'd ever allowed anything to come between them.

After a moment she smiled through her tears and ran her hand down one of his plaid shirt collars, letting her fingers trail over the neat, starched surface. Brock always did such a nice job of ironing his shirts.

Amanda had a vivid mental image of him standing in his kitchen, quiet and lonely, ironing his shirts and worrying about his financial problems, wondering how he could ever offer her the kind of life that she evidently wanted.

A sob caught in her throat. She dropped the shirt collar and turned away, wandering restlessly through the empty rooms to the kitchen. She considered driving into Crystal Creek, turning up at Zack's and surprising Brock at the party, but she decided against doing anything so dramatic. Brock hated drama.

It would be better for her simply to snuggle into his bed and be there waiting for him when he came home. He'd arrive feeling lonely and miserable, and when he climbed into bed she'd open her arms and draw him into a warm embrace, and then she'd say...

Her fantasy was interrupted by a sound at the kitchen door. Amanda frowned and hesitated, listening. The noise was louder now, a kind of furtive clatter and scratching, like raccoons running along the wooden floorboards outside.

She hurried through the kitchen and opened the door a crack, then gasped in astonishment as Alvin pressed against the door and tumbled inside, falling in a weary heap at her feet.

"Alvin," she murmured, reaching down automatically to pat him. "What's the matter, Alvin? Poor baby, you're so tired...."

Indeed, the little dog seemed exhausted. His coat was dirty and matted, even more unkempt-looking than usual, and both his front paws were bleeding. He held one of them up off the floor, gnawing at it repeatedly. Amanda saw a couple of broken cactus spines protruding from the soft pad of flesh.

She gathered up the little dog and sat in a chair, holding him tight in the crook of her arm while she tugged at the spines and worked them loose. Normally Alvin would have made a tremendous fuss over an operation like this, but now he seemed too weary to object very much. He lay with his head over her arm and his tongue lolling, waiting stoically for her to be finished. Occasionally his body was racked with a long shudder, and once or twice he yelped weakly in pain.

"Poor little sweetie," Amanda whispered, stroking the silky skin behind his ears with a slow, loving gesture. "Where have you been, Alvin? You're so dusty. Have you been rolling in the dirt somewhere? Was something chasing you? Poor baby..."

Still murmuring in concern, she set the dog gently on the floor and moved across the room to fill his food and water dishes. Alvin looked a shade more lively when he heard the sound of running water and the rustle of the feed sack. He followed her, walking gingerly on his lacerated paws, and pressed against her legs, lapping greedily at the fresh water in his dish.

Amanda sat back in the chair to watch him, smiling, though her brow was still furrowed with anxiety. There was something strange about Alvin, something she couldn't quite put her finger on.

She stared hard at the little dog, and suddenly realized that his collar looked different. He was eating now, and when he lifted his head something dangled from his throat, almost obscured by the metal tags on his collar.

"Alvin?" Amanda muttered, getting up and moving toward him again. "What on earth..."

She knelt beside the dog and tugged at his collar. Alvin growled low in his throat, annoyed at this interruption of his meal, but Amanda knew him too well to pay any attention. She continued to work at his collar where a small pouch, like the kind used to carry a stopwatch or compass, was attached to the leather strap with a series of tight knots.

The pouch was grayish plastic, difficult to see against Alvin's ragged fur, with a black drawstring that closed the neck tight. Amanda finally worked it loose and let Alvin return to his meal. She carried the pouch back to her chair and sank down, staring at it, trying to remember if she'd ever seen it before.

When she untied the last of the knots and opened the little plastic sack, her heart beat faster and her throat tightened. Inside the pouch were a couple of tightly folded sheets of paper, covered with handwriting.

It was a message from Brock, she thought with a surge of excitement. Why hadn't she thought of it before? After all, this wouldn't be the first time Brock had used his dog to send her a message. In the past, during happier times, she'd received a number of whimsical love letters tied to Alvin's collar....

But when she unfolded and smoothed the dusty sheets of paper, then reached in her handbag for her reading glasses, Amanda frowned in confusion.

This wasn't Brock's handwriting. And one of the pages was a map of some kind, a complex topographical drawing covered with arrows and compass points.

She looked blankly at the map, which meant nothing to her at all, then began to read the letter. After a few moments her face turned white and her eyes widened with horror. She read to the end of the page, folded the two sheets and placed them carefully on the table, staring at Alvin.

Finally Amanda got up, threw on her jacket and hunted frantically in the back closet for Alvin's leash, which was hardly ever used.

She snapped the leash onto his collar while he rolled his eyes up at her with sudden deep suspicion and slunk closer to his food dish.

"Sorry, darling," Amanda told him, "but I can't risk losing track of you again. Did you know that you hold somebody's life in your paws, Alvin? You really do."

With that, she bundled the dog into her arms over his strenuous protests, locked the house behind her and hurried out into the moonlit ranch yard, heading for her car.

IT WAS CLOSE to midnight when a strange procession appeared on the rocky trail, moving slowly in the moonlight along the limestone ridge at the back of Brock Munroe's property. Four vehicles bobbed and churned over the rough grade, their headlights winking in the darkness, while a helicopter churned noisily overhead.

The lead vehicle was a rugged four-wheel-drive emergency van belonging to the sheriff's department. Wayne Jackson, in uniform, was at the wheel, his face hard and worried in the silver light. Amanda sat next to him on the front seat, with Brock at her other side.

She and Brock had hardly exchanged a word since she'd arrived at Zack's with her incredible story, and set the merry group scattering in confusion. Brock glanced down at her delicate profile, aching to gather her in his arms and hold her. He wanted to know why she'd forsaken the party in Austin, and what her presence at the ranch really meant.

Was she here to make up their quarrel, or was this going to be the final showdown? Most of all, he desperately wanted to know what had happened to Judd Hinshaw.

But now wasn't the time for dealing with their personal matters. All that would come later, when those poor kids in the cave were safe. Brock dropped an arm around Amanda's shoulders, drawing her a little closer to his side when he felt how she was trembling. She nestled gratefully, but didn't look up at him.

Alvin whined a sleepy complaint from the back seat. Brock looked at the dog over his shoulder.

"Our hero's missing his beauty sleep," he commented. "Alvin's gonna be real cranky in the morning."

"If we get those people out in one piece," Wayne said, "I'll take Alvin into the Longhorn tomorrow and personally buy him the biggest, juiciest steak they've got. Hear that, Alvin?" he called to the sleepy dog, who regarded him with cold suspicion from the shadowed back seat.

"Oh, that sort of thing doesn't impress Alvin," Brock said. "Alvin's a very light eater."

Wayne chuckled. "Yeah, right. Meaning he only eats when it's light out? I've heard a story or two about Alvin."

Brock grinned in return, then looked down at Amanda. She sat tensely in the circle of his arm, holding the gray plastic pouch and worrying it between her fingers.

She was always so softhearted, Brock thought with a wrenching flood of emotion. Amanda was feeling all the fear and pain of the girl in the cave, and she could hardly bear it.

"It's going to be okay, sweetheart," he whispered. "It really is. We'll get them out soon, thanks to you and Alvin."

She gave a brief nod but said nothing.

Wayne picked up his mike and spoke to the vehicles that were following. "Jim, this grade's getting too rough," he told the ambulance driver. "You better park and wait. We'll get back to you. Warren, stop and pick up the stretcher, okay? Manny, can you all handle this trail? Over."

"Lead on." Manny Hernandez's voice sounded confident through the speaker as he maneuvered the truck that followed them. "We can handle anything you can, old hoss. Over."

Both Brock and Amanda wore jeans and denim jackets. Brock had decided before going to Zack's that he wasn't in the mood for a costume party, but the people in the rest of the procession were another story. Brock shook his head briefly when he thought how this rescue team would appear to a casual onlooker.

Behind them, Manny drove dressed in his matador outfit of red velvet tights, gold-trimmed bolero jacket

and a lace fichu. Tracey was with him, fetchingly cos-
tumed as a Spanish señorita with a rose in her hair.

Cal McKinney rode in the back seat of Manny's vehicle, dressed in a tight black spandex suit with a
ghastly skeleton outlined on the front in fluorescent
paint. Serena, his wife, was a prim Mary Poppins, accurate right down to the umbrella.

Manny and Cal had been allowed to join the rescue
party because, surprisingly, both had confessed to doing quite a lot of amateur spelunking during their earlier years. At this point, Wayne needed all the
experienced help he could find. And if the medical details in Neale Cameron's letter were accurate, they
probably didn't have time to wait for a trained group
to arrive from the city. Following Wayne and Manny
was a heavy van driven by Warren Trent, dressed as
Zorro, with a dashing hat and mask. The quiet, taci-
turn Warren was always a useful man in a crisis, and
Wayne had accepted his offer to drive Marjorie Perez
and Virginia Parks to the cave entrance. Marjorie was
an impressively beautiful witch in a glamorous black
cape and a pointed silk hat, while Virginia appeared to
be a sunflower. She wore brilliant green tights and a
hooded pullover with a stiff framework of yellow fabric petals that surrounded her sweet face.

Everybody in town wanted to be in on the rescue, but
Wayne had limited his backup to these two vehicles,
both of them rugged enough to handle the terrain on
Brock Munroe's ranch, and the ambulance, which now
pulled off and parked along the trail.

Tyler McKinney, looking tense in a black gorilla suit and cowboy hat, flew the Double C Ranch helicopter overhead, hovering just above the line of vehicles.

Wayne looked back over his shoulder at the lights of the trucks behind him. "How much farther, Brock?" he muttered, bumping his way up over a steep rise. "This is getting damned rough."

Brock peered out into the moonlit expanse. "God, Wayne, it's so hard to know for sure. If I'm reading that map right, they must have entered way over on the other side of the ridge, a few miles away from where I first saw Clint that day. I can't think of any other place where they could go in, head steadily downward like he shows on the map, and still be fairly close to another opening lower down."

"And you figure that lower opening would be somewhere in this valley floor?"

Brock studied the isolated valley with its rugged thatch of brush. "I think it's got to be, Wayne. Unless we're on the wrong track altogether. Maybe they're over on the other side of the ridge, dammit. I just can't think of any other landform that fits the description on this map."

Wayne hesitated briefly at the edge of the valley, frowning and tapping his fingers on the steering wheel. After a moment he sent his truck bumping down toward the valley floor. "Well, we've come this far. Might as well try it," he said. "Alvin, you ugly little sucker, pretty soon it's all up to you. I surely do hope you know what you're doing."

Alvin glared at the sheriff and lowered his head onto his paws, looking increasingly obstinate and sulky.

The three vehicles rocked down onto level ground and lined up, spilling their strange array of occupants into the cool moonlight. Tyler set the helicopter down nearby and came running toward them, moving awkwardly in his bulky costume.

Brock watched while Amanda gathered Alvin in her arms, attached the leash to his collar and kissed him, murmuring something into his floppy ear.

Warren Trent, dark and handsome in his dashing costume, looked quietly around at the moonlit valley. "If there's a cavern opening down here, it's sure well disguised," he muttered. "There's nothing visible in the face of the cliff."

Manny shrugged. "It doesn't have to look like a cave. The opening could be a hole in the ground right under that thicket. Could be a vertical shaft dropping straight down into the first chamber."

Serena McKinney poked her umbrella nervously at the ground and glared at her husband, whose eyes sparkled with excitement.

"Cal McKinney," Brock heard her whispering furiously, a little apart from the group. "A trained spelunker, for God's sake! You've never been inside a cave in your whole life, and you *know* it."

Cal gave her his most charming grin and leaned to kiss her, splendid in the tight black skeleton suit, with the bones glowing luridly on his chest. "Hell, darlin'," he whispered, "if ol' Alvin can do it, I guess I can. I wouldn't miss a party like this for anything."

Meanwhile Manny was preparing his equipment in a calm, professional manner. He tied a nylon rope around his red velvet waist and attached it to Cal's, while the onlookers waited tensely.

"I guess it's time," Wayne said, nodding to Marjorie, who stood quietly nearby in her witch's costume with her arms around Virginia. "You can go ahead, Marj."

"Here, Alvin," Marjorie called to the little dog in her sweet, clear voice. "Come here, sweetie. Come and smell this."

She knelt and held out a wad of flowered cotton.

"This is Neale's nightgown," she told Alvin as he edged forward reluctantly and sniffed at the fabric with a noticeable lack of interest. "This is the nightgown she wore the night before she...she left. I want you to smell it, and go find Neale. Find her, Alvin," Marjorie finished, patting the dog and getting to her feet again.

Her shoulders began to shake and she turned to Virginia, dissolving in sobs as the older woman held her and murmured to her.

Listlessly, Alvin nosed a couple more times at the nightgown on the dusty grass. Brock watched the dog, his hands clenching automatically into fists. He looked down at Amanda, who stood tensely next to him, her eyes also fixed on Alvin.

"Please, Alvin," she whispered, like someone chanting a prayer. "Please, please, please..."

Alvin sat back and gnawed one of his hind paws, then licked at the sore pad where Amanda had removed the cactus spines. He looked sullenly at the assembled group of anxious faces, then gazed for a long, thoughtful moment at the fading moon.

Brock felt himself growing wild with impatience. He was about to yell at the dog when Amanda slipped her hand into his with a gentle pressure. He held her hand gratefully and subsided, forcing himself to wait.

At last Alvin sniffed once more at the nightgown in casual fashion, looked at Brock and Amanda, then started off hesitantly toward the dense thicket at the base of the cliff. He ducked to avoid an overhead tangle of branches and vanished into a small animal trail that ran through the base of the thicket.

Cal stood staring in dismay at the overgrown thicket with its bank of wicked thorns, and the disappearing end of Alvin's leash. But Manny had already dropped to his knees and grasped the trailing leather cord, his tasseled black patent slippers glistening brightly in the moonlight as he crawled along the path.

Cal sighed, dropped to all fours and shouldered his way into the dense growth behind Manny.

Soon the two men and the dog were lost to view, and the valley was plunged into silence. The group by the thicket waited tensely, straining their ears to hear the faint sounds of rustling leaves and the snapping of twigs. At last even those were gone, and the stillness was so profound that a flight of birds passing overhead sounded almost as loud as the Double C helicopter.

Brock stood with one arm around Amanda's shoulders, staring at the narrow path in the thicket. This moonlighted tableau was like something from *Alice in*

Wonderland, he thought a little wildly. Maybe all of them would disappear, one by one, into some enchanted hole in the ground, and find themselves in a bizarre world that they could never escape from....

Amanda looked up at him, her face pale in the silver light. "It's all so weird, with the moonlight and the costumes," she whispered. "I almost expect to see the White Rabbit come hopping by, don't you?"

He smiled at her, overcome with love. She was the only person in the world who understood him completely, and shared his thoughts on such a deep level. If he lost this woman, there was no way he would ever survive the loneliness.

They heard a distant bark from Alvin, and then a shout of triumph, strangely muffled and faraway. After a few moments Manny's voice came ringing through the thicket, sounding much more distinct.

"Hey, Wayne!"

"Yeah? We hear you, Manny!" The sheriff leaned close to the bushes.

"We've found a cave opening down here."

"Does it look passable?"

"It's pretty steep," Manny called through the darkness. "But I think we can get through. Alvin's fixing to guide us inside. He's a real good dog, Brock."

"If you say so," Brock muttered, trying to smile. "Good boy, Alvin! Good dog!" he added, in a louder tone of hearty encouragement.

"Wayne!"

"Yeah, Manny?"

"Cal's waiting for me down in the first chamber. We're going in now. Get Warren and Tyler to haul that stretcher up to the opening, would you? They'll be able to see it clear enough inside the thicket. We'll come back up for the stretcher if we find them."

"Sure thing, Manny. Take care, you hear? She says there's a waterfall down there."

"You bet. Hey, Tyler?"

"Here I am, Manny."

"You got anything on under that damn gorilla suit?"

"Just my shorts," Tyler called.

In the stillness, they heard the reassuring sound of Manny's chuckle. "Better leave your hide on, then, old son. We wouldn't want to scare the ladies."

The group outside smiled nervously and shifted their feet in the grass. Warren hurried to his van to lift out the lightweight metal-and-canvas stretcher while the women stood watching him with wide, frightened eyes.

NEALE WOKE from a haunted dream of suffocation, gasping and clawing for air. She lay back in the clammy darkness, breathing hard.

She'd started turning the lantern off while they slept to preserve the batteries, but the utter blackness when she woke was terrifying to her. There was nothing to help her get her bearings or position herself in space, and she had the frightening sensation that if she moved or rolled over, she'd slip off a narrow ledge into some kind of bottomless pit where she'd just keep falling for eternity.

With shaking hands, she fumbled for the lamp and switched it on, grateful for the weird orange glow that suddenly illuminated their cavern. Clint lay beside her, muttering and tossing in his sleep. Neale struggled to her knees and leaned over him, gasping with alarm when she touched his forehead.

He was on fire, worse than he'd ever been. His skin felt dry and papery, and when his eyes flicked open from time to time, his stare was glassy and uncomprehending.

Lovingly, Neale stroked his dark, curly hair, his finely molded cheeks and mouth and chin. She poured a bit of water onto a cloth and wiped his face and neck, then pressed more water against his fever-chapped lips, trying to moisten them. "Clint," she murmured. "Clint, can you hear me?"

"Thirsty," he muttered. "So thirsty."

But when she tried to lift his head and trickle some of the water into his mouth, his head rolled away and his eyes dropped shut again.

Neale sobbed aloud, then cupped his flushed face in her hands. "Clint, I have to go away," she whispered, though she knew that he could no longer hear or understand. "I hate to leave you alone, darling, but I have to try to find a way out of here. I can't just sit here any longer. I have to try, even if I don't make it."

She wet the cloth and placed it on his lips again, then moved the pillow into a more comfortable position under his head, covered him well and got up, shouldering her backpack and taking a careful drink of water to ease the dryness of her throat.

Their food was almost gone, and the water supply was dwindling as well.

Neale knew that the cave was full of water, dripping and trickling everywhere, gathering in murky pools within the narrow passages. But she was afraid of the cave water, not sure if its high chemical content might be hazardous, even poisonous. She was reluctant to use any of it as long as she could hoard the precious bit remaining in Clint's canteen.

She lifted the helmet lamp and fitted it on her head, regarding Clint with sorrow as he lay in the sleeping bag.

"I've just found you," she whispered to his still face. "And now I might never see you again. But I love you so much, darling. I really love you."

She bent to kiss him tenderly on the lips, knowing that what she said was true. These few days of terror and isolation had brought them closer than months of ordinary courting. The man felt as near to her as her own heartbeat, and leaving him alone and helpless was an agony almost too great to bear.

Neale got to her feet again, looked at him one more time and then turned hastily, picking her way across the uneven floor of the cavern toward the maze of passages.

After a brief hesitation, she entered the tunnel where she'd met Alvin, trying to retrace her steps through the winding labyrinth. In her hands she clutched the spool of cord that was still attached to Clint's boot, holding it like a talisman as she climbed and twisted her body along the cramped passageways.

She reached the spot where the dog had visited her, then paused, staring blankly at the warren of passages. They opened everywhere, sloping up and down, leading off in all directions. There was no way to guess where Alvin might have gone, and nothing to hint at an outside opening. No matter how she tried, Neale couldn't smell fresh air in any of the tunnels, or see a hint of outside light, or hear anything but the ominous rumble of the distant waterfall.

She stood tensely in the passage, trying to pretend that she was a small dog. Where would she go?

"Please, God," she whispered aloud in childlike supplication. "I probably don't deserve anything for myself, but for Clint's sake, please show me which way to go. Please, because he's going to die otherwise. I love him so much, God. I don't want him to die."

She held her breath and inched along one of the tunnels, shining her lamp nervously into the yawning blackness, knowing that a single false step could send her plunging over some invisible precipice and into that roaring waterfall.

Neale was concentrating so fiercely that at first she didn't hear the faint sound approaching along the length of the tunnel. Gradually it grew louder, a frantic clattering noise followed by a muffled bark. Suddenly Alvin was at her feet, looking up at her.

"Alvin!" she whispered, bending to touch him, feeling faint and dizzy.

Even when she felt the dog's coarse fur, she wasn't sure if he was real. She was so hungry and thirsty, so weakened by trauma that she might be having fantasies, like a wanderer in the desert.

"Alvin, is it really you? Oh, Alvin..."

The dog squirmed away from her hand and cocked his ears, as if listening for something behind him. Neale noticed for the first time that Alvin had a leash attached to his collar, with the end trailing loose on the rough floor of the tunnel.

She stared at the leash. Her mind moved sluggishly, trying to decide what it meant. Maybe he'd been tied up at home and broken loose....

Suddenly she screamed aloud and put her hand over her mouth, gasping with horror. A skeleton came slithering over a dark ledge nearby and loomed upward in the gloom, its bones shining a lurid green in the glow of her helmet. Neale shrank back against the rock wall as the skeleton advanced slowly toward her, carrying a lamp in its bony claw.

"Hey, Manny," it called in a jubilant masculine voice. "Over here! I found her! Alvin's here, too."

"Coming," a voice called.

Neale watched in rising disbelief, clutching the damp wall to steady herself as a dapper figure in red velvet and glistening lace came sliding into view and grinned at her with a flash of white teeth.

It must be a nightmare. She was still lying next to Clint, sleeping in the big cavern, and she was dreaming. She had to be dreaming.

"Hey, kid, don't be scared," the bullfighter said gently. "We've come to help you. Alvin was bringing us in here when he pulled the leash out of my hand, and it took us a while to catch up.''

She crouched in the shadows as the two specters moved toward her. When they got close enough, she could see that the skeleton had a tanned face and a friendly smile. And the elegant toreador wasn't some monstrous phantom of the depths. It was Manny Hernandez, the local veterinarian.

Neale crumpled in a heap on the rocky floor and started to cry.

CHAPTER THIRTEEN

BLACK CLOUDS MASSED on the hills and drifted across the moon. A heavy rain began to fall a few hours after midnight, rustling in the tree branches and pattering noisily on the porch roof. Amanda woke in the darkness and lay still, frowning in confusion, surprised to realize that she'd been asleep.

Brock had left her at the ranch with Alvin when they came back from the limestone ridge. Then he'd driven on into town with the others and she'd gone to bed, hoping to sleep because she couldn't bear the tension of waiting in the darkened house for news of Neale and Clint.

She rolled her head on the pillow, wondering if Brock had returned and slipped into bed next to her while she was sleeping, but there was no sign of him. She was alone except for Alvin, who lay in an untidy heap on the quilt next to her.

Amanda smiled and reached down to pat him, but he didn't stir.

"Good boy," she murmured, stroking his head gently. "Good dog, Alvin. I love you."

She lay back and looked at the window, where raindrops glistened and streamed down the glass. She couldn't seem to free her mind of haunting images, pictures that kept flashing at her with painful vividness.

Serena McKinney in her quaint outfit, staring fearfully into the thicket where Cal had vanished, clutching her umbrella with her heart in her eyes. Marjorie Perez, majestic in cape and hat, weeping in unrestrained joy when she heard that Neale had been found.

Above all, Neale Cameron's dirty face as Warren helped her out of the thicket, and the way the girl stood, pale and rigid, to watch while the stretcher carrying Clint's still body was lifted out behind them. . . .

Amanda shuddered and reached toward Alvin once again, pulling him a little closer and snuggling beside him for comfort.

She heard a door open and close at the other end of house. Amanda tensed, waiting while Brock tiptoed down the hall and appeared in the doorway to the bedroom.

"Hi," she whispered.

"You're awake?"

"I think the rain woke me just now. I can't believe that I was able to fall asleep at all."

"Well, you've had a pretty long day, honey."

Brock hesitated, then began to undress, stripping off his shirt and jeans while Amanda lay watching him. The scene was domestic and cozy, like a hundred other times they'd gone to bed together, but she knew that both of them could feel the underlying tension.

She waited in silence while he vanished into the bathroom briefly, then came out and padded across the room to slip into bed next to her.

"Damn!" he muttered suddenly. "That dog's in the bed again. Alvin, get down!"

"Let him stay, Brock," Amanda murmured. "He's so tired, poor baby. And he's a hero, after all."

Brock switched the lamp on. Both of them looked at Alvin, who lay between them in a drowsy lump, with his nose tucked under his paws and one ear turned inside out.

Brock chuckled. "You know, I think old Alvin's all done with his wandering. I'll bet he's going to stay home from now on."

"I hope so. Although things could have been pretty grim if he hadn't been out roaming the countryside the past few days, couldn't they?"

"They sure could." Brock turned to look at her in the shaded glow of the lamp. "Neale's fine, just a little dehydrated and worn out. Nate checked her and sent her home. She said she wanted to soak in a hot bubble bath and sleep for a week, but you know what? I'll bet she's back at the hospital by the crack of dawn."

"She really loves him, doesn't she? I can't stop picturing her face when they brought him out."

"I guess those two kids fell pretty deep in love while they were stranded down there. Neale says there's quite a story to tell, but she wants to wait until he's stronger before she talks much about it."

"How is he?"

"He's got three broken ribs, a badly bruised spleen and an internal infection. That's what caused the fever. They put him on antibiotics as soon as he got to the hospital, and Nate says his condition is already stabilizing. I guess he's a pretty tough hombre. Nate figures he'll likely be up and around in less than a week."

"I'll bet he won't be climbing into any more caves."

"Are you kidding? Neale said they're going back in as soon as he's strong enough. They're going to cooperate on an article she's writing for a big travel magazine."

Amanda stared at him in the darkness. "Neale's going back into that cave? Marjorie said she's been claustrophobic all her life."

"I guess she's cured." Brock grinned. "I think if Clint Farrell goes anywhere, Neale's going to be right behind him. I don't think they plan to let each other slip away."

Amanda moved her head on the pillow. "I keep thinking about all the terrible possibilities," she murmured. "What if Alvin hadn't been out there wandering around? What if I hadn't been here to let him in and see that pouch on his collar?"

"But you were," Brock murmured, reaching out to touch her cheek.

She nodded again, close to tears. "Yes," she whispered. "I was."

"Why, honey?" he asked huskily. "Why did you come out here tonight? What happened to your party at the governor's house?"

"Funny thing about that party," Amanda said, trying to keep her voice light. "You know, I was all dressed and ready to go, and then somebody dropped in to see me."

"Yeah? Who was it?"

"It was Millie. She and I have gotten to be pretty good friends."

"No kidding!" Brock turned to look at her. "I didn't know Millie was planning to stop and visit you. She's on her way home, you know."

"I know." Amanda smiled privately. "But she's coming back at Christmastime."

"Is she?"

"Yes. I invited her to our wedding."

The room was suddenly so quiet that they could hear the raindrops pattering against the windows, and the soft rustle of the cedar tree outside the window.

"Our wedding?"

"We're getting married at Christmas," Amanda told him calmly, though her heart was pounding so loudly that she was afraid he could hear it over the sound of the rain. "Won't that be nice?"

"I'm surprised that you still want me, girl." Brock glanced at her soberly. "I haven't been acting like much of a prize lately, have I?"

Amanda smiled, then shivered when she thought about Neale's face as she looked at Clint on the stretcher. "It's so frightening," she murmured. "Just the thought that we could have lost each other, Brock. I'd die without you."

"Me too, darling. But I don't know why you want to marry me. I can't..."

Amanda rolled over and threw herself into his arms, pushing Alvin gently aside so she could get close enough. "Don't say it, Brock," she told him urgently. "Don't you dare say another word. Millie told me all about your money troubles and why you were reluctant to marry me, and it makes me mad!"

"Why?"

"Because it's so damned unfair! Brock, what if my business suddenly went downhill? What if all my clients went somewhere else and nobody wanted my outfits, and I could hardly scare up enough cash to pay my bank loan?"

"What about it?"

"Would you stop loving me because I was having problems?"

"God, what a question," he said, laughing. "Of course not. How could I stop loving you over something like that? Don't be ridiculous."

Amanda leaned up on one elbow and glared down at him. "Then why can't you give me credit for the same depth of loyalty? How come you get to stand by me through thick and thin, but I'm not allowed to do the same for you?"

His eyes widened and he looked at her thoughtfully. "You know, I never thought about it like that."

"Well, maybe it's time you did," Amanda said, still glaring at him fiercely. "It's pretty insulting, you know, this whole idea that I'm too shallow to share your hardships as well as your prosperity."

He was silent, his eyes on the ceiling, his arms folded behind his head. "Maybe we shouldn't rush into things," he said at last. "Neale thinks that property could be worth a lot to the government now that they've discovered the cave. Maybe I'll be rich after all, if you just give me a year or two."

Amanda gasped and stared at him, ready to shout in fury until she saw the sparkle in his eyes and realized that he was teasing.

"No way," she said calmly. "I'm not waiting a minute past Christmas. I feel just the same as Neale does. I'm not letting you out of my sight, Brock. We're getting married at Christmas, and we're going to be married forever and have a bunch of kids and grow old together, and you'll just have to learn to live with that whether you like it or not!"

Brock chuckled and switched off the lamp, then drew her into his arms and bent to kiss her mouth, her eyelids and earlobes and throat. He pulled aside her lacy nightgown and his mouth moved to caress her breasts while she shivered with pleasure.

"So, we're getting married, are we?" he asked lightly, running his hand over the curve of her hip and thigh.

"Well, maybe," Amanda told him, suddenly demure. "If you ask me and I decide to accept, that is."

"Amanda," he whispered huskily while his hand moved lower, slipping between her thighs, "will you marry me?"

She pressed herself against him, shameless with joy. "Oh, Brock... only if you promise you'll never, ever stop doing that."

Brock laughed and hugged her, moving his hand with more purpose. Alvin woke and yawned drowsily, then displayed a rare degree of tact by climbing down off the bed. He tumbled in a heap onto the braided rug and moved toward the door without looking back.

The little dog sat for a while in the darkened hallway, listening to the murmurs and sighs of passion coming from the big bed. Eventually the springs began to creak, and Alvin felt a deep satisfaction.

Everything was all right. The world was back to normal, just the way he liked it. He wandered down the hall to the kitchen, his toenails clattering softly on the hardwood floor. For a moment he paused by the door, listening to the cold rain falling, but he no longer had the slightest desire to go outside.

At last he trotted into the living room and scrambled up onto the couch. He turned around a couple of times, then dropped among the heaped cushions with a sigh of contentment and fell heavily asleep, while the rain slashed and pounded on the roof, and the autumn wind sighed through the trees.